Grace pulled her hand back to rest on her stomach, and Mrs. Clay's mouth tightened. "You're not the first young woman of your class I've seen in here, heavy around the waist. However that child was got on you, your family will want you back once it's gone. You storing everything up on your insides won't do you no favors once you're past these walls. Find something outside to bring you back to the world, or you may end up here for good."

Grace's eyes returned to the window, where a light morning rain began to seep through the layers of grime, allowing splashes of color from the outside world into the gray interior. Mrs. Clay sighed heavily and rested a hand on her shoulder.

Kind as they were, Mrs. Clay's words were lost on Grace. She knew the baby would be born, and with its exit would come her reentry into the world she'd known. They would sew her back into her red velvet dress she'd arrived in. Her father's black lacquered carriage would gather her after hours, the rolling wheels taking her back home to her own room, her own bed. Her own terrors.

She had already decided she was never leaving.

Also by Mindy McGinnis

In a Handful of Dust

Not a Drop to Drink

A MADNESS  SO DISCREET

MINDY McGINNIS

KATHERINE TEGEN BOOKS
An Imprint of HarperCollins Publishers

Katherine Tegen Books is an imprint of HarperCollins Publishers.

A Madness So Discreet
www.epicreads.com

Library of Congress Cataloging-in-Publication Data
McGinnis, Mindy.
    A madness so discreet / Mindy McGinnis. — First edition.
        pages   cm
    Summary: Near the turn of the nineteenth century, Dr. Thornhollow
helps teenaged Grace Mae escape from the Boston asylum where she was sent
after becoming pregnant by rape, and takes her to Ohio, where they put her
intelligence and remarkable memory to use in trying to catch murderers.
    ISBN 978-0-06-232087-2
    [1. Criminal investigation—Fiction.   2. Physicians—Fiction.
3. Ohio—History—19th century—Fiction.]   I. Title.
PZ7.M4784747Mad   2015   2014041255
[Fic]—dc23   CIP
                                                                AC

Typography by Erin Fitzsimmons
18 19 20 PC/LSCC 10 9 8 7 6 5 4 3
❖
First paperback edition, 2016

For all who struggle in darkness

ONE

They all had their terrors.

The new girl believed that spiders lived in her veins.

Her screams sliced through the darkness, passing through the thin walls of Grace's cell and filling her brain with another's misery to add to the pressures of her own. Grace pulled her pillow tight over her ears, ignoring the feather shafts that poked through the cheap muslin and pricked her skin. On the other side of the wall she could hear Mrs. Clay shifting in her bed, sleep stolen from both patients by the new girl, who hadn't learned yet that screaming didn't bring help.

Quite the opposite.

The ward door crashed open, the metal clanging against the stone wall and bringing cries from all corners as patients rushed away from the noise and whatever fresh hell it brought. The girl screamed louder, ignorantly drawing her tormentors to her. Grace identified the dragging gait of the women's ward administrator as they passed her cell, followed by Dr. Heedson's lighter step.

An unintelligible string of words from the new girl was silenced by a sharp crack. Another slew of syllables that meant nothing brought the harsh snap of a kick. Grace jammed her fingers into her ears until all she could hear was her heart as it pushed blood through her body, no matter how she wished for it to stop. The new girl wasn't learning the efficacy of silence, the art of invisibility. Grace had given up speech long ago. Once the words *no* and *stop* had done nothing, the others refused to come out, their inadequacy making the effort necessary to voice them an equation too easily solved. Grace curled into a protective ball as Croomes and Heedson left the ward, the whimpers of the new girl trailing in their wake. Grace could deafen herself with her own hands and squeeze her eyes shut so tightly that the muscles in her face twitched in agony. But the acuity of her memory was a dark artist at work in her mind, painting pictures without her permission.

She moaned, pressing her forehead into the sharp ridges of her kneecaps. They poked through her threadbare nightgown into her eyelids, sending sparks across her sight, defying her dearest wish— to stop seeing. Faces were the most painful and the most likely to surface in the dark hours of the night. The spider girl's moans had conjured her mother's face in exquisite detail, each finely etched wrinkle apparent as she grimaced under whatever new indignity had been brought upon her, the edges of her lips permanently stained with wine.

Grace turned her head from the apparition, tentatively drawing her fingers from her ears. The ward had returned to silence, but her brain would almost welcome strings of gibberish in the dark, anything to send her thoughts on another avenue than the one it had chosen. It barreled on, resurrecting her father's face twisted into a paroxysm no daughter should ever witness.

Her cry broke the stillness, bringing movement from Mrs. Clay's cell. A soft humming threaded through the air, the only comfort her friend could offer through the walls that separated them. Grace latched on to the notes, following the pattern until she learned it. She joined in soundlessly, the silence she'd enveloped herself with too sacred to break. Her mind toyed with the notes, happy to be busy. She relaxed as it allowed itself to be bent to her whim, tracing the pattern of the lace cloth at home instead of the faces around the table. Grace's hand fell to her belly as she drifted into sleep, cradling the life that grew there.

They all had their terrors, but at least the spiders that lived in the new girl's veins were imaginary. Grace had learned long ago that the true horrors of this world were other people.

TWO

I t was still dark outside when they were called to breakfast by the sound of Miss Marie walking the hall with her cowbell. Even though the clanging noise seemed to perforate her lips and bounce off her teeth while she dressed, Grace preferred Marie's method of waking the inmates as opposed to Croomes's; she was more likely to unlock the door and barge in, hoping to catch some infringement that she could punish.

Grace's nightshirt went over her head, a flimsy shift taking its place. There were no undergarments to bother with; she'd been stripped immediately after her admittance, her corset, chemise, and petticoat whisked from her bare skin to reveal the guilty bulge of her belly while she was given a bath, Croomes scrubbing unnecessarily hard over her tender abdomen.

The lye soap had left burn marks on her skin, some laced with the deep scratches from Croomes. They scabbed over while she lay crying that night, the last of her voice seeping out of her while the Grace Mae who had worn a red velvet dress hours before fell asleep to wake only as Grace. Her family name had been stripped from her along with her clothes. There would be no record of a person with the last name of Mae in Wayburne Lunatic Asylum of Boston. Her father wouldn't stand for it.

As her first days in the asylum had passed, she began to think of her body as a scab that served only to protect the tiny movements inside of her. Eventually she would be able to protect it no more; it would be forced into the world kicking and screaming, wanting nothing more than the protection and silence that the darkness had offered.

She understood babies now, and their reluctance to be born. Once hers was forced into the light and taken away, her body would be of no more use. She could only hope it would be allowed to slough off the world, unnoticed. Until then, she had only to wait.

Grace combed her light hair roughly with her fingers, catching the split ends in the ragged tips of her nails. Miss Marie gave a perfunctory tap on the door before unlocking it, taking one glance at her, and saying, "Well, you're one less I'll have to help dress, at least," and moving on.

Mrs. Clay was in the hall, deftly working her dark hair into a bun with the pin she was allowed to keep even though it was against the rules. Grace stepped over a writhing woman, well aware of her own untidy hair and what price Mrs. Clay paid for her small luxuries. To be an exemplary patient meant she was paraded about when the Board came to inspect the asylum, her hairpin a prize won at a carnival where she was the animal on display.

"Hello, dear." Mrs. Clay smiled, the tiniest of lines around her mouth edging more deeply as she did. "I hope you slept well."

Grace shook her head as Mrs. Clay tucked her hand inside of Grace's elbow to steer her toward the dining hall. Unperturbed by her walking partner's continued silence, Mrs. Clay kept on. "Come and have your food before there's none left for you or the babe."

Food was a constant struggle. The kitchens provided only what they could afford for the day, regardless of how many mouths there were to feed. Many inmates never made it to the tables in time to see food but made the best of it with crumbs and scraps that fell to the floor. If not for the driving necessity of eating for two, Grace would've been happy to be a forgotten one who died quietly in her cell.

But for now her appetite was a pit, and she fed it with the abandon of the desperate. They made for the tables and the food piled there, the press of unwashed bodies on all sides of them breaking any pretense of a line. Mrs. Clay snatched two slices of bread, rolling one into a ball and hiding it in the folds of her skirts for Grace later.

Grace dove for her own piece, slapping away the filthy hands of the girl on her right, who hissed at her. She jammed the bread into her mouth, ignoring the threat.

Grace chewed as quickly as possible, grinding the heavy bread with her teeth and peeling it off the roof of her mouth with her tongue. Even without knives and forks, her training wouldn't allow her to stuff her fingers in her mouth. Across the table from her, Cracked Pat had no such compunctions. Fingers caked with food went into her mouth, along with fistfuls of her hair that she'd managed to pull free from her head. Grace turned away, her delicate stomach turning. Mrs. Clay followed with the concealed bread, and they retreated to a corner by a window rendered nearly opaque by streaks of bird droppings.

"Here then, eat up," Mrs. Clay said, passing the bread tightly in her fist over to Grace. She leaned against the window and watched as Grace devoured it. "Whoever thought the idea of sitting while you ate your food would seem like a treat, eh?"

She was rewarded with a tiny smile, but Grace's thoughts slipped away again, to the days when sweet Alice's angelic face was what she saw across the table, not Cracked Pat's bleeding scalp.

"Fresh bruises on that one." Mrs. Clay jerked her chin toward the door where a patient not much older than Grace was making her unsure way to the table. "Must be the new girl that was screaming about the spiders."

Grace nodded but didn't turn her head to look.

Mrs. Clay reached out and touched her chin, pulling Grace's blue gaze to her own. "Have a care, girl. Show me you'll take an interest in something around you, bleak as it all may be. You can keep your words inside if you want, but I see your eyes looking far off and your arms crossed over your belly. They'll take it from you when it's born and after that I won't see you again even if I should get out of this place. I don't think my kind is welcome at your home address."

Grace's eyebrows drew together.

"It's your hands that give you away," Mrs. Clay said, taking one of Grace's in her own. "All smooth and lily-white, never done a lick of work in your life. I've got the calluses of twenty years at the plow, and every penny earned from it right into the husband's pocket once he shucked me in here."

Grace pulled her hand back to rest on her stomach, and Mrs. Clay's mouth tightened. "You're not the first young woman of your class I've seen in here, heavy around the waist. However that child was got on you, your family will want you back once it's gone. You storing everything up on your insides won't do you no favors once you're past these walls. Find something outside to bring you back to the world, or you may end up here for good."

Grace's eyes returned to the window, where a light morning rain began to seep through the layers of grime, allowing splashes of color from the outside world into the gray interior. Mrs. Clay sighed heavily and rested a hand on her shoulder.

Kind as they were, Mrs. Clay's words were lost on Grace. She knew the baby would be born, and with its exit would come her reentry into the world she'd known. They would sew her back into her red velvet dress she'd arrived in. Her father's black lacquered carriage would gather her after hours, the rolling wheels taking her back home to her own room, her own bed. Her own terrors.

She had already decided she was never leaving.

THREE

"Water treatment for you today?" Mrs. Clay asked, as they strolled arm in arm through the halls, stepping over inert bodies.

"For you today? For you today?" Cracked Pat kept pace alongside them, echoing Mrs. Clay's words. Grace nodded as Cracked Pat reached up and plucked at Grace's blond hair, which Mrs. Clay had neatly tucked into a bun using her pin.

"There's the little lady," Croomes's voice bellowed down the stony hall, as she waddled toward them. "Keeping time with the farmer's wife, a fine pair of friends they are. I'm sure the two of you are plotting rather a nice picnic. Perhaps you'll go for an afternoon ride on your matching ponies afterward? In the meantime it's my clock you're on, and it says you're next for your treatment." Croomes made a mock bow.

"I'll remind you that I am not a farmer's wife," Mrs. Clay said, her voice cold.

"That a fact?" Croomes asked.

"It is," Mrs. Clay said. "My husband divorced me soon after shuttling me in here. One word from him and the signature of a judge and I'm insane. My lands became his, the judge's sister his wife, my children now hers."

"Sad story you got there," Croomes said.

"I am not a farmer's wife. If you call me that again, they'll have good reason to put me in solitary and you'll be missing an eye."

Croomes watched Mrs. Clay for a moment, her jaw grinding her teeth together. "I've got a fine list of things I'd like to call you. How about I try some of those?"

"I am not a farmer's wife," Mrs. Clay repeated.

"All right then, get an idea stuck in there much, do you?" Croomes said. She gave Grace a push on the backside to move her along, but Grace noticed that she never turned her back on Mrs. Clay. Another small smile played on the edge of Grace's lips and she squelched it quickly. It was the little battles that got them through their days. All in preparation for the bigger ones to come.

To kill yourself in an asylum is a thing easily done.

Plenty who wished to stay alive found themselves dying of neglect, while those who prayed for death woke each morning to the sun's rays filtered through greasy windows. Grace had thought through her options more than once; to slide beneath the freezing waters during a treatment while the attendant's back was turned or to simply cease eating.

But Grace had sat through many sermons by her father's side, heard about the perils of hell and the fiery brimstone that surely awaited her if she took her own life. She doubted that hell was hot and sulfuric. Instead, she imagined it was comfortable and smelled like her own bedroom. If fear kept her from ending herself, she'd be neatly deposited back between those sheets, as confining as any chains. An ethereal hell or the one she'd already lived through were her options. Croomes twisted Grace's wrist, bringing her thoughts back to the body she was stuck in for the moment.

"My, my, but you do walk pretty," Croomes said. "Not a bone out of place on you. Forget balancing the book, I bet we could put a whole bookcase on your head, couldn't we? You look like a picture in one of them lady's magazines, except for that bit." Croomes flicked Grace's pregnant belly as they turned the corner to the baths. "Nothing much ladylike about that, is there?"

Grace had buried the urge to speak so deeply that most words from others meant nothing, but Croomes's voice always crept through the safe fog she'd veiled her mind in, demanding to be heard. Grace set her jaw and went to a tub already half-filled with freezing water. Miss Marie was dumping buckets over another patient, but moved to help Grace take off her shift.

Marie offered her a hand as she stepped over the porcelain rim, and Grace took it, leaning heavily on the girl's arm as she lowered herself into the frigid water. Though she'd forsaken sound, she couldn't stop her teeth from chattering.

"Right then, help her on into the tub. Let's see if we can find some scented soaps while we're at it," Croomes said, crossing her arms. "'Course, Marie here would be wanting to make sure you get through everything safely. Did she tell you she's taking your baby?"

Grace's head jerked at the words and her wide eyes met Marie's, who flushed and turned to hiss at Croomes.

"What'd you have to go and do that for? No need to upset the girl."

Croomes produced a half-smoked cigarette from her pocket, struck a match on the stool, and lit what was left of it. "You going to pour it over her head, or am I?"

"I will," Marie said, fetching her bucket from the other tub, where the patient's head lolled to the side, lips blue. "Though I don't know as I see much of the point of it."

"And where's your medical degree, I'll ask you? Heedson says it's too much heat in the brain that makes them crazy, and so we douse 'em."

"If that's the case, this girl here should be talking normal as you or me right now. She's as cold as the dead."

Croomes blew smoke out of her nose and watched as Marie

poured the first bucketful over Grace's head, the water loosening the pale bun and turning it into dark streaks that clung to her skin. "This one's as cold as the water she's sitting in, down past her bones and into her soul. Nothing wrong with her brain. It's her heart that's got no life in it."

Grace sat, letting the water numb her skin and apathy numb her ears as Croomes rose from her stool. "I've got Cracked Pat to tend to. Never comes to her treatments without my special encouragement."

"I'll finish here," Marie said as Croomes walked past Grace's tub. "No need for you to trouble yourself."

"No trouble," Croomes said, digging her fingers into Grace's bun and pulling out the pin that held it in place, sending the loose hair cascading down her shoulders. "I'll make sure this gets to its rightful owner," Croomes said, lifting a hank of Grace's dripping hair and grinding her cigarette out on the pale expanse of her neck.

Words boiled in Grace's stomach as she clenched down on the pain, her teeth grinding together to keep from rewarding Croomes's cruelty by crying out. Marie gasped but cut it short at a glare from Croomes. "Anybody hears about that, I'll know who did the talking, won't I?"

The only warmth left in Grace's body slid down her face in the form of tears, which Marie brushed away with her callused fingers once Croomes's footsteps had receded down the hall. "I'm sorry about that, miss, really I am. Way I look at it, most of you've got big enough problems without the likes of Croomes on your tails all the time."

Marie fell silent, her gaze cutting to the door and the other, unconscious patient floating in her freezing water. "I'll just do one more bucket and leave off the rest, no one needs to know. Besides, a bit of the cold might feel good on that burn."

The frigid water cascaded over Grace's features once more, the icy fingers digging into the singed pink flesh of her neck where Croomes had burned her. Numbness crept in, a heavy weight that began in her legs and moved up her torso. She rested her head against the rim of the tub, cramped muscles crying out as she did.

Marie pulled up a stool next to her and began running her fingers through Grace's hair to untangle the wet ends. "You do a fine enough job of keeping yourself clean," she said. "But without no brush I'm sure it's difficult."

Grace felt the slightest relaxation spreading through her shoulders as Marie finger combed her hair. "I'm sorry about the other thing too, miss," she said after a while. "I don't think there's no reason to tell you I'll be the one taking your baby from you. Croomes did that just to satisfy the meanness in her.

"My Andrew—that's my husband, see—he's always been wanting a wee one and I . . . well, I guess there weren't such a thing in the cards for me. My own ma says we've not been married all that long, and you can't hurry nature, but I got this feeling inside of me that I can't shake. Like an emptiness where nothing's ever gonna grow. I tried to say so to my ma and she said I'd best keep that talk to myself if I don't want to end up in—"

Marie stopped short, her fingers pausing for a moment. "Well . . . I guess it's no secret that some of you are just as sane as me and maybe that works the other way around too, sometimes."

Her fingers picked up their work, sliding freely through Grace's hair. "So when you came in here with your belly, I had a talk with Heedson and it was decided upon. I told my husband that our prayers had been answered, and he'd best be sleeping in another room for the time being just to be careful, and . . . I suppose it's a horrible thing, miss, but I've been padding my skirts so that my waist matches your own, and I'll be doing it right up until—"

Marie's words stopped and Grace stared forward, giving no indication that she'd heard any of it.

"Aye, well," Marie said. "If you want to hate me for it, you can and that's your choice. I can't say as I feel like it's a good thing to do, but I promise I'll give your babe a good home, and it'll be loved as if it were my own."

The numbness had spread to Grace's thighs and midsection, but she could still feel the kick inside of her. Slowly she reached up, entwining her freezing fingers with Marie's and bringing them down into the cold water. Marie gasped at the shock, but then Grace cupped the nurse's hand on the swell of her belly to feel a kick so strong it sent ripples to the sides of the tub.

They held hands under the water. Their cold fingers sheltered the tiny life, their combined tears the only heat in the room.

FOUR

When Grace woke in the morning her hair was frozen to the floor. Croomes had returned to the baths to find Marie combing it rather than administering treatments. Grace had been dragged to her room, her only dinner a day-old piece of bread tossed through the door before it was locked again. Grace had fallen asleep, her still-dripping hair hanging over the edge of her bed. The night temperatures froze them in place, and she had to pull herself free at sunrise, leaving her hair torn at the ends.

She was inspecting the unevenness when Croomes burst into her room. "That's a downright shame," the nurse said, rubbing her shoe over the ends left behind on the stones. "You've got a fancy dinner tonight and here you've left most of your hair on the floor."

Accustomed to the teasing, Grace kept her face blank.

"No, girl," Croomes went on. "I'm not having a go at you. Heedson gave me a list of what he claims is the 'well-mannered ones,' and I've got to get you looking respectable. You get a new dress and everything. I think you'll even get to have some silverware. Make sure you hold your fork right, now. And no elbows on the table." Croomes laughed at her own joke and slapped Grace's backside on her way out.

"You too, farmer's—" Croomes's voice broke off in the hallway as she reconsidered. "Mrs. Clay," she finished. "You're on display often enough to know the drill. God knows how Heedson's deemed you respectable, the way you go about swearing to tear the eyes out of God-fearing folk."

"If you fear God, that's more to do with your actions than mine," Mrs. Clay said.

Croomes huffed and her footsteps receded down the hallway before Mrs. Clay appeared at Grace's door. "I tried to squirrel away a bite for you last night, but they were watching me pretty close," she said.

Mrs. Clay pulled the younger girl's hand into the crook of her own elbow. "So what's this dinner, do you think?" she asked, knowing full well that there would be no answer. "I don't see any room for kindness in this place, but let's put a good face on it and see, shall we?"

There was silverware. Grace was unprepared for how much it set her back to see a table set properly, and she stood still in the doorway for a moment before entering. Mrs. Clay gave her a slight push to get her into the dining room, followed by two other women she didn't know, faces pink from fresh scrubbings and wet buns pulled tightly back from clean scalps. Already seated were three male patients, who rose when the women entered, although one of them lagged slightly behind the others, not accustomed to the tradition.

"Mr. Baltingham, Mr. Crow," Mrs. Clay said congenially, nodding toward them before she sat down. Grace followed her cue, lowering her eyes when the men glanced toward her and staring at the plate setting in front of her. It was heavy and awkward, nothing like the slight china she'd had at home, but it meant that there would be real food to eat, not only bread to grab and run with.

"I'm sorry, I don't believe we've met," Mrs. Clay said to the third man, who reddened under her attention. "It seems we're allowed to pretend to be civilized this evening. You may as well tell me your name."

"Moore, ma'am," he said.

"Hello then, Mr. Moore," she said. "I am Mrs. Clay and these ladies are Miss Holstein, Mrs. Ubry, and . . ." Her hand fluttered to Grace's shoulder for one second. "I'm sorry, I don't know our young friend's name."

It pulsed in Grace's throat for one second, the syllable that meant her. Yet it remained halfway up, lodged like a chunk of her supper from the evening before.

There were murmured hellos around the table, and then Mr. Baltingham cleared his throat. "What's this about, then? Anybody know?"

"I believe you're all going to be used like I am, shining examples of—" Mrs. Clay began, when the dining room door blew open and Dr. Heedson came in, a half-empty wineglass in hand and one of the cooks at his heels with a tray of ham.

Heedson took his seat at the head of the table, to Grace's right. "Looks like you're all here, then," he said.

The cook moved between Mrs. Clay and Grace to set the ham-laden platter on the table, and the wafting scent filled Grace's mouth with saliva. In her belly, the baby awakened and kicked hard, its tiny foot striking the edge of the table.

"I've handled the introductions, Dr. Heedson," Mrs. Clay began.

"I believe I'll do my own version, nonetheless," Heedson said, unfolding his napkin into his lap before pointing at the patients in turn. "Moore here is a syphilitic; Crow went after his wife with a pitchfork after catching her in the haymow with his brother— which hardly makes him crazy, to my mind. Baltingham's an alcoholic, Ubry's a nymphomaniac, Holstein insists that her menstrual blood is made of demons, Mrs. Clay is a cast-off wife, and little Grace here is an aristocrat of loose morals."

"So much for a pretense of civility," Mr. Baltingham muttered.

Mrs. Clay's fingers found Grace's wrist. "Hello, Grace," she said, her voice quiet and kind under the mutterings of the other patients. A shy smile swept Grace's pale features.

"All's I said was that my monthlies hurt like the devil," Miss Holstein said, her napkin twisted tight in her hands. "And my stepfather takes me to a judge—"

"And a hundred years ago you'd have been burned at the stake," Heedson said, cutting her off, as the cook brought out a fresh glass of wine and set it before him. "So shut your yap."

"And if we could please not speak of such things at the table," Mr. Baltingham added.

"Hardly a shocking thing that women menstruate, I suppose. We're not fighting for our food or being kicked at the moment. I'm happy to talk about it," Mr. Moore said.

Heedson continued. "If I may go on—I'm confident that the group of you here are intelligent enough to understand what I'm about this evening."

He snapped his fingers and more of the kitchen staff appeared, bringing with them food that the patients had not seen or smelled in a long time. Green beans, potatoes, gravy, warm bread, and a tray of real butter were spread before them.

"I want you all to understand one thing first and foremost,"

21

Heedson went on. "I'm not a bad man. I'm a man of limited capabilities in a bad situation. This hospital holds hundreds of patients, many beyond any hope of recuperation. Old methods of bleeding and starvation are not means of a cure, but rather methods of weakening the patients so as to make them more manageable for the staff."

"Well, cheers to him who's not the bad man, then," Mrs. Ubry said, raising her water glass in a mock salute.

"This hospital is unmanageable," Heedson said as if she hadn't spoken. "Many of Boston's unwanted end up here; the difficult, the slow, the savage, and the truly insane all sharing space, and myself given the task of keeping the peace."

"Can we eat?" Miss Holstein asked.

"When I'm finished speaking."

"He's cutting us a deal, missy," Mr. Moore said. "There's something he wants from us. And once we agree to it, we get to eat what's been put in front of our eyes, though our bellies will be yelling louder than his words here in a minute or two."

"As I suspected," Mrs. Clay said.

Heedson polished off his wine, leaning across Grace and toward Mrs. Clay. Grace shrank away from his shoulder and the fumes rolling from his mouth.

"What I need is simple. Mrs. Clay and the group of you here are the sanest I've got. You're the cleanest. You speak tolerably well and you can be reasoned with."

"'Cept for Grace down there," Mrs. Ubry chirped up. "She don't speak none."

Heedson turned to look at Grace, his elbow touching hers. She pulled it away quickly, skin crawling where it had touched his. The glassy tint of his eyes was too familiar, and she leaned back in her chair as he spoke, the sweetness of his wined breath choking her as he followed her movements.

"Ah, but our Grace here is such a sight. Don't you think, gentlemen?"

Heedson rose somewhat unsteadily from his chair, running his hand up her arm as he moved behind her. "True, she doesn't speak, but when the Board comes to inspect this place you'll tell them what they want to hear, each of you with a sad story about your lives and how you've found refuge here. A new family, a home when you thought you'd lost anything of the sort."

Grace's hands were in her lap, pinching each other in their effort to keep still while Heedson ran his hand up her arm, to her neck, his thumb brushing over the burn Croomes had given her. Pausing. Touching it again, with the slightest bit of pressure this time.

"Grace won't tell her story, but she hardly has to, does she? It's right here in the wideness of her eyes, the innocence of her expression, and the bulge of her belly." His hands cupped either side of her neck, and Grace's breathing came in short gasps, even those tiny bits of air reeking of wine and his cologne.

"Dr. Heedson," Mrs. Clay said. "I think you would do well to take your hands off the girl."

"She inspires protection, doesn't she?" Heedson leered toward Mrs. Clay, losing his balance slightly and bracing himself against the table with one hand. "The Board will take one look at her and say to themselves, 'What's the world to do with poor little birds like this one? Surely she's better off here than in the streets.'"

The hand still covering her burn tightened and Heedson leaned against Grace's back, his stomach pushing against her. "Someone knew well enough what to do with you, didn't he, little chickadee?" Heedson whispered in her ear.

The smell of him, the maleness surrounding her, the wine-soaked words in her ear flowed through Grace, filling the gaping hole of herself that she had trained to become only a shell, a carrier for the life within. Horror filled the chasm that had been, and every word, every utterance, every time she had stamped down her own name or bit back a cry of pain came pouring out in an incoherent shriek as she grabbed her fork, slamming it through the web between his thumb and forefinger, straight down into the table below.

FIVE

Grace expected blood, but there was none. Whatever word she had meant to shriek had scraped the inside of her throat, and every breath she drew burned like fire creeping through the divots left behind. She counted two dragging breaths before Heedson started screaming. The others pushed away from the table, Mrs. Ubry going over in her chair and upending her water glass. Holstein had pulled out her bun and was wrapping her hair around her face in an effort to hide. Shocked into stillness, Grace could only stare as Heedson jerked the fork free from his impaled hand, blood finally flowing between his fingers.

Mrs. Clay was at her side, urging her from her chair while keeping a wary eye on Heedson. "Dear . . . Grace . . . ," she was saying, the name still unfamiliar on her tongue. "Come along now, you've had a shock."

Mrs. Clay had her by the elbow when Heedson backhanded Grace hard enough to send both women to the floor in a pile of skirts. Her belly struck first and Grace cried out as the impact rolled through her body, the baby kicking in feeble protest.

"You little bitch . . ." Heedson lunged for Grace, yanking her to her feet. Two more practiced swipes of his hand sent her head ricocheting back and forth, his blood spattering across her cheeks, her hands still protectively clutching her belly.

Mr. Baltingham grabbed Grace from behind, backpedaling her out of Heedson's reach, while Mrs. Clay wrapped her arms around the doctor's knees to stop him from following. Croomes burst in from the hallway, skidding to a halt at the sight.

"Christ in heaven, what's happened here?"

Heedson yanked a napkin from the table and began wrapping it around his hand. "Grace is what happened here, Mrs. Croomes. It appears I made a mistake when compiling the list of those I deemed reasonably sane."

"Or maybe two," Mr. Crow added while he calmly filled his plate, gesturing to where Holstein lay, her face wrapped in her own hair.

Marie appeared behind Croomes, red and out of breath. "I heard the fuss . . . ," she began, then saw the blood-spattered table. "What on earth?"

"Miss High and Mighty has gone and stabbed Heedson," Croomes said.

"That's nonsense," Marie argued. "She's not got a violent bone in her—"

Grace's newfound voice burst forth again, feral and wordless as she bucked in Baltingham's arms. Though he meant only to steady her, he'd not released his grip and she fought against him. He let her go and she slid to the ground, wrapping her arms around her midsection.

"Get her up," Heedson said, tucking the ends of the napkin into a makeshift bandage. "Croomes, Marie, take this girl down to the laundry and sheet wrap her. She is a harm to herself and others."

"Dr. Heedson, please," Mrs. Clay said, pulling herself into a chair. "Send her to the infirmary. She's had a fall and in her condition—"

"Been bashed a bit about the face too," Mr. Crow added around a mouthful of ham. "Though that's not got much to do with the fall."

"I'm the one who needs a doctor," Heedson screamed, brandishing his hand as he did. "She's insane. She'll be treated as such. Croomes." He snapped his fingers and the nurse was happy to comply, peeling one of Grace's arms away from her midsection while Marie wrestled with the other.

Grace moaned, no longer able to keep sounds inside of her now that pain was filling her core and pushing everything outward. Croomes bent her arm awkwardly at the elbow and forced her to her feet. Marie was on her other side, her grasp not unkind but tight enough to be sure she wouldn't slip free.

"Grace . . . ," Mrs. Clay said, fingers brushing Grace's skirt as she was led from the room.

"Knew there was fight in you," Croomes said as she propelled Grace to the laundry, her feet giving out underneath her as another wave of pain racked her torso. "No point tussling with us, missy. You done wrong and you're gonna pay.

"You," Croomes snapped at the young girl working at the mangler. "We need us some sheets for a wrapping."

The girl bobbed her head automatically. "Will you be wanting hot or cold, mum?"

"Oh, I think this one here is a rather hot little dish herself. Why not treat like with like? You've got some fresh on the steamer, I see. Let's put them to good use."

The girl's eyes went wide. "Oh no, mum. Those just now went through, they're almost too hot to touch, let alone wrap a body in."

"Nonsense," Croomes spat. "Is it a punishment, or ain't it?" She tore the sheet from the steamer, hardly able to hold it for more than a second before it fluttered to the ground. "It'll do nicely. Hand me a pair of gloves, girl. Marie, strip the patient and hold her arms down. I imagine she'll kick up a bit of a fuss once I start the job."

Grace's new dress was yanked over her head, the undergarments she'd been allowed for the evening rudely pulled off. Her hands snaked after them into the air, modesty still a convention she clung to. Instead, her hands met Marie's midgrab.

"I'm sorry, girl. Truly, I am. But I have a job, and it's the job I do." Then Grace's wrists were pinned to the cold floor above her head and an envelope of heat closed around her feet.

She kicked out instinctively, her heel hooking the sheet and sending it arcing over Croomes's face before the woman could react. The nurse snagged her foot and turned her ankle inward until Grace quieted and the wrapping began.

Croomes spared her not an inch, and her practiced hands bound Grace's legs together so tightly that her kneecaps dug against each other while the heat pressed in. Steam rose from the sheet as Croomes worked, covering Grace up to her belly before calling for another sheet, hot from the steamer.

Sweat sprang from every pore, rolling down her face as her body tried desperately to shed heat anywhere it could. A fresh sheet, even hotter than the one before, draped over her belly and was pulled ruthlessly tight against the flushed skin. Marie moved Grace's arms to her sides, and they too were pinned to her ribs. Croomes worked toward her neck, wrapping Grace's hair, now wet with sweat, into the sheet. Fingers worked between the folds near her mouth, pulling apart an opening for her to breathe through.

"It's a fine mess you've got yourself in, little lady," Croomes said. "You've had better treatment than most up till now, but stabbing a man will rouse his temper."

The gas lamps were extinguished, one by one, the pale haloes of light disappearing from her shrouded eyes as the women's voices receded. The darkness was complete when the first contraction came. The shock of it squeezed the first word she'd uttered in a long while past her lips as the excruciating wave rippled through her.

"No."

I'm going to die.

She had denied language for so long, shutting down not only her tongue but her mind as well so that no thoughts could form. Her life had become a fog, one that would end soon if she found a way, yet as she writhed on the edge of true madness, her brain rejected the safety she'd made for herself, patching together a sentence to shock her into action.

I'm going to die.

The voice of her own thought was oddly familiar, like seeing an old friend on the street after some time apart. Grace stilled, listening to her consciousness, and found herself rebelling against the conclusion it had come to.

I'm going to die, and my baby with me.

Grace screamed in agony, against fate and futility, against the life she should have lived versus the one she'd been delivered into. Her cries rolled down the darkened hallways, only to dissipate before reaching anyone's ears.

SIX

When they pulled the sheets from her, the shock of the cool air was almost painful. Grace heard Mrs. Clay saying her name, but she could only moan. Her hands fell away from her sides and her fingers went instinctively to her belly, digging into the loose skin that hung there.

"Grace," Mrs. Clay said. "Can you hear me?"

She nodded, fingertips still buried deeply in her malleable belly. "B-b—" She tried to speak, but the word she needed most wouldn't come.

Mrs. Clay pulled her hands into her own. "The baby's lost, dear, I'm so sorry. Listen to me—listen!" she said, clamping Grace's fingers together as the girl's mouth contorted into a soundless cry. "Heedson has to make sure you're going to be all right after losing

31

the baby. I've seen a few women on the farms get sick after, and I can tell you it's not the way you want to go."

Grace barely nodded, her dilated pupils fixed firmly on Mrs. Clay's. "I . . ."

"You're doing brilliantly, dear," Mrs. Clay encouraged her, wiping cold sweat from her brow. "To hear your voice is a lovely thing. Keep trying. You what?"

Heedson came through the door, rolling his shirtsleeves up to his elbows. Grace cried out, whatever hard-earned word she'd been trying to form lost entirely as she scraped the sheets into a pile to cover her nakedness.

"Spare me, girl," he said. "My only interest in you now is seeing that you don't die on my watch. Your father would have my head."

"A fine thought," Mrs. Clay said through clenched teeth. "After what she's been through on your orders."

Croomes and Marie filed into the room behind him. Marie's eyes were swollen from crying, and she wiped them with her apron as she set instruments on the table next to the bed, their metal edges banging against each other.

"What—" Grace's panicked eyes shot toward the noise.

"Ah, talking now, are you?" Croomes asked. She pulled Grace's wrists above her head and pinned her arms back in a meaty grip. "You'd best sit quiet while the doctor looks after your welfare. I'm happy to put you back in the sheets."

Mrs. Clay cradled Grace's face in her hands. "Listen to me, Grace. This needs to happen. You can die if you're not looked after properly."

"Enough," Heedson said. "Grace, the less you squirm, the quicker I can be," he said as he worked a hand between her knees. She lashed out instinctively, the sheet sailing with her movements as she kicked. Marie yelped and slipped sideways, sending the instrument tray to the ground amid a clattering of metal. Croomes's grip bit down on her wrists, and Grace's hands tingled as the nerves sang, but she didn't stop fighting. Her blood-smeared feet scissored in the air, striking the doctor's hands and knocking Mrs. Clay aside.

"God damn it," Heedson yelled. "Have it your way, then, idiot girl. Let her go, Croomes. Let her rot from the inside out if that's what she wants."

The second the pressure released her wrists Grace lunged for the doctor, humiliation fueling her past the bounds of energy. She dove for a metal instrument and lashed it across his face in a vicious arc, sending his spectacles flying.

Then Croomes was on her, throwing her to the ground and grinding her face against the cold rock as if she would make flour out of her cheeks. Mrs. Clay struggled to her knees, picking her way over strewn instruments to Grace's side.

"Grace," she whispered. "What have you done?"

"What's she done?" Heedson said, his voice towering over the women huddled on the ground. "She's earned herself a place in the cellar."

"Oooh." Croomes leaned over to crow in Grace's ear. "That'll be a treat. Not quite the European tour, but a sight you've not seen yet, nonetheless."

"Dr. Heedson, please." Mrs. Clay struggled to her feet. "In her state . . . it'll kill her."

Heedson wiped the blood from his cheek, fingering his swelling lower lip. "The Board is coming for inspection tomorrow, Mrs. Clay. I've been attacked by a demented patient who's been given every chance to show that she can behave better. One look at this exhausted, bleeding slip of a girl and they'll have my certificate. She's going with the worst, down to the cellar, where the Board won't think to look for patients."

Grace lay flat on the floor, all of her fire spent on the attack. Croomes didn't bother to help her to her feet, simply dragged her into the hall. Grace watched dispassionately as her toes trailed through her own blood and the sound of Mrs. Clay's crying dissipated in the dark.

"Nobody's gonna look after the welfare of people in a place where ain't no person able to live," Croomes said, when they came to the cellar door. "You done sealed your fate. He don't care who your daddy is now."

The door yawned open with a creak, its black shadow creeping over Grace. She was a chasm, her baby gone, her revenge spent. Croomes would take her to the darkness and it would match her insides. She would blend with it, absorbed into nothing.

"Good-bye then, highfalutin lady," Croomes said. She took Grace's wrists again, and they passed into the blackness.

SEVEN

There was a voice in the darkness. It slipped through the shadows to find her ears.

"Get up, love. Get up or the rains will kill you."

Grace opened her mouth and cold water flowed in. It slipped over her parched tongue, leaving behind a gritty aftertaste. She gagged, the convulsion pulling her into a sitting position as she struggled for air, water pooling around her.

"That's something, anyway," the voice continued. "I've listened to more than a few unconscious drown slow, not even knowing they're dying. The rains slip through the walls down here and the reaper comes quiet with them."

Grace's hands sank into the floor, mud squeezing between her fingers as she pushed herself against the wet stone walls, panicked breaths wheezing into the pitch-black.

"It's all right, it's all right," the voice said again, low and smooth. "I'm not going to hurt you. Even if I should want to, there's bars between us, love, and more than that. My conscience is stronger than they, and you've got the smell of young flesh about you."

In the darkness all she could tell was that his voice came from the right. She pushed herself away from it, her feet digging into the muck for traction.

"Shhhh, shhhh," her fellow prisoner went on. "Don't get yourself out of sorts. Lose your breath and you're likely to go over into the wet again. Calm yourself. Sit still and let me learn from the air you've brought with you."

Shivering and streaked with mud, Grace found the corner of her cell. Pressing herself against it until her shoulder blades dug into the rock, she heard a deep breath from his direction, then silence. Seconds later, an exhalation, followed by another audible intake.

"Now then." His voice reached for her again across the black, drawing her head up from her chest, where it had begun to sag in weariness. "Yours is a story whose events happen more often than are told. Tales like these belong to the black, do they not? Where they can't be seen or heard. But I can smell it out quick like the devil.

"You've got the smell of man on you, faded but there, a scent still strong enough to tell that it matches your own, like to like. Fresh blood—I imagine even you can smell that, all coppery in the back of your throat—but I can say where it's come from and know the harm done to you. And the babe . . ."

Another sniff, this one soft and delicate.

"Gone to the permanent darkness now. Sorry, love."

A fought-for breath stuck in her chest, and Grace forced it outward, then another in, to keep herself going. Her arms crossed in front of her empty belly, their duty failed, nothing left to protect. A sob stuck in her throat, lodging itself halfway on its path to the dank air.

"There's the blood of another on you, though. I smell a spatter or two, underneath your own. You didn't come down here without a fight, did you? And who was your tormenter?" An inhalation, this one drawn deep inside of him as if his lungs were digesting the air.

"Ahhhh . . . Heedson, you are a vile thing."

Grace rested her head against the stone wall, letting the cool fingers of the stone sink into her temple as his words flowed over her, drawing her into a deep calm.

"There's your voice, love. It's small and cold, tucked down under all else. I can smell it, like a river stone it is. Smoothed out and polished into a nothing it's jammed down under something else . . . something hot. There's a touch of brimstone in you, there is. And it's putting up the smoke that's got your voice trapped underneath.

"And the smoke and the—" Another sniff. "The sweat. Your anger sweated you out. It's gone and opened up all your pores, and I can smell that dainty lavender soap you used to use, though I imagine it was a good long while ago.

"What a shock you've had. Taken from that world into this. You used to move about in light and lavender, with the laughter pouring from you, and now it's all blood and darkness, with your throat closed so tight your own breath is choking you."

The truth of his words wrapped around her, and Grace gasped for air, letting it out in a deep rush as if to release the smoke he spoke of and give her voice freedom.

"That's right, keep doing it. The in and the out of the air. Your lungs know the job, know it well enough to do it without being told, and likely won't stop even if you want them to. You're alive, girl. And it's been a good long while since I've had an interesting person in the darkness with me. And you'll stay alive, for Falsteed is not about to let those that have the brimstone in them die while he's near. No, not me."

There was a scraping noise of wood against rock and something nudged against her foot in the filth. "Grab the end of that, and feel about on the wall in the corner. There's a bit of rock that sticks out just enough to rest the board against. I'll put the other end on my knees and take the weight of you on myself, for the night. You've got to get out of the muck, your lower parts anyway. There's dirt and filth ankle-deep everywhere down here. The last fellow that had that cell was none too gracious about using his bucket. That's not only mud you're wallowing in."

Grace felt around for the board poking at her toes and found the ridge in the wall easily. She felt the other end of the board lift along with her as she put it in place, rain trickling over her fingers. Her hands came away with the sweet smell of outdoors, only slightly fouled by the cellar walls. She pressed her hands against her face, the rainwater cooling her swollen eyes.

She sat on her makeshift bench and felt it settle on Falsteed's end as he adjusted for taking her weight on his knees. Grace curled into the corner of her cold darkness, resting against the wall and feeling the rain seep through the rocks. Her eyelids sank and she felt her jaw fall slack right before sleep brought the darkness from outside into her mind.

As she settled into its comfortable grip she heard Falsteed's voice once more. "Dear child, do you even know all the rage that is inside you?"

EIGHT

Whether her eyes were open or closed, she could not tell. Sleep and reality melted together until she saw a streak of light in the darkness, a cascade of blond hair that flowed over a white linen pillowcase leading to a pair of bright blue eyes. Grace's memory provided the details, down to the pattern of broken blood vessels in the whites of her little sister's eyes, red from crying.

"Alice," Grace said, the name slipping through the slit between her teeth. "Alice. You can't be here. You don't belong in the darkness."

Her sister smiled, the pearly white of her childish teeth bright against the pinkness of her lips. But it was Falsteed's baritone that came from her mouth, bringing with it a swirl of black that pulled her to consciousness.

"Wake up, love. Reed's brought you clean clothing. Heedson fancies that Reed's our jailer, and though he may collect an asylum paycheck, I've given him something more than money in the past. You can trust him."

A flicker of light caused her to cover her eyes, the anonymity of the dark lost.

"S'all right, then, girl." A new voice came from behind the lantern. "I've not come to look upon ya. Come and take the clothes I've snatched up, and you can toss the old once yer decent."

Grace stretched her legs hesitantly, feet sinking ankle-deep into muck before finding the stone beneath. She heard Falsteed shift in the cell next to hers as her weight came off the board, both knees popping audibly. A hand beckoned to her from behind the lantern, and she approached cautiously, eyes still shaded against the light.

"C'mere then, and back to the shadows with you for the dressing part."

Grace's fingers closed over the clothing, the dryness of the fabric drawing a sigh from her as she took it. Back to the darkness of the corner, she let the filthy sheet fall away, wadding it into a pile at her feet. The clean clothes fell over her shoulders, fitting awkwardly around the new laxness of her belly, empty without the life she'd come to know.

"Step out into Reed's light, love," Falsteed's voice directed her from his cell. "Let me see your color."

Grace did so, though Falsteed remained anonymous in the dark, light flickering off the iron bars that separated them. "Well enough, then," he grunted. "You've not got a fever. Reed, take the filthy clothes out and come back with a stool, if you can pilfer one. I don't think a bite of food would come amiss to the girl, either."

"Grace," she said, her name bubbling up from her mouth into the dimly cast rays of Reed's light. She spoke toward Falsteed's voice, her own stretching out wearily toward his to bridge the gap. "My name is Grace."

"Hello, Grace," Falsteed said, a smile evident in the twist of his words. "And welcome to my asylum."

Silence hung in the air while she reasserted her grip on the smoothly polished river rock that he had called her voice. She found it, the words tripping over it roughly as they scratched their way upward. "Your asylum?"

"Yes, love. You'll find that Reed here keeps me well apprised of the comings and goings above our heads, the matters that happen in the light. Meanwhile, I pull little strings like a cunning spider and wait for the throbs to come back and let me know what's about. And speaking of what's about, Reed, how goes the convalescent in the men's ward?"

"Still not so much of a flicker of his eyelids, sir."

"And there was no fall, no injury to the head?"

"Not that anyone knows."

"Next time you get a chance, bring me a clipping of his hair. I'll give it a whiff. If something's gone amiss inside his skull, that'll tell me all I need to know."

"Yes, sir. And I've brought you the pillowcase of the newest, a girl what claims there's spiders in her blood."

"Give it here, then." Falsteed's hand appeared between the bars, and Reed handed over the linen, his features briefly in the light. Reed wasn't much older than Grace, but his face was already lined with the weight of life. The sound of Falsteed breathing deeply filled the air, and Grace listened intently for his recommendation, intrigued after he'd learned so much from her scents.

The linen sailed back through the dark, landing neatly into the waiting hands of Reed. "What do you think, Dr. Falsteed? Any hope for her?"

"That one is lost. She not only claims her veins are full of spiders but truly believes it. And once we are convinced of something, no matter how ludicrous, it becomes a fact. If you cut her she'd see eight-legged creatures pour forth rather than a crimson tide, and who is to say that we are only all agreeing on the same perception when we say it is blood, and not arachnids, moving through us?"

"I'm afraid I don't follow, sir."

"Do you believe in God, Reed?"

"Yes, I do. And our Lord and Savior, Jesus Christ."

"As I said, you are convinced and so it is fact. When in reality, I am your savior, the one who cut the abomination from your side and gave your life back, to live and to love and to make your children, is that not true?"

In the meager light from his lantern, Grace could see Reed's cheek muscles jumping as his teeth gritted. "You did, sir, saved my life and rightly so. Yet you are not the son of God."

"Unless I believed myself to be so, and then it would be so. To me, at any rate."

"I'm not sure what you're wanting me to say, sir."

"Say that you'll bring Grace a stool, and be on your way. I've taxed you enough for the day. And when you send for Dr. Thornhollow, ask that he may stop and pass the time with me as he goes about his bloody business."

"Dr. Thornhollow, sir? The surgeon over at Mayfaire?"

"Yes, Reed. We've come to that time again. Grace's arrival says the Board is coming. We've a new patient whose screams smell of delirium and by the scent of Heedson's blood he's nigh in a panic. He'll call for Thornhollow. He'll call for the one that wields the knife."

NINE

The girl with spiders for blood came into the cellar like a typhoon, her screams breaking the companionable silence that Falsteed and Grace had established. In her own panic, Grace moved the low milking stool Reed had brought her from the stables next to Falsteed's cell, her hand groping for his in the darkness. The iron bars pressed cold against her shoulder, and she was about to call for him when she felt his dry, warm hands close over hers.

"Needing some support from the sane, love?" His voice was almost next to her ear, but she didn't shy away from it.

"Do you call yourself sane?"

He chuckled, a sound of true mirth that flowed low under the high-pitched screams of the spider girl.

"I do. I'd put the same label on yourself, though I sense you'd deny it."

Her hand pulsed in his, and he squeezed her back. "Do I have a right to claim sanity?" she asked, her voice still hoarse from disuse. "I'm cursed with a perfect recollection of all things and have seen things no one should—even once. To have it shown to me again and again, eyes open or shut, would truly make one mad."

"Maybe," Falsteed said. "But I've smelled you, smelled the wrongness of all that's been done to you by hands familiar and those of strangers. You chose to stop acknowledging a world that has treated you foully. What's saner than that?"

Grace sat still in the darkness, allowing the screams of the spider girl to roll over her from the cell opposite hers. The truth of Falsteed's words rang deep inside of her. Her voice flowed again, more easily with practice.

"And yourself? You are a good man, yet you are in the darkness here with me."

"Sane and good are not the same thing. Yes, I'm sane. What of it, if I can smell the sickness of others? The flavors of their feelings rich in my nostrils? It was a boon to my medical practice, for certain, but I've got other proclivities you need not know of. No, in the end . . . I am not a good man.

"But that's neither here nor there in the darkness. This particular darkness, anyway, the one you and I find ourselves denizens of. We are here because we're the sanest people in this establishment, so they put us down here as the bedrock on which to gain a foothold for the wanderings of their own minds. They call us insane, then feed their own insanities on our flesh, for we are now less than human. Heedson and Croomes are but examples of the greater world, love. They work their discreet types of madness on us, power and pain, and we hold to our truths in the darkness."

Grace considered his words, her hand small and cold still resting inside Falsteed's warm one. She could feel his breath on her ear but didn't mind his closeness or the hint of warmth that emanated from him as their bodies pooled their resources in the cold.

"Who is this Dr. Thornhollow you spoke of?" she asked.

"Him? He's the sanest of us all."

"Why is that?"

"Because he knows he's insane."

Grace moved to pull her fingers from his grasp, but Falsteed stopped her with his words. "I'm sorry, love. I'm not teasing the words from one who kept them buried so long. I mean what I say. Thornhollow . . . he's a special bit of a man, and that's the closest I can come to explaining it."

"How do you mean?"

"You wouldn't have to go far outside of Boston and mention my name to find someone who knows it, none of them remembering it for the lives I saved. It's the other they remember. But Thornhollow, he's safely anonymous for the moment. Passes through halls like this one with his dark gift and leaves those that he touches silent and still, fragile as the day they were born. Quiet like doves they are, placated with warm milk and sleeping the night through.

"You can always count on a visit from Thornhollow when the Board is about to visit. Heedson feeds the worst of the lot down here, slick as a laundry chute, and Thornhollow, he . . . well, I guess he does the laundry, in a sense. Sends it back upstairs nice and clean, a blank slate for the Board to look upon with approval when they make their rounds."

"A blank slate . . . ," Grace repeated, her words lost in a renewed shriek from the spider girl. She rested her head against the cold stones behind her. "Do they forget?"

"I can't say for sure," Falsteed said. "There's a little room down the hall. You'd never see it in this pitch, but Reed comes down with his light when Thornhollow makes his rounds. The violent ones and the screamers, they go in there loud with the doctor, and they come out smelling like blood and metal and, yes, I suppose a type of forgetfulness. Although I'd say it's more of a removal, a permanent state of that which you're only now emerging from."

Grace kept silent, not trusting her throat to handle the voice now running rampant inside of her. All the things she had kept silent boiled inside. The burning rage that Falsteed had diagnosed plummeted into the cold river of her voice and produced a harsh smoke, one that filled her lungs and pushed to overflow from her mouth.

It enveloped her brain, burning off the fog that she'd allowed to settle as easily as the sun ripped the mist away from the morning. She knew it all again, footsteps in the dark and her father's face looming in the bedroom doorway. It was all seared into her memory, and she knew it as perfectly as she knew the cracks in the ceiling of her cell. All the details of her life, caught forever in her mind. Inescapable.

The blood had slowly ceased to flow down her legs, the fear that came with each drop lost losing its bite as Falsteed had talked to her in the darkness, his voice her anchor. The dress Reed had brought already fit less snugly, the extra flap of skin that had once held her baby evaporating. She'd woken from sleep once to see that Heedson had come to check on her, the bandage on his hand bright in the darkness.

The baby was lost, the purpose of her body gone as it returned to its normal shape. There was nothing to keep her here now, no stain on the family name in the form of a widening waistband. As soon as the scratches from Croomes's fingernails on her wrists were healed, the bruises on her cheeks from Heedson faded, she'd be returned. She clutched onto Falsteed in the anonymous dark, both her arms slipping between the bars that separated them and clasping on to his broad shoulders and finding bare flesh.

"Is Thornhollow coming for me?"

Falsteed was silent for a moment, and she felt his body rise and fall as he breathed in deeply. "Dearest," he chided. "You smell of hope. You smell as if you want him to."

Her small hands clenched, her fingernails digging into Falsteed's skin. "Maybe I do."

TEN

Fingers of orange light threaded through the darkness from Reed's lantern as he approached, bringing muted noises from the spider girl. Falsteed moved to a corner of his cell where the flickering could not reach him, but his voice covered the distance between him and Grace, its low whisper meant only for her.

"Hang back a moment, dear one. I'd have you draw the measure of the man while he's still in ignorance of you."

An irrational fear sliced through Grace as she saw two shadows cast in the dim lamplight. Her world had shrunk into a place populated only by herself and Falsteed, the pitiful complaints of the spider girl underscoring their existence, punctuated by visits from Reed. The arrival of a new person, and one who Falsteed had spoken of in awe, sent Grace fleeing to her stool in the corner.

"I apologize for the dank, sir," Reed said. "Once the weather gets a mind to start raining, the cellars don't stand much of a chance of drying themselves."

"Interesting choice of words, Reed," a new voice said. Grace's ears perked up, even though her hands began to tremble.

"How's that, sir?"

"You've given the weather and the cellar—entities that don't make choices or take action on their own—precisely the qualities that the humans in your care lack."

"I suppose I did, sir, though I had no intention of doing it."

"All the more telling, that your mind would subconsciously choose words to allocate control to things that lack exactly that."

Grace pressed her bare toes against the stones, bracing her body against the cold wall. The stranger's voice was low and melodious, wandering through sentences as if assured it would find the end victoriously, though the path was unsure. His shadow stretched beside Reed's as they came nearer, the serpentine voice easily supplying answers to Reed's nervous chatter.

"Nonetheless, I'm sorry for the state of things down here, and you with a surgery tonight, sir."

The pair stopped outside of Grace's cell, and she examined the newcomer in the sickly light of the lantern, his deep-set eyes lost in the shadows, his doctor's bag slung over his shoulder almost haphazardly.

"Why do you call me 'sir'?"

"Well, I suppose because you're a surgeon, Dr. Thornhollow," Reed said, his hand trembling on the lantern as he held it aloft.

"Yes, but I'm no greater than you. In fact, I'd venture to say you're probably the better person, if it came to a matter of weighing souls."

"I don't see how one would weigh a soul, sir, or what bearing it would have on the argument."

"For example," Thornhollow continued as if Reed hadn't spoken, "I can see my mother's house from my office, yet I only visit her once a month or so, and then only under duress. The last visit occurred because I had a bit of glass buried at the base of my spine—never mind how—and had to find someone to pull it out. Even considering that, I think I went there because it was the only house that had a light at the time. I could've very well asked a stranger in the street to oblige me—would have, in fact, saved time if I'd done exactly that."

"Saved time, sir?"

"Yes, of course. Because once I was back in the house of my birth, much the worse for wear for having been out of the womb for some twenty-plus years, my mother had to fuss and pick. Nonetheless, she's a well-intentioned person and I did get a good dinner out of the whole escapade. I suppose I just don't go in for that sort of thing."

"What? Dinners?"

"No, well-intentioned people. Speaking of, where's the poor soul I'm meant to see to?"

"To the left, sir. Just follow what little noise she's able to keep making."

The men moved from Grace's sight, and she shifted silently, tip-toeing along the edge of the wall. The pale glow cast around them by Reed's lantern sank to the floor with them while the men knelt beside the spider girl's cell, one pleading white hand stretched between the bars.

Dr. Thornhollow's fingers closed around her wrist, and the faded mewlings that she'd been making intensified, like a starving cat in an alley that spotted hope in a stranger. "You can open the cell, Reed. She's no danger to anyone in this condition."

"True enough at the moment, but she's down here because she nearly took the upper lip off of Croomes."

"Only fair. I assume Croomes has been giving lip to people long before someone accepted her invitation to take it."

Reed's keys clanked and the cell door swung open. Thornhollow beckoned for him to follow as he propped the girl against the wall. Her eyes were dark circles, her hair a tangled cloud that moved in a perpetual storm above her head, but she offered no resistance when the doctor touched her, placing his palm against her forehead gently.

"What's your opinion in this matter, Dr. Falsteed?" Thornhollow asked, raising his voice so it would carry.

"It's a sad case, Dr. Thornhollow," Falsteed said, his voice assuming a professional tone Grace had never heard from him before.

"She came in recently, claiming that there's spiders in her veins for blood. Reed said the constables found her in an alleyway, slicing at her wrists with a bit of glass so as to let them out. Nobody's had a word from her about anything other than the spiders, not even her name."

Thornhollow nodded, pushing the girl's hair out of her face. "What's been done to you, then?" he asked, as if expecting an answer. "Or what have you seen that you've gone to the abyss so young?"

Grace's throat constricted, her words piling on one another in her gut as she yearned to answer the questions that weren't asked of her.

"It'll be a mercy, Thornhollow," Falsteed said. "We both know she'll get no true care here, and there's no one to speak for her on the outside. She's another lamb to the slaughter, and it's better you wield the blade and bring her the blackness than allow her to know the injustice of this life."

Thornhollow remained crouched in front of the girl, his hand in her hair and his gaze searching her blank face. Her fingers drummed a rhythm on the stones beside his foot, and her eyes rolled.

"Seems a bit calmer, almost," Reed observed, leaning toward her.

"Yes, they do that sometimes when you treat them like people," Thornhollow said, rising to his feet. "All right, Reed. Take her by the hand, please. I believe she'll follow easily enough. We'll use the same room as before. If you'll fetch another light, I believe we'll need it."

Grace watched as the doctor stepped out of the cell, all semblance of emotion now stripped as he pulled his doctor's bag from his shoulder. "Falsteed, what are your feelings on additional patients? I'm surprised at Heedson only requesting one procedure with the Board's arrival imminent."

"I imagine one or two more will be along," Falsteed said. "He always overestimates his capacity for generosity before the panic sets in."

"Panic indeed," Thornhollow said, pulling a wooden box from his satchel. He sank to his knees on the stone hall, oblivious to the wet as he flipped the lid. It came open like a jewelry box, compartments unfolding in the faint light of Reed's fading lantern as he led the spider girl away. Grace's hands went to her ears, remembering the jewels that had hung there once upon a time and a similar box on her nightstand at home.

But what emerged from Dr. Thornhollow's box was nothing to ornament a woman or anything to be spoken of at parties. Glass bottles clanked against one another and metal scraped as he rummaged in a lower drawer. "I don't suppose the kitchens would begrudge me an egg or two, Falsteed? I seem to have broken mine." Thornhollow distastefully flicked something off his fingers.

"Trying something new?" Falsteed asked.

Footsteps signaled Reed's return, along with the gradual lightening of the hall. Grace could see one of the doctor's eyebrows raise.

"I hardly think you're one to condemn a little experimentation, Falsteed," Thornhollow said.

"Just a professional curiosity," Falsteed said. "I find it hard to remain at the top of my field when I'm always . . . kept in the dark."

Thornhollow's mouth barely twitched at the joke. "I highly doubt that. Reed keeps a steady stream of information directly to your ear. As far as the darkness goes, I'd welcome an excuse for isolation."

Falsteed grunted in response, and Grace squinted as Reed leaned over the still-kneeling Thornhollow. "I think you'll find her quite ready for you, sir. I dosed her with ether and the poor bird flew off into the oblivion like she'd been pining for it."

"Like I said, Dr. Thornhollow," Falsteed said. "It's a mercy."

"No doubt. And yet only hours after I carve into the brain of a lost girl whose name we'll never know, I'll be seated next to the recognizable names of society with my hands itching to give them that same mercy so as to stop their ceaseless words."

"You've evaded their clutches quite a while. A young man of your position can only escape his social duties for so long. I imagine they're hoping to affiance you to a daughter before you leave for Ohio?"

Thornhollow snapped the box closed. "Reed really does keep you up to speed on current affairs," he said stiffly. "As to the daughters, society will have to learn to live without air if they're holding their breaths for my marriage." He rose holding only a glass vial and a slim blade. "Reed, if you'll humor me by going to the kitchen for two eggs and an apple corer?"

Grace could see Reed's face pale. "Y-yes, sir," he stammered, leaving the lantern on the floor. The light pooled around the doctor's feet, his features lost into a smeared blur once again.

Falsteed cleared his throat. "Thornhollow . . . if I could speak with you about something, when you're finished?"

"Of course. I have to meet with Heedson to see if he'll have me deliver any more of his patients from ever having to be aware of his presence again, then I'll be back down to check on the girl. Unless you needed something from me immediately?"

"No, Doctor, just a moment of your time after the procedure. And if we can agree to something, perhaps a favor after the fact."

"A favor? I don't recall you ever asking anything of the kind from me before."

"And I wouldn't, if the situation weren't dire."

"For a man who's been sitting in darkness for years with none but the mad for company to suddenly find his situation dire makes me quite worried for him."

"Not for myself, Thornhollow. My lot is my own," Falsteed said.

The doctor rose to his feet, lantern in hand, as the sound of Reed's footsteps advanced down the hall. "I'll speak to you of it afterward," he said. "Your protégé returns much more quickly than he left. I imagine he's been told to set to. Which means I've got more than our poor lost lamb for my night's work."

Reed burst into the hall, two eggs in one hand and the apple corer in the other, sweat beaded on his upper lip. "I'm sorry, sir, it seems there'll be two more at least tonight."

Thornhollow rolled his sleeves to the elbows. "Your favor, Falsteed, it will keep?"

"All the night long, Thornhollow."

The doctor nodded sharply. "Right then. Reed—gather some more eggs from the kitchen and a pot of boiling water. And I'll have to bother you to send my regrets to the governor's mansion. It seems I won't make dinner this evening."

Reed's mouth gaped open, more horrified at dispatching the news than retrieving the apple corer. "And what do I say to the governor, sir?"

Thornhollow slid two of his blades together; the metallic zing of their meeting brought a smile to his face. "Tell him I'm working."

ELEVEN

The first man came down like a demon being cast back into the hell he'd escaped from. The lanterns in the hands of the male assistants swung crazily as they dodged his blows. Shadows leaped across the walls and Thornhollow emerged from them, his white shirt now spattered with blood.

The knot of male bodies twisted outside Grace's cell, but he slipped in between them easily, wrapping his forearm across the patient's neck. Thornhollow was not a large man, but Grace could see the knotty muscles at work as the patient realized he could not escape the doctor's grip.

Grace could see that force was not the only thing bringing the man's struggles to an end. Thornhollow's voice rose and fell rhythmically, his mouth moving next to the patient's ear as he made promises that no one but the two of them would ever know. The man slumped in either agreement or defeat. Thornhollow released him and the orderlies moved him farther down the hall into the promising dark. As the doctor moved away from her she caught the faintest whiff of a scent from her former life, one so reminiscent of luxury that it was difficult to place amid the foulness that surrounded her. It lingered even as the doctor disappeared into the surgery, and Grace raised her hands as if to follow its translucent path.

The only thing to answer her silent supplication was the emerging face of the spider girl, almost unrecognizable. Her features had worn a mask of misery for so long that the slackness of peace made her almost beautiful as Reed guided her to her cell. A bandage held the hair back from her cheekbones no longer clenched in pain. Her eyes were wide and bright, the sheen of suspicion and fear vanished. She looked at ease for the first time; whatever her horrific past had been wiped clean with a flash of Thornhollow's blade.

The scent flowed from her too, heavy and redolent in the mire of the cellar, bringing with it the memory of warm baths. Grace watched the girl lean against the bars of her cell for support as she slid to the stone floor, her gaze blank and satisfied, the smell of luxury drifting from her corner.

"Thornhollow," Grace cried, when she heard the hollow banging of the door at the end of the hall. "Come here, Thornhollow!" All the authority she'd carried in the time before swelled her vocal cords, and her voice came out stronger than it had been in months. He came out of the depths, a question stamped on his features.

"Here," she called. "Next to Falsteed."

Thornhollow carried a lantern, and though her voice was strong, Grace flinched when the light fell on her. He studied her for a moment, and she fought against the years of training that told her to not meet his gaze.

"Hello there," Thornhollow said. "And what demand do you make of me?"

"I only wish to know, sir," Grace said, "why is it that you should bring roses to only one lady when there are two who wish to receive them?"

"Roses?" Thornhollow's eyebrows rose in surprise, and she heard Falsteed move closer in the adjoining cell, though he did not come into the light. "What do you mean?"

"Oil of roses," she said. "You reek of it, as does she, though she went in smelling like the rest of us. Whatever you've done to her to bring forgetfulness, the roses play a part. Give me the same, so that I may know less."

"You do not know what you ask, though I'll show you," Thornhollow said. "Falsteed—"

"Yes, Doctor?"

"I assume this is your favor?"

"Not what she is asking for, no. Our Grace has a quick mind. I'd not see it incapacitated."

"Mmm..." Thornhollow held the lantern close to the bars of her cell and peered deeply into her eyes, as if to illuminate her brain and make an assessment that moment.

"Quick or not, she'll have to wait. There's a man down the hall who is quite insane and needs me immediately." He gave her one last look before pulling the lantern away, the coldness of the cell instantly sapping all the heat her cheeks had gained from it. His footsteps receded and Grace sank to the floor, all initiative gone now that she had his attention. He would be back, and she would make her plea.

"Grace," Falsteed chided in the dark. "No."

"The roses," she said, sighing. "The smell of the roses, it undid me. How can I call it a life when I curl in the darkness, covered in my own filth? I was once surrounded by light and smelled as lovely as a garden. I'd rather forget both than remember either."

"Oil of roses," Falsteed said. "You've got a good nose."

The second patient was brought down before Thornhollow came to her. Grace watched with a keen eye as the insane went into the dark room at the end of the passage like feral animals and walked out led by Reed, simple and trusting as children. If the slackness of their faces was off-putting, the dead calm of their eyes offset it, promising that the tumult that had once raged within was now at rest.

Thornhollow followed on the heels of the last patient, arriving at Grace's cell with fresh blood spatters speckling his bared forearms. She rose when he came close, moving into the light of the lantern with a calm determination. His eyes searched her face before he spoke.

"You've seen it three times now, and you'd still know what goes on in the shadows where Heedson has me do my work?"

"I would," Grace said, her voice unwavering.

Thornhollow produced a key. "Courtesy of Reed," he said, unlocking her cell door. The hinges protested as the door moved, and Grace felt the first rush of apprehension. She hadn't left her safe square of life in the days since she'd been brought to the cellar. She knew the stones under her feet well—her hardened soles had traced their edges in the blackness many sleepless nights. And now her cell had been opened by a man who wielded forgetfulness with a blade.

She stepped out and heard Falsteed's murmur of disapproval.

"Enough," Thornhollow snapped. "I'll show her, and she'll make her own decisions." He beckoned with the lantern for Grace to move down the hall and she went, the pale circle of light barely casting a few inches of sight past her grimed toes. Thornhollow followed behind her, his shoes ringing out on the stones.

The hall had always been shrouded in darkness, his earlier patients seeming to evaporate into an unlit hell to rematerialize as tamed demons. The door was not far. Thornhollow reached past her and lifted the latch.

The room was sparse, holding only a bed and table. The bright-ness of the linens leaped at Grace's eyes as if there were a phantom in the room, except for a few dark drops that appeared nearly black in the dim light. She crossed to the opposite side of the table, enjoying the feel of the clean stone under her feet. On the table was Thornhollow's toolbox, the meticulous order now in disarray, along with the apple corer and broken eggshells.

"I suppose to the unpracticed it seems a bit more of a kitchen than a surgery," Thornhollow said as he set the lantern on the table.

"Explain it to me, then," she said, running her finger through a trace of yolk.

Thornhollow crossed his arms and studied her for a moment before speaking. She stared back, savoring the appearance of a new face after being denied company for so long. The meager light could hardly penetrate the hollows of his eyes, but she could see the muscles of his jaw tensing as they studied each other, the slightest tic beneath his red sideburns giving him away.

"First you'll show me why Falsteed thinks your mind is quick. It's not a compliment he pays easily and I'm intrigued. You caught on quickly enough about the oil of roses, but it takes more than that for me to call you clever." Thornhollow leaned against the wall. "So, impress me."

"I . . ." Grace's recently found voice died inside of her, unable to find proof of her intelligence on demand. "Georgia was not present at the First Continental Congress."

Thornhollow laughed at the trivial fact, a harsh sound that echoed in their small chamber. "Tell me something I'll find interesting."

Grace dropped her eyes, gaze going to his shoes, which were splattered with the blood of those gone before her. She closed her eyes, allowing a picture to be drawn there. "The man who came in here before me was very large, but you overpowered him with words more than strength. He had a tattoo . . ." She turned her body as his had been positioned in front of her cell as he struggled with the doctor. "It was on his left bicep. It was of a letter *M*."

The doctor said nothing, and she took encouragement from that. She squeezed her eyes tighter in search of the smaller details. "He was missing two teeth on the right side of his mouth, a third turned inward at an awkward angle. And his eyes were blue."

The silence continued and she opened her eyes. "Doctor?"

"Very good," he said, though his face didn't change expression. "I did indeed find that quite interesting. Since you seem to have some interest in knowing what happens in this room and have asked for the same treatment for yourself, I'll explain. But I warn you, it's not a pretty story."

"Then it's the kind I've grown accustomed to."

"Very well, then. Have you ever heard of a fellow named Phineas Gage?"

Grace blinked. "I don't believe so, should I have?"

"In your circles? No. In mine he's a miracle, but I shall have to acquaint you with him. Some forty-odd years ago Phineas Gage was a railroad worker. His specific job was a blaster, which means that he would drill holes into bedrock, fill them with gunpowder, add a layer of sand, and then press the charge down into the rock with his tamping iron before igniting it. Now, a tamping iron is—"

"Doctor," Grace interrupted, "I have to struggle for every word I speak and only wish to know what you've done to the others. Must you tell me these things?"

"No, but I'm answering questions you haven't asked yet. If I do it in a circuitous manner you'll have to suffer through it. I only have a short time to inform you about the history of my medical practice and then offer my services to you, should you be so inclined."

Grace wordlessly settled back into the chair, crossing her ankles beneath the filthy dress, a mannerism that had been ingrained in her by her governess, which the doctor's quick eyes took in.

"As I was saying," Thornhollow said, his tone warning her not to interrupt, "Phineas worked with a tamping iron, a long metal rod with a sharp tip. Something like a spear, but a heavy one at that. Phineas had his made to order, and it weighed about thirteen pounds, which you'll understand why I make a note of its heft in a moment."

Thornhollow laced his hands behind his back, his feet wandering the stones as his story flowed.

"One day, his fellow workman failed to put the sand on top of the gunpowder, which is why anyone even knows the name of Phineas

Gage. He struck with the dull end of the tamping iron directly onto black gunpowder, triggering an explosion that drove the tamping iron through his skull."

Thornhollow's steps brought him behind Grace. "It entered here," he said, suddenly jamming his fingers under her cheekbone below her left eye. She jumped at his touch, but he casually traced his finger along her head as if she hadn't moved. "It passed through the roof of his mouth, behind his left eye, and exited through the top of his skull, here." He tapped her hairline, but she sat still this time.

"Amazingly, the man didn't die." Thornhollow's hands spread out, framing her face, his own lit with the excitement of his tale. "Gage was thrown onto his back, but only a minute after the explosion he was up and speaking, despite the fact that the tamping iron had passed cleanly through his brain.

"Luckily for Gage, the nearest doctor actually knew something about treating head wounds, and his injured brain had room to swell thanks to the opening in the top of his head. With a little time Phineas healed completely, and yet those who knew him said that Gage was . . . no longer Gage."

"What do you mean?" Grace asked.

"Gage was a kind, well-mannered man before the tamping iron passed through his brain. After his recovery he was rude, ill-tempered, and vulgar with women. The man who struck that tamping iron was not the same man who left the doctor's office healed.

The injury to his brain had altered his personality."

"Altered," Grace echoed, thinking of the shrieking men who had passed by her cell hours before, only to leave this room tame as lap kittens. "And so you've done something similar, haven't you? But in reverse. You've found a way to . . . to . . ." Her gaze slipped to the apple corer, and her stomach rolled.

"Don't leap to conclusions yet, though I see Falsteed was right in calling you clever. It's not a simple chore, and I'm sure you've noted by the size of my valise that I'm not driving thirteen-pound tamping irons into people's skulls."

"I'd imagine not," Grace said, but her eyes were still on the apple corer.

He followed them and picked up the tool. "What I did was combine the knowledge of what we learned from Phineas Gage with the common practice of trepanning. As I said before, Gage was lucky in that his wound was an open one, allowing his brain to swell. Most patients with injured brains don't know they're in danger until it's too late. A kick from a horse or a fall from a ladder may jar them, but they don't realize that their brain is swelling inside their skull, pressing against the bone and cutting off blood flow.

"It's long been a common practice to cut a hole in the skull of such a patient, allowing the brain to swell as it needs, then closing the wound. Different doctors use all manner of different things to pack the wound with, but I prefer lint soaked in—"

"Oil of roses," Grace interrupted again, rolling her fingers together, still coated in the residue from the table. "And the eggs?"

"I'm guessing you've never had to wash your own breakfast plate. If you had you'd be well aware that a dried egg is almost impossible to remove from anything it's adhered to. I've not found its equal for closing up wounds that shouldn't be stitched."

"So you . . ."

"It's quite simple," Thornhollow said, advancing on her again. "I make two triangular incisions on the forehead—here and here." He tapped her sharply on the temples right at her hairline. "Cut through the dura to the skull." He increased the pressure on her temples from both sides, his fingers digging into her scalp.

Grace stiffened. "And then?"

"And then"—Thornhollow released the left side of her skull to reach for his bag, producing a blade and a circular tool—"I cut to the bone on both sides of the temple and punch through the skull with a trephine, which leaves a neat little circle in the bone. The apple corer is to destroy the frontal lobe of the brain. This is where you live. Every gesture, every skill you've perfected and experience you've had is wiped clean, like my breakfast plate once I managed to get the damn egg off of it."

"And memories?" Grace asked, refusing to smile at his joke. "What of them?"

"Gone, I suppose," he said, his eyes no longer jesting. "I don't

70

know for sure. Most of them lose the capacity for speech and can't say. For all we know they're living in their own private hell that I delivered them into."

"They're not," Grace said swiftly. "Their eyes tell the story. They're calm and contented."

"But"—Thornhollow raised a finger in warning—"I would never claim they are happy. I think they lose the ability to feel anything. I've only been experimenting with this for a short while, but the asylum administrators thank me for it. They believe I'm doing them a favor by turning violent patients into timid lambs. But in truth I do it for the afflicted, to ease their suffering and the weariness of the world they've been born into, where we have yet to understand or truly help them."

He fell silent, his eyes on his hands, now balled in his lap. Grace watched without speaking, willing him to come to the same conclusion she had hours before.

"This is what you ask of me, then?" He raised his eyes to hers. "You want me to cut into you, tear away your skin and your brain, and leave you a desolate, incoherent mess that feels no more?"

"Yes," she said, the one word heavy in her throat as a tear slid down her cheek. "Yes, I would have that."

The lantern flickered, sending his face into shadow and back into stark illumination for a moment. "I don't need to ask why," he finally said. "You're an attractive girl, obviously well-bred by your speech and mannerisms. The poor excuse of a rag that you wear can't hide where you used to carry a child. Any society family would have a sharp eye on an attractive daughter your age, and you wouldn't have the freedom to pursue any males you find yourself drawn to and so . . ." He paused, watching her closely. "I assume that in order for you to become with child it would have been at the hands of someone with the freedom to roam the halls of your own home."

Grace dropped her gaze. His fingers went under her chin and drew her eyes back to his own. "And so," he continued, "once your condition was discovered there was no acceptable way to explain it other than to disappear you for a while, am I right?"

"I'm on my European tour at the moment," Grace said. "Due to return in a few months."

Thornhollow nodded and then glanced about the room. "You should register a complaint about the lodgings."

A bubble rose up in Grace's throat, erupting in the form of a laugh, and she clasped her hand down on her mouth in astonishment. Thornhollow smiled.

"That's the game, then?" he continued. "You return home, undoubtedly back into the nest of the viper himself?"

Grace nodded, all laughter gone.

"We can't have that."

She reached for him, and it was his turn to flinch. "This is why I ask for it, Doctor. I cannot go back. If you change me permanently,

I won't be wanted at home. They can say what they like about my fate, I'll live and die here, happily unaware of the present, and all traces of the past taken from me."

"As well as your propensity for thought," he argued. "Grace, so few people in this world have any skills worth speaking of. You've learned that beauty can work against you, and your build is so slight you'll never be able to defend yourself. Your brain is your strength, your quickness of wit the one thing that will deliver you from the damnable life of the dull."

She yanked her hands from his, balling them into fists at her temples as she realized he was refusing her. "No," she cried. "Doctor, it is my weakness. I see everything; I notice all and I remember—the beautiful and the horrific alike I can recall as easily as a daguerreotype that can't be unseen. It will be the death of me, this remembering."

"No, Grace," Thornhollow said, pulling her hand away from her face. "Utterly to the contrary, this curse of *seeing* will do you well."

"You won't do it, then?" she asked, hot tears streaming down her cheeks. "You won't cut me?"

"No," he said. "There's a much better use for you."

TWELVE

"She'll go with me," Thornhollow said, casting the words into the darkness of Falsteed's cell. "You were right in your estimation of her quickness, and I can use her in my new endeavors. She'll be safe, far away from the brute who did this to her. Not to mention Heedson."

"He'll never let me go," Grace said at the mention of the director's name. "My father is paying him well to keep me here and for his silence as to my condition."

"In your current state, no, he wouldn't let you go," Thornhollow said. "But you came across the solution yourself. Your family's story about your absence being due to a long holiday won't hold up if you come home scarred."

"Thornhollow, you wouldn't!" Falsteed cried from the darkness.

"No, he wouldn't," Grace said. "I'm of no use to him without my mind intact."

"Quite right," Thornhollow agreed. "I'm not in the practice of smuggling privileged young women out of asylums, even if they are as sane as a field mouse. She'll be put to use and earn her keep with me at my new assignment."

"And getting her out of here?" Falsteed asked.

"Your man, Reed, he's dependable?"

"As the dawn."

"He'll be the perfect player in our little ruse, then," Thornhollow said. "Now, Grace, I imagine you'll want to say a little something to Dr. Falsteed. I'll give you some moments alone. Join me in the surgery when you find yourself quite prepared."

Thornhollow disappeared into the darkness, his footfalls echoing after him.

"Prepared for what, young one?" Falsteed asked, his voice heavy.

Grace took a deep breath. Even though their plan was her only hope of salvation, she was worried that Falsteed would disapprove.

"We've worked it out," she said softly. "If Heedson believes Thornhollow has cut me and I'm unrepairable, he'll panic at the thought of my father's wrath."

"I should say. For you to enter the asylum healthy and with child and walk out a drooling idiot would hardly be to Heedson's credit."

"Precisely." Grace wrapped her hands around Falsteed's cell bars, wishing her friend would come into the light before she left him forever. "He'd go to any lengths to cover the enormity of such an error. Bruises and cuts for his own sadistic pleasures will heal, but if I'm permanently damaged he'll have no choice but to aid in my escape."

Falsteed sighed heavily, the warmth of his exhalation reaching her but not the sight of him. "And what am I to do after you're gone? Wait for a new prisoner and hope they're interesting?"

The second smile of the day spread across Grace's face, her stomach now alight with the possibility of a future. "They could only be so lucky, to have you with them here in the dark."

Fingers closed around hers, but she couldn't see past his wrist. "Write to Reed here at the asylum under the name of a Miss Madeleine Baxter. He'll get the letters to me. I would know how you fare."

"Good-bye, my friend," Grace said, her throat tight once again. His fingers gripped hers, stopping her from moving away at the last second.

"Be wary of Thornhollow, Grace. He's a good man, by all measures. You have nothing to fear from him that you would from other men. But that is precisely why you must guard yourself. He does not understand human nature, our emotions and attachments. He's made a place for himself among the insane because it's easier for him than moving among society. People are a mystery to him."

"They are to me as well," Grace said, squeezing his hand before she followed Thornhollow into the dark.

"You've said your good-byes?" Thornhollow's back was turned to her when she entered the surgery, his hands busy sharpening a scalpel.

"I have," Grace said. "Shall I sit or . . ." Her voice trembled as she motioned to the bed.

"Sit," Thornhollow said. "Obviously, I won't be coring your brain. Triangular cuts at your temple should be enough to convince that witless Heedson that you've been damaged. You do realize you'll be scarred?"

"Yes," Grace said as she settled into the chair.

Thornhollow nodded. "Very good. As to the cutting itself, I'll be dosing you with ether, so there will be no pain."

Grace's hands grasped the seat of the chair. "No, Doctor."

"I'm sorry?"

"I'll take no ether, sir."

"Grace, you must understand—"

"No, *you* must understand. I'll not be witless for a moment."

Thornhollow frowned, his brows drawing together. "Do you not trust me?"

"I trust you with my life. Nothing more."

The blade hovered in the air, the slightest tremor betraying him. "I'll need you to be utterly still through the pain. You're no use to me if you twitch and I accidentally put your eye out."

Grace sat straight in the chair. "I've been still through worse."

Thornhollow nodded his assent and moved behind her. "All right then, look up at the ceiling, if you please."

The first cut brought a slice of heat near her eye; a second slice came close to her hairline, followed by pressure as the doctor pressed a clean rag against the wound. "Hold this," he said, drawing her hand up to the wad of cloth. "Tightly as you can stand," he added when she gripped it.

Grace concentrated, all sense of self lost as he moved to her other side, and the pain, bearable in its familiarity, flashed again. Thornhollow pushed against the wound with one hand, the other reaching for a ball of lint on the table.

"I'll soak this in the oil," he said, "and dress the wounds with gauze. I doubt Heedson would go so far as to flap back the skin to see if I truly punctured your skull, but I wouldn't put it past my bad luck to have him decide to suddenly take interest in his patients when I need him at his most incompetent."

Grace nodded her understanding but said nothing. Black spots had started to float in her vision as a stream of warm blood trickled down both cheeks. "Is it . . ." Her voice floated off, lost in the darkness of the room beyond their lanterns.

"Is it . . . ? Whoops-a-daisy," Thornhollow said, righting Grace as she slumped in the chair. "Steady now, girl. Almost done."

With his hands flashing about the work and oil of roses following in the wake of blood, Grace felt the warmth returning to her hands, now resting in her lap. "I'd not thought there'd be so much blood," she ventured to say when she trusted her voice again.

"Head wounds do tend to bleed," the doctor answered, his eyes not leaving her bandage as he tied it securely about her head. "There," he finished, patting her crown like a child. "Nicely done. No bow, but I suppose you'll not mind the fashion faux pas. Rest a moment, then we'll go about our little ruse."

"Doctor," Grace said as he leaned back against the table to rest. "I have a friend here, in the ward. A woman named Mrs. Clay. There's nothing wrong—"

Thornhollow waved her words away before she could finish. "It cannot be done."

"But I owe her—"

"That may very well be, and I'm sure she's a fine sort. One finds many unfortunate women tucked away in places such as this. But she's of no use to me, and I'm hardly running the Underground Railroad for Insane Women."

"I don't under—"

Thornhollow raised his palm. "Getting you out of here will be difficult enough, and I stand to gain by your release. Attempting to rescue the ill-fated Mrs. Clay would be sheer madness, if you'll allow me the use of the phrase."

Grace bit down on her lip to stop the flow of words, finding it difficult to cut them off now that they had begun.

"You're unhappy with me, I see," Thornhollow mused. "It can't be helped. For the sake of our working relationship it would be best if you didn't dislike me, but I won't take unnecessary steps to ensure your goodwill, either. We'll be clear about that with each other from the outset. If you'd like I can return you to your cell with nothing to show for this misadventure other than a bit of scarring."

Grace felt her teeth grinding together, stopping the vowels and consonants that she wanted to spew at him. For a moment she remembered the meaty give of Heedson's hand under her dinner fork, but she cut the thought cleanly from her head as if wielding a scalpel of her own. "No, Doctor," she said. "You don't need my goodwill for us to work together, as I don't need your friendship to facilitate my escape."

Thornhollow clapped his hands together. "Good. Onward, then. Are you steady enough on your feet? Wobbling a bit is perfectly fine, but if you fall I can't be expected to catch you. It won't do to scramble your brains in the end, would it?"

"No, Doctor," Grace said, rising despite the black swell that threatened her vision. "I can stand perfectly fine."

"Excellent." He reached into his valise for a flask, the smell of alcohol overtaking the lesser scent of roses in the room as he splashed his shirtfront with it before taking a pull. He ran his fingers through his hair, yanking the red locks in all directions. "And now, Grace, if you would please poke me in both eyes."

"I'm sorry?"

"No need to apologize, you haven't done it yet," he said as he snapped his kit shut. "Now come here and have a go at me. If you need me to antagonize you a bit first, I can certainly do so."

Grace thought of Mrs. Clay. "I don't believe that will be necessary," she said, stepping toward him as he matter-of-factly held his own lids open.

"No gouging. I simply need you to—CHRIST!" He wheeled away from her, hands up to his face. "Well done, well done," he muttered, still covering his eyes with one hand as he leaned against the table. "I'll be asking you to do worse things than that shortly, so it certainly bodes well that you're willing."

Grace rubbed her hands against her skirts to rid the feeling of his eyes from the tips of her fingers. "Are we ready, then?"

"I believe so." Thornhollow pinched the bridge of his nose. "Do I look quite disreputable?"

Grace looked him over, from his red-rimmed eyes to his disheveled hair. "Quite."

"Very well. You've no doubt made a study of my patients as they exited this room. The better you can make yourself like them in the coming minutes, the easier a time we'll have of it."

Grace nodded, stamping down the rise of apprehension in her stomach.

"Think of the door of your own cell shutting," he said, when he saw the tremor of her hands. "Put your thoughts and feelings away for the moment and bar them in."

"I'm long familiar with shutting out the world, Doctor," Grace said. It was not her cell she thought of, though, which had ironically offered its own type of protection, but the sound of familiar footsteps in the middle of the night, followed by her doorknob turning.

The click she heard in her mind was as audible as if it were in the room with her, and Grace let her emotions leave her in a rush, all cares exiting with her exhalation, not to return until she allowed them. Even her outer appearance changed, though she hardly knew it, and the doctor watched, fascinated, as her eyes glazed over, her muscles became torpid. She slouched as if her soul had left her body, leaving behind only the warm flesh that appeared as lifeless as a bag of water.

"Very . . . good," he managed to say, but she did not respond. "Reed," he called as he opened the door to the surgery, and the assistant appeared from the darkness, his gaze flicking to Grace's bloodied bandages and back to the doctor's face without flinching.

"You're set, then?" Reed asked.

"Good man," Thornhollow said. "Falsteed's brought you up to speed?"

"I'm to make a ruckus and bring Heedson straightaway," Reed said, as if reciting his lessons.

"Come along, then, Grace," Thornhollow called. "Let's see if

Heedson is as pliable as you pretend to be."

Grace followed Reed and the doctor down the dark hall, allowing the safe detachment to envelope her as she emerged among the cells. Even Falsteed's murmur at the sight of her bandages slid off her consciousness like rain on a windowpane. She was a receptacle only, storing facts and impressions to sift through at a later date.

"Go to it, then," Thornhollow said to Reed, who sprinted for the stairs.

"Heedson! Dr. Heedson!" he bellowed, his voice echoing back to them as he ascended. "Thornhollow's cut one too many!"

His cries faded. Thornhollow examined the bloodied cuffs of his sleeves as he casually unrolled them. Grace watched blankly, her brain sopping up details like a sponge but rejecting all reaction.

"It's on you, girl," Falsteed said gently, his voice rolling from the dark. "The ruse is his, but you're the player. And the punished, for that matter, if Heedson smells the plot."

"He won't," Thornhollow said. "And she's the last person you need to remind of the risks we run tonight."

"THORNHOLLOW!" Heedson's bellow filled the basement. He erupted from the stairwell, dressing gown flapping around him like badly clipped wings. "What have you done?" he demanded, his cheeks red with the unaccustomed exertion.

Reed followed behind Heedson. "I said it was so. You believe me now, Doctor?"

"Dear God," Heedson cried at the sight of Grace, blank and staring. He approached her warily, as if she were a wild animal that might erupt into life and injure him when he let his guard down. But she only stood, shoulders slumped, eyes riveted to a point on the ground.

When his searching hands touched her face, she slipped deeper into her mind, to a place no touch could follow. Though she refused to feel it, she could draw every line of Heedson's palm if she were asked to. The tiniest gradations of the rock she'd affixed her gaze to were forever stamped on her memory. The smell of drunkenness that wafted from Thornhollow as he stumbled toward her imprinted itself thoroughly on her mind.

"Hands off the patient," Thornhollow slurred, awkwardly knocking Heedson's hands away.

Heedson gripped Thornhollow's shoulders as if he would shake him to sobriety. "I did not order this girl to go under your knife, sir," he said, biting off each word. "I said the girl in the cellar and the two men that I would send. That was all."

Thornhollow wiped his nose on his sleeve and rocked back on his heels. "You said *girls*."

Reed held his lantern close to Grace, but she didn't react to the heat. "Ordered or not, it's a thing done now, Dr. Heedson. And no undoing it."

Heedson turned pale in the lamplight, cold beads of sweat

standing out on his forehead in the damp. His fingers slipped under her bandage, and Grace held her breath for one instant as he lifted it. His own exhalation in her face when he saw her matching incisions was rank with defeat. "That's the case, is it? You can't . . . fix her in some way?"

Thornhollow chuckled as he swayed on his feet. "I guess I could scrape the bits of her brain that's on the table into a pile and shove 'em back in."

Falsteed's voice interrupted from the shadows. "Even you're enough of a doctor to know that won't do much good, Heedson. The brain's damaged and there's nothing left of that girl other than what you see before you. What's another lifeless patient to you, anyhow?"

"She's not just anyone," Heedson said, neatly tucking Grace's bandages back as if healing her wounds could undo the surgery. "This girl is Nathaniel Mae's daughter."

"Nathaniel Mae the senator?" Reed asked, true surprise ringing in his voice.

"The same," Heedson said, nodding. "She's here because of her former delicate condition, under my direct care until she was able to return home. How do I explain this?"

"Tell 'im you've got a surgeon that's overly fond of brandy and doesn't understand plurals, for all I care." Thornhollow slapped him on the back. "The road is long, gentlemen, and I need to be on it. I'll send you a bill, old fellow," he said as he disappeared into the dark hall to collect his valise.

"Thornhollow!" Heedson yelled after him. "You can't leave me in this position!"

"Nonetheless, I am leaving," Thornhollow said as he emerged from the shadows, bag in hand. "The girl is your problem. Ohio needs me, and I must go."

"Ohio," Heedson said, his beady eyes shooting back and forth as he thought. "Reed," he said quickly. "The girl hasn't spoken since she came here, correct?"

"Not a word, sir. I'd give her some bread and she'd eat it just fine, but never a thank-you or request for something more did I hear."

"Indeed," Thornhollow said. "I'm not sure I'd have needed to use the ether on the girl; she was as compliant as a lamb. I did, though. A blade has a way of bringing one to wakefulness."

Heedson closed his eyes. "Reed, do you feel that I pay you well?"

"Well enough, sir. You do know that Maggie's got another little one on the way, and I can't say there's meat on the table every day."

"If I were to make your life more comfortable, do you think meat is a good replacement for the memory of this night?"

"More than enough, sir," Reed said. "I've no liking for Nathaniel Mae as it is. He seems as like to spit on the poor as to feed them. If you'll put food in the mouths of my own and I can pull the wool over his eyes at the same time, I call it a deed well done."

"And do we still have any empty tins at the moment, for the ashes of the dead?"

"Yes," Reed said slowly. "But I'll not let you kill her, sir. Trickin' a man is one thing, but killing a girl to cover your mess is beyond me."

"And I'm not so drunk that I'd allow it, either," Thornhollow added.

"Jesus, what do you take me for?" Heedson asked. For the slightest moment Grace saw in the depths of his eyes a hint of sadness, a reflection of a man who had once truly wanted to give care to the insane, now dampened and dulled by years of discouragement.

"Mae will rant and rave at me," Heedson continued. "But in the end, what can he do? I know the reason why his daughter came to be here in the first place, and he'll not threaten me for fear I'll share the story. We'll give him a tin of ashes with her name printed on it, along with apologies. The girl disappears and no one is the wiser for it."

"Disappears to where, sir?" Reed asked.

Heedson turned to Thornhollow. "You've landed us in this fine mess—you'll be taking the girl with you."

"With me! And what am I supposed to do with her?" Thornhollow bellowed, his drunken indignation echoing around them.

"Heal her up and sell her to a brothel for all I care," Heedson said. "Her story's sealed inside that ruined mind and the truth dies with it. You and I have our careers to think of, Thornhollow, and you'll not want it getting around that you hit the bottle before surgery, I don't think?"

"I take a nip or two to get me in the right frame of mind. I don't think you'd hold it against me. My work is not pleasant," Thornhollow said, smoothing his ragged hair and straightening his sleeves as he pulled on his traveling coat.

"Not pleasant, indeed," Heedson said, his eyes returning to Grace once more. "Reed, bring the girl a decent dress, a coat, and some shoes if you can manage some."

"Straightaway, sir. I believe a girl's come in just about her size the other day, died soon after. I'll just lift her things out of the belongings room." He disappeared again, returning with a bundle of clothes and a pail of water.

Heedson looked at Grace dubiously over the lantern's glare. "Can she dress herself?"

"Doubtful," Thornhollow said, hiccupping into his hand. "Reed, take her into the surgery and burn the filthy rags she's wearing."

Grace let Reed take her by the hand, his touch cool and light. He shut the door behind them and laid a bundle of fresh clothes along with a pair of shoes onto the table.

"I snagged them from the laundry this morning," Reed said, pitching his voice low. "The shoes may rub a bit, but they'll do in a pinch. Go on then, make it a quick wash. I'll not look."

Grace took a minute to resurface, letting her body know she

needed it to perform a duty again. Feeling returned. The warmth of the lantern was a welcome thing, slipping past the darkness of the basement that had permeated her skin. She stripped the nightgown away, scratching her nails along the filth that coated her arms. A ragged cloth and a bar of heavy white soap floated in the pail. The water was cold, but Grace welcomed it the same. She brought a froth from the soap and dragged the cloth over her skin, passing over the sag of her belly with care.

It was quick indeed, nothing like the steaming baths at home, where she had taken care to clean under her nails, scrubbing imagined dirt away. She'd never known what it was like to be truly dirty until she came here, and she washed away the asylum as best she could in the dark with a stranger only a few feet away.

The dress was a shapeless thing but clean, and she held her breath against the smell of the laundry's soap, too familiar after her wrapping. The top was too big in the shoulders, the sleeves passed well below her fingertips, and the shoes did pinch. But she had on real clothes, her footsteps rang when she walked once more, and there was no layer of dirt on her skin.

"You can turn," she said softly, and Reed faced her in the lamplight, offering his hand to lead her back out. She took it, but her mind had retreated before she'd even finished the gesture, the darkness always more welcome than the light.

They emerged into the cell block, where Thornhollow was

slouched against the wall, his eyes closed in a half daze. Heedson raised the lantern to give Grace one more inspection. "You'd best change these bandages before you go, Thornhollow. She's apt to bleed right through them on the road."

"No need for that," Thornhollow said, pulling himself to his feet. "The early morning hours are the darkest, and the best ones for secreting the girl away. If she dies on the road it's all the same to you and lends truth to your tale."

"Here she is, then, Dr. Thornhollow," Reed said. "Have a safe journey and take care of the girl. I'd like to believe that lost ones such as this find a good end, no matter how unlikely."

"A lovely thought, Reed," Heedson said. "But I'll be happy to never see that face again, pretty as it is."

"I'll keep her from harm. That's all I can promise," Thornhollow said. "To claim that any who follow in my footsteps will find something good isn't a safe bet."

Thornhollow peered into Grace's eyes and shook his head. "How I've found myself the guardian of a young woman, I'm not sure I'll ever know." But he took her hand and they climbed the stairs together, her steps ringing out strong and sure beside his own.

The night air was clean and sharp, almost painful for her to breathe in. Grace gasped at the stab of fresh air, and Thornhollow rounded on her in the street.

"Quiet," he warned with a hiss. "I've got a horse and carriage along the alley, with a blanket or two inside. What you're wearing won't keep you warm for long in this weather."

The horse nickered at their approach and Grace reached up to touch its velvety nose. "In, in," Thornhollow urged, brushing her hand away.

She climbed into the carriage and wrapped herself in the blanket he'd promised. He clicked to the horse and they were moving in an instant, the clip-clop of hooves and the swaying of the carriage lulling Grace into a stupor. She slipped onto her side and pulled the blanket over herself, the smell of clean air mixing with the scent of roses as she left the city behind her.

THIRTEEN

It was dark work, as he'd warned her.

A week on the road, being jostled from carriage to shady hotels, hadn't prepared her for the luxury of a soft bed. The asylum in Ohio was like a castle in a fairy tale, even if she did approach it on a dark night with lightning streaking the sky and fresh blood dotting her bandages. Although the scene was from a nightmare, her head rested easy on a clean pillow, in a room she was to have all to herself.

Only hours into a well-deserved sleep her door banged open and Thornhollow was at her bedside, shaking her awake.

"Come on, girl. Time to earn your keep."

Pulled from the sacred confines of sleep she lashed out, but the doctor was ready for it, well outside of her reach when she swung.

"Sorry," he said, from a safe distance. "I've yet to find a good way to wake someone."

"There isn't one," Grace complained, one hand dragging across her eyes. "It's the black of night, besides."

"Our work isn't done in the daylight," Thornhollow said, rifling through the closet for clothing, which he tossed at her head. "Or rather, their work isn't. If we're to catch them while the deed is still fresh, we must keep the same hours."

"What's this?" A voice came from the doorway and Janey, the head nurse for the female ward, came into Grace's room, confusion making lines on her otherwise young face. "Doctor! I know this girl is under your special care, but you'll not be barging into her room in the middle of the night. Not in my ward, no, sir."

"I apologize," Thornhollow said, though he hardly sounded contrite. "However, we must work quickly to—ouch!" His sentence was cut off when Janey grabbed his ear.

"And I must work quickly as well, sir. You're the doctor, and I'm to take your orders. But in the night these women are under my care, and I will not have a man walking among them, no matter how many degrees he has!"

"Grace," Thornhollow said calmly as he was led from her room, "if you could meet me outside?"

She nodded dumbly and looked up to find that Janey had remained behind with her. "The rest of the staff said you don't speak a word, but you can move your head yes or no as to whether or not you want to go with the doctor?"

The young nurse's lips twisted when Grace acknowledged that she did. "All right then," Janey said. "If it's your will, I'll not go against it. The superintendent said that the new doctor has some interests that might be taking him about in the middle of the night and you in his wake."

The clothing Thornhollow had thrown at Grace now rested on her lap. Janey began sorting through the items. "Although I'd advise you to manage your own wardrobe from here on out. He's given you three undergarments."

Grace smothered a smile and let Janey help her dress in more suitable clothing, then followed the ward nurse to the lobby, where Thornhollow waited for her, his ear still red. They walked outside, where his carriage was ready and waiting, a driver in place.

"Doctor," she said quietly once they were safely ensconced inside. "You said we must move quickly in order to catch them while the deed is still fresh. Who are *they*?"

"My dear Grace," Thornhollow said. "I thought you understood. We're going to catch murderers."

It was a gruesome scene, lit by the flickering lamps of the policemen and the flashes of lightning that still ripped through the night. Thornhollow pulled his valise out of the carriage and held a hand out to help her down, while their driver hunched himself awkwardly against the pelting rain. Grace stymied the rush of nerves as she reached out of the safe anonymity of the gig for his hand, her face going instantly slack as soon as she passed through the doorframe. Even the mauled body on the pavement did not move her as she alighted from the carriage, each footstep as light and quick as a ghost's.

"Gentlemen, what is the situation?" Thornhollow asked.

"You the fellow playing policeman, are you, then?" a portly officer asked as he stepped over the blood pooling in the rainwater. "You've still got a bit of a baby face, yet you want to be a doctor and policeman both? Want to take your paycheck from the asylum and mine alongside it?"

The younger policeman nodded toward the carriage. "A gig as fine as that, with a nice shiny horse . . . he doesn't make that money up on the ridge."

"And a driver too," his partner added. "What you pay him to bring you out here this time of night? More than I make, I wouldn't wonder."

"Per my agreement with your commanding officer—decided upon when I applied for the job at the asylum—I'm being afforded every opportunity to learn more about the criminal mind," Thornhollow said patiently. "Gentlemen, your job is nothing more than my hobby."

"As to my driver, his name is Ned, and he manages the asylum's stables. He was kicked in the skull some years ago, bringing about the damage that made his new residence a necessity, though he harbors no ill will toward the species that brought the fate upon him. He chooses to live in the stables and spends his days carving small figurines of horses, as if in worship of the animal that delivered him from the necessity of having to interact with people such as yourselves. If I need him in the night, he's there, without complaint. So, if you'll step aside so that I can satisfy my curiosity, I'll take myself and my assistant out of your immediate area as soon as possible."

"I'd heard that about the asylum up on the hill," the heavier man said, his gaze still on the driver. "That you give 'em regular jobs. I never heard the like of it."

"Yes, we do give them regular jobs, and as I said, they do them without complaint, making them much more effective than any rational workingman I know."

"Your assistant?" the younger man asked, peering at Grace. "How come we don't have pretty girls to follow us around and carry our nightsticks, George?"

"I bet the doctor sees to her nightsticks, sure enough, Davey."

Their words were lost on their target. Grace remained as she was, empty gaze riveted on the dead body, sketching the details of the scene onto the blankness that she had created inside herself.

"Don't talk much, do you?" Davey snapped his fingers in front of her, but she didn't so much as blink.

Thornhollow didn't look up from where he knelt beside the corpse. "I wouldn't antagonize the girl too much, if I were you," he warned. "She's a mental patient as well."

"She one of them that just stares?" George asked, all attention on Grace so that he didn't notice Thornhollow going through the victim's pockets.

"Stares, yes," the doctor said. "Although every now and then a fit of violence takes her. The staff has yet to figure out what causes them. The other day they sent her out to milk the cows and she ripped two teats clean off one of the heifers."

Davey eyed Thornhollow with suspicion but edged away from Grace nonetheless.

"She get tied down a lot, eh, doctor?" George asked, his eyebrows up near his greasy hairline.

"I don't know her history," Thornhollow said as he touched an open wound on the dead man's face. "Although the asylum practices the most humane type of medicine, so I severely doubt this young woman has ever been bound against her will."

"Seems complacent enough," Davey ventured again, curiosity overcoming caution as he moved around Grace in a semicircle.

"They should all be done in, make no mistake," George said, his beady eyes narrowing on Grace. "Even the ones with the sweet faces such as hers. You don't know what devil lurks inside if it's like you said, tearing into a milk cow who done nothing wrong that day.

"You'd do better to practice your medicine on them that can be healed, Doctor. The works of such as goes on up at the asylum is an offense to nature. Ain't no survival of the fittest at work anymore when we're housing the idiots and stocking their kitchens with the food from our own larders. I work hard and I earn my bread for me and mine and seeing the likes of her staring there into the ground as if she don't know up from down and she's got a better roof over her head tonight than my little ones opens up a hole in my heart, it does."

"The existence of said organ still being under great question," Thornhollow said under his breath.

"What's that?"

"I said this man suffered some damage to his organs."

"That he did," Davey agreed. "Some of us do take an interest in the mad, you know, sir, having so many here in our own town." Thornhollow made a noise in his throat that was hardly encouraging, but the officer continued. "My papaw said he's seen a time or two when more than one person from the same family ends up there on the hill. What you say to that, Dr. Thornhollow? Does madness run in the families? Or is it all skewed, and you never know who's going to . . . to tear the tits off a cow, or something the like?"

"I think it's a good bet that you never know who is going to tear the tits off a cow on any given day."

George hawked and spat in the street, the stream landing near Grace.

"Them's that's mad should have the surgeries so's they can't have babies. We could put an end to it in a generation or so, if just one person had the bollocks to say we should cut off theirs."

"On the contrary," Thornhollow argued, "I've seen plenty of perfectly healthy children born to those deemed insane and decidedly insane progeny of the most normal persons imaginable."

"I still says there should be the surgeries," George said.

"I find that very odd indeed," Thornhollow said, coming to his feet.

"Why is that?"

"I think you should thank me for arguing against the castration of idiots." He tipped his hat at them. "I have all I need, thank you, gentlemen."

He passed by Grace, and she turned to walk beside him as they left the policemen in their wake, jaws working awkwardly as if they belonged in the barn beside the fictional, mutilated dairy cow. A smile lurked on Grace's lips, which she barely managed to contain until comfortably seated inside the carriage.

"I rather enjoyed that," she admitted to him as their driver touched the reins to the horses and the hoofbeats carried them into the night, thunder rolling to catch up to them.

"I'm a bit surprised to hear it," Thornhollow said, his face lost in the darkness. "I'd no doubt that you could look upon the horrific without flinching, but to actually enjoy it makes me wonder if perhaps I should truly shield poor ignorant men such as those we're leaving behind us from you in the future."

"I'd not hurt them," Grace said. "But men are always so—" she broke off, correcting herself. "Most men are always so proper in the presence of a lady. To hear men speak to other men as they would if I weren't there was enlightening."

"And not to my gender's credit, I'm sure," Thornhollow said. "However, what you say is true and part of the reason why I agreed to take you with me from Boston in the first place. Your mind is quick, your attention to detail established, your memory infallible. But the bandages on your forehead—and the scars that will form—provide the perfect cover for all your assets. It's established; you're insane."

"And therefore I am not human," Grace finished for him.

"Precisely. Most people will assume you lack reason. They're bound to say anything in front of you. Words that might pass when I'm out of earshot will be trapped by your meticulous mind. Within the bounds of the asylum you're free to be more expressive, establish some relationships however you can without using your voice. But among the public you're my fly on the wall, a carrier of all the information I can't possibly collect alone."

"And all my information, Doctor? All the things I glean while I stand in the rain pretending to be dull and staring at a corpse, what shall we do with them?"

"Dear girl, I'm a doctor," Thornhollow said as they crested the hill to the asylum. "What else will we do with them but dissect them?"

FOURTEEN

Thornhollow said a good dissection must be done while the subject is still fresh. He brought a steaming pot into his office, the warm scent of coffee following while Grace chafed her hands together for warmth.

"I'd apologize for dragging you out on a night such as this," the doctor said, "but this particular crime being as straightforward as it is affords the perfect opportunity for you to cut your teeth."

Grace accepted a steaming mug and settled onto a leather chair. "Straightforward?"

"Yes, quite, as I'll explain," Thornhollow said as he rolled a chalkboard to the front of the office, knocking askew a few piles of books as he did. "I'd apologize for the mess as well, but it's not likely I'll ever clean the place."

Grace looked around his office, which was rather a mess. Piles of books fought a tottering battle against gravity, unaided by their own weight whenever his relentless wanderings shook the warped floorboards. His coat was flung across the desk, and he'd set the coffeepot on top of it.

"Now to work, young Grace, before sleep claims you again."

She shook her head to clear it, already lulled by the warmth of the fire. The loose end of her bandage had unwound itself and flapped against her cheek. She tucked it back in, her fingers adept at the movement, now so familiar. "I'm ready when you are, Doctor."

"Good," he said. "Tonight, a brief primer. We'll see if you're able to draw any conclusions." He turned to the chalkboard, but his fingers played with the chalk as he spoke.

"Do you remember the Ripper killings in London a few years back?"

"I remember everyone talking about them," Grace said. "But I don't know much about the murders. Mother said it wasn't a fit topic for me, and she wouldn't allow the newspapers in the house for fear that . . ." Grace's throat closed, as if a valve from her former life had turned, not allowing her to speak of it.

Thornhollow nodded, all his attention on her words, not her emotions. "I'm not surprised she'd shield you from such events. It was a nasty business. The papers would have you think it was a new type of person altogether, or a demon at work. But there are those of us who've seen dark things long before the Ripper took his night-time walks. The only thing new in this story was a method that the police used in an attempt to find the killer.

"Most crime solving involves a very simple approach, Grace. Who? When? Why? How? That's it. These questions are pivotal and have done their duty for a long time, and done it well. But in the case of the Ripper they weren't doing the trick. Some scientists started looking at the behavior of the criminal *before* and *after* the crime, not just during, in order to collect information about who this person might be, what their profession is, their connection to the victim, even what their emotional state was like at different times before, during, and after the event. All these things can help establish a pic-ture of your criminal well beyond the simple monosyllabic questions we've been asking for centuries."

Grace sipped her coffee, letting the warmth soothe her vocal cords and the rough spot that had opened up when she spoke of the past. "That's all very well, Doctor, but I have to point out that the Ripper was never caught, new method or not."

Thornhollow stopped pacing and bit his cheek. "True. However, I became somewhat entranced by the idea and have spent years in study, gathering information about individuals that are known mur-derers so that we may have a collection of facts to draw from when we don't know who we're looking for. We're drawing a picture, if you will, of what kind of man—or woman—would do certain deeds, and how they'd go about doing them."

"So, you work backward, in a sense," Grace said, her eyebrows drawing together as a headache began to form at her temples, pulsing against the bandage. "Instead of learning their biography after you catch them, you put together a story about who you think they are, and then use that to track them down."

"Precisely."

A flush of pride flowed through Grace at his word, a warmth in her belly not provided by the coffee.

"In the case of the Ripper, you're right. He was never caught, but I believe the methodology is sound and have used it myself multiple times to aid the police in Boston. Coming to Ohio means I'm casting my net in a smaller pond, no doubt. Boston was so full of murders some nights, I hardly knew which crime scene to attend, but the hospital here is the most humane I've seen, and I grew weary of operating in darkness both day and night."

"Don't be deceived by a pleasant setting, Doctor," Grace warned. "Sometimes the loveliest places harbor the worst monsters."

"Very true," he acknowledged. "With that in mind, I'll ask you a straightforward question. If you were to murder someone, who would you kill?"

"My father," she said promptly.

He nodded, as if he'd expected the answer. "And how would you do it?"

She answered immediately, allowing the smoldering feeling in her belly to take control of her vocal cords before giving any thought to the words. "I'd scratch his heart out of his chest and stamp on it. Then I'd gouge out his eyes."

"Oh," Thornhollow said, after a pause. "That's . . ." He cleared his throat. "It definitely serves to prove my point."

Grace tightened her hands on her coffee cup. "Forgive me, Doctor," she said, the heat from her words lighting her cheeks a bright red. "I didn't mean—"

"No," he interrupted her. "Do not apologize. You *did* mean. You meant every word exactly as you said it. And no one, least of all me, will ever judge you for that."

She looked down into the swirling dregs of her coffee, as the headache gained traction. "Thank you," she said.

"As I was saying, your proposed actions illustrate my point very well. And now a second scenario. I want you to imagine that you need money. You're a poor girl on the streets and you may starve before the day is out. You see a well-dressed man on the corner in the dark of night. You're going to kill him and take his money. How will you do it?"

"I . . ." Grace's voice faltered as she pictured the scene. Though she came from wealth, she understood desperation, and her mind picked over the imaginary scene.

"I'd pick up a brick, I suppose, or a rock. I'd sneak up on him, hit him on the head, and take his wallet."

"Precisely," Thornhollow said. "In our first instance you have a personal connection to the victim—your father. You are motivated by emotion and revenge. You commit the proposed crime with your bare hands, even mutilate his face in order to strip him of the power to look at you as he's dying."

"But with the man in the alley I don't care," Grace said, filling in the gaps on her own. "I'm killing him because I need his money, not because I want to hurt him. It's not . . . it's not personal."

Thornhollow nodded. "Spot-on. Falsteed was right to call you a quick study. Now, earlier I said that tonight's murder was a simple one. Why?"

"Because—"

"Wait," he said, stopping her. "Don't be too hasty. Close your eyes and see."

Grace did so, letting her mind slip back into the moments where she'd stood immobile on the wet bricks, the rivulets of blood trailing past her shoes.

"He was shot in the head," she said, her eyes roving over where the body lay on the ground. "In the face," she corrected.

"And so?"

"So . . . the killer probably knew him. They wanted to disfigure him."

"Not only that"—Thornhollow's voice sidled into her reverie—"but the killer also wanted to be seen by attacking from the front. The killer wanted the victim to know who was taking his life."

"They knew each other," Grace said, her eyes still closed while internally roving over the picture in her mind. "He was married," she said quietly, when she spotted the ring on his left hand.

"He was," Thornhollow agreed.

Her inner gaze left the body, traveled over the surroundings, lit only by the sputtering gas lamps and the feeble light streaming from the windows of the building the victim was killed in front of. "Why was a married man at a pub in the dead of night?" she asked.

"Why indeed?"

Grace opened her eyes. "You searched his pockets," she said. "Why?"

"To see if he was robbed. Which he was not."

"So a married man is shot in the face by someone he knows when leaving a pub in the middle of the night, but he's not robbed," Grace said. "His wife killed him."

"My thoughts as well," Thornhollow agreed. "For what it's worth I imagine that in an establishment as run-down as that particular one seemed to be, the women probably serve more than drinks if the price is right. I can't imagine a wife killing her husband for being thirsty at an inopportune time."

Grace set her now cold coffee on the edge of Thornhollow's desk. "You said this was simple, but how do we know if we're right?"

"I'll follow up with the officers in the morning. Even they will be smart enough to identify him and go to his house. It's an unfortunate side effect of matrimony that the majority of people killed participating in it were brought to that pass by their other half."

"I see," Grace said, her fingers going to her bandage, where the headache had laid full claim.

"Are you well?" Thornhollow asked.

"Doctor, I've been cut to my skull on both sides of my head, traveling with a strange man for days, and pulled from my bed in the dead of night to view a corpse. Oddly, I feel fine except for this headache."

Thornhollow laughed, a full sound that echoed off the windows and made Grace smile in its unmitigated loudness.

"Grace," he said. "Not only do you have a unique gift suited for these dark purposes, but I think your nature is as well."

"And what becomes of a girl such as that?" Grace said, her tone somber.

Thornhollow's smile fell. "I admit I didn't have a lot of time to think ahead when we scuttled you out of Boston. The staff here believes you are a patient under my express care who I have done an experimental surgery on. The charade of muteness is one you will have to maintain. For that I apologize. I'm the only person who can know that you have use of your voice and mind. If anyone were to suspect who you really are—"

"I understand," Grace said. "I don't mind being silent in exchange for what I've been delivered from."

"Yes, but I'm afraid it'll be no kind of existence for you."

"No," she said. "What I came from was no kind of existence."

"Not much of a compliment, since you were living in a dungeon."

"That's not what I was referring to, Doctor," Grace said, but her thoughts had drifted back to the darkness of the asylum and Falsteed's voice comforting her.

"Well"—Thornhollow brought his hands together in a clap—"it's been a long night, to say the least. You should get to your bed. I'll let the staff know that you were out assisting me and should be allowed to sl—"

"Doctor, why was Falsteed in the asylum?" Grace asked suddenly.

"For a girl of good breeding you certainly do interrupt often."

"And your answer?"

"I . . ." Thornhollow ran the toe of his shoe over a spot on the floor. "I'm not sure I should provide it."

"Why?" Grace demanded. "Falsteed was my friend."

"Which is why I'm not sure I should answer you."

"I'm hardly naive. Falsteed was not only an inmate but one relegated to the bowels of the dungeon. I know he must have done something horrid at one time. I would know what it was."

Thornhollow sighed and looked at the floor. "You've had all the benefits of a good life. I suppose you've been inoculated against smallpox?"

"I . . ." Grace trailed off, suspicious. "Yes."

"Do you know much about what the smallpox vaccination does?"

"No," she said. "Only that once I'm inoculated I cannot catch the disease."

Thornhollow nodded. "It's a simple enough concept. Once your body is exposed to certain illnesses it learns how to fight them and remembers so that you cannot be afflicted again. The smallpox vaccination is actually a bit of cowpox entered into your body at a low dose. Your body reacts, learns to fight it, and while you may get a headache or slight fever, you will never be afflicted by the more lethal cousin, smallpox.

"While medical science has come far and accomplished much, there is little we can do against the malignant beast of cancer. Falsteed has lost more than a few patients to the monster, and I'm afraid he developed a . . . bit of an obsession."

"I hardly think he can be called obsessive by wanting to treat the afflicted," Grace said.

"It is not treatment Falsteed delivers. When he was still a free man practicing his trade, Falsteed was known for searching out those who suffered from cancerous tumors. He performed surgeries for free, his only payment being that he kept the offending growth."

Grace shrugged. "Where is the crime in that?"

"And then he ate them," Thornhollow said.

Grace felt the blood flow from her face. "He did what?"

"He ate them," Thornhollow repeated. "In a foolhardy attempt to inoculate himself against cancer. His actions landed him in the asylum, and I don't mind saying that he rightly belongs there."

"Dear God," Grace said, her hands fluttering to her face. "But he saved me."

"He did," Thornhollow said. "And despite these things, he is your friend and you owe him much." The doctor came to the side of her chair, resting a hand on the back of her head. "These are your friends now, Grace Mae. A madman who eats cancer in the dark and another who searches for a different kind of killer, the kind who smiles at you in the light of day. This is your new life. I hope you can stand it."

FIFTEEN

"She's wakin'." An Irish lilt drifted into Grace's dreams, followed by a much softer voice.

"String says to let her sleep."

"Stuff you an' your string."

A slight gasp followed that comment and Grace felt herself swimming toward consciousness, despite the ever-present pressure at her temples.

"Ohhh, there ye are now," the brogue continued. "Open up them pretty peepers and let us have a look at ye."

Grace came fully awake to find herself face-to-face with two girls her age, both dressed in the drab gray of inmates.

"Blue," the Irish girl declared, after shoving her face up next to Grace's. "Ye owe me your dessert at suppertime, Elizabeth."

The smaller girl squeezed her lips together in annoyance. "Why couldn't your eyes have been green?" she demanded of Grace. "It would've looked so nice with your hair."

Luckily for Grace she could come up with no words to defend the eye color she'd been born with, and the Irish girl's voice filled the void.

"Ain't no use asking questions of 'er," she said. "Janey said this one's not got 'er voice about 'er."

Elizabeth's eyebrows drew together in confusion, and she turned her head as if to consult something on her shoulder in a whisper.

The Irish girl stamped her foot. "I told ye there's to be no talkin' to the string while yer with me. And scarin' the new girl, no doubt."

Elizabeth drew herself up to her full height—which wasn't much—before speaking. "Janey told *me* she came in with that Dr. Thornhollow late last night, and we weren't to wake her. But you've gone and done it anyway, Nell, as is your pleasure."

"Oooooh," Nell said, her eyes popping wide and matching the form of her mouth. "Dr. Thornhollow, eh? I wouldn't mind letting 'im know me pleasure, if you get the meanin'."

"One look at your chart and he'd be disinterested, I'm sure," Elizabeth said.

"You leave me chart out of it," Nell said, eyes narrowing.

Grace sat up in bed, bringing both girls' attention back to her. "Sorry, luv," Nell said, throwing herself onto Grace's mattress with a huff. "Elizabeth and I, we know each a bit too well. Sometimes we 've conversations that get temperamental."

"Yes, a bit like sisters, I suppose," Elizabeth said. "Affection tinged with suffering."

"Suffering." Nell rolled her eyes. "Elizabeth's a wee bit of a wet blanket. But ye get used to 'er. She'd pass for normal if she didn't insist 'er string tells 'er all she knows."

Grace smiled tentatively at Nell, wondering what had landed her in the asylum. Her black wavy hair flowed freely, setting off a porcelain-white face and eyes that Grace's mother would've said would lead a man to trouble.

"It is *String*," Elizabeth corrected her friend. "Not *her* string, or *my* string. Simply String," she said with a dignity that her friend waved off casually.

"Aye, it's got a name all right," Nell said. "And if ever a string was too big for its britches, it's that'un."

Elizabeth gave up the argument with a wave of her hand and sat by Grace's head, burying her hands in Grace's hair and weaving tiny, delicate braids without another word.

"Don'tcha mind wee Elizabeth," Nell said, shaking her head. "She gets a bit puckish when you insult String, beings as it tells 'er all she knows. She's terribly attached to it, though it landed 'er in this 'ere place."

"I'd say you're a bit attached to your own cause of residency," Elizabeth said.

"Aye, well." Nell sighed and reached between her legs suggestively. "There's no separatin' me from it, is there?"

Even though Grace heard Elizabeth sigh in frustration, she could feel repressed laughter running through the other girl's fingers as she tied off one of Grace's braids. "There you are," Elizabeth said, patting her on the head.

"Enough of this fanciness," Nell said, raking her hands through Grace's new braids so that her hair fell wild like Nell's own. "Janey— she minds our floor of the women's ward—she said we was to show you the grounds."

Grace rose from her bed, eyes searching for the dress she'd worn the night before.

"We sent your dirty linens down the chute in the hall," Elizabeth said, pulling Grace to her feet. "Although how you managed to dirty three pairs of underwear in one night is outside my knowing."

"Maybe she's like that Mr. Feiffer over in the men's ward, can't 'old his piss," Nell said.

"Enough," Elizabeth said. "We took a guess at your size at the laundry." She smiled at Grace. "Brought you some fresh things. They're not particular about how you dress here. If your family sends you something lovely, then you can wear it and no one will fuss at you. But Nell and me, we . . . we . . ."

"Neither of us got nobody," Nell said. "None that care fer us, anyway. Why do ye stand there a-starin' like ye got no sense? Up and over with the shift. We're the all of us lassies." Without any further preamble, Nell jerked Grace's nightgown over her head.

Grace immediately crossed her arms in front of herself, but Nell and Elizabeth kept up a lively chatter between the two of them while they dressed Grace in the clothes they'd brought her. Nell glanced up at her skeptically while she buttoned Grace's boots, fingers dexterously looping each button. "Janey said the doctor claims yer bright, but I'm beginning to wonder, meself."

Elizabeth slapped her friend's hand lightly. "You've only awakened her, made lewd suggestions, and stripped her in a matter of minutes. If you've driven the sense from the girl, there's no wonder in it."

Nell stepped back and took in Grace from head to toe while Elizabeth combed out her hair with her fingers and wrapped it into a bun. "You'll do," Nell said. "Though I don't know about this no-talkin' business."

Elizabeth put her hand on Grace's elbow. "Can you write?"

Eager to please the other girls, Grace nodded before considering if Dr. Thornhollow would want her communicating with the other patients at all. But the smile that lit up Elizabeth's plain face told her she'd made the right answer regardless.

"We'll get you a slate then and some chalk. Then you can say whatever you like."

"Aye, it's a fine plan for them's that can read," Nell said.

"I'll tell you what she says," Elizabeth said, steering Grace toward the door.

"And who's going to keep ye honest?"

Elizabeth came to a dead halt and stamped a dainty foot so hard Grace jumped in alarm. "Nell O'Kelly, if you're suggesting that I would tell a falsehood—"

"Ooooh, a false'ood, is it?" Nell said, throwing her hands in the air. "As long as the first thing the poor vacant dearie 'ere says is tha' I'm the prettiest girl she's ever seen, then I know you're sayin' it true." She took Grace by the other elbow and the two of them walked her out into the sunlit hall.

Grace had escaped Boston under the cover of dark. When the other girls dragged her outdoors into the sunlight she recoiled as if struck, her hands going up to her eyes.

"Is it your bandages?" Elizabeth asked, misjudging Grace's pain.

Grace shook her head, though she kept one hand on each of the girls' shoulders for her first few steps. She blinked quickly, allowing her eyes time to adjust.

"'Ave ye got somethin' wrong with yer 'ead?" Nell asked, peering at Grace's temple. "On the outside, I mean?"

"Nell, shush," Elizabeth said. "There's no point pestering her with questions she can't answer without a slate."

"True enough," Nell said, removing Grace's hand from her

shoulder, but not before giving it a squeeze. "I'll be back, and when I do I'll be expectin' ye to write me a fine story."

Elizabeth frowned as the other girl disappeared into the towering expanse of the asylum. "She'll get a slate off one of the boys, no doubt. And I pity him if he takes any more in return than a smile."

Grace tucked her hand into Elizabeth's elbow and raised an eyebrow in question.

"Nell is a syphilitic," Elizabeth explained, her mouth forming the word with distaste. Grace looked down at her shoes as they walked across the gravel path, accustoming herself to the unfamiliar pinch of having any to wear. "Don't think worse of her for it," Elizabeth added quickly. "She's not had an easy life—" Elizabeth cocked her head suddenly as if she'd been interrupted. "String says it's not my place to say more."

Grace was happy to take in the grounds in companionable silence. The asylum in Boston had worn a skin as ugly as the heart beating inside of it, the darkness seeping from inside and staining the bricks that contained the mad. But this asylum was beautiful, its bricks an honest red that soaked in the sun's rays and reflected the heat back onto those inside during the night. Even in the darkness of her room Grace had felt a calm that the building itself seemed to translate into her skin, a tuneless melody that sang her fevered brain into sleep.

Acres of green grass rolled beneath her feet, and Grace strayed from the gravel path with Elizabeth as a silent shadow. Green leaped at Grace's eyes, and though the sun had slipped behind a cloud, the healthy colors beat into her pupils like a pulse she'd been separated from too long. The air was so fresh that Grace could feel it cleansing her lungs of the last fetid gasps of Boston air and could only wonder what secrets Falsteed could pull from it.

The faintest wisps of rose oil leaked out from under her bandages. The itch of healing had settled in, and Grace knew that soon her wrappings could go. Everyone would see her scars then, but she could wear them with pride here in this new world where the insane wandered freely in their own clothes. The pair crested a hill to see a rippling expanse of water below them and Grace gasped, almost exclaiming out loud to her new friend before she remembered herself.

"It's a sight, is it not?" Elizabeth said, smiling as if she were responsible for it.

Grace smiled in return and spotted a man over Elizabeth's shoulder who had his arms wrapped tightly around a tree. In her current state, she almost felt like hugging one herself. She'd been so long separated from anything except the dark that words wanted to trip out as they piled on top of one another in her throat in their need to proclaim the joy of finally feeling safe.

"You make good time, fer a pair of idiots." Nell huffed over the hill, hot spots of exertion on both her cheeks, slate in hand. "I even cut short makin' eyes at Charlie when I saw ye comin' fer the lake.

You coulda waited," she chided Elizabeth. "I woulda liked to seen 'er face."

"She lit up like a candle," Elizabeth said, her own eyes glowing. "As does everyone when they see it. String says the power of—"

"Yer claptrap can go on," Nell interrupted. "Or we can see what the new lassie has ter say."

She handed the slate and a piece of chalk with teeth marks in it over to Grace, who pinched it between her fingers for moment, the well-rounded tip poised inches from the slate.

"Well," Nell prodded her. "What ya got ter say?"

Grace thought for a moment, then she wrote as the breeze pulled the edges of her bandages away from her temples, the faintly bloodied tips flapping around her face. She held up the slate for both girls to read, hoping that her new friends would ignore the sheen of tears over her eyes.

MY NAME IS GRACE

SIXTEEN

She did not see the doctor that day, except as a tall, silent shadow that stalked the grounds with others in attendance as they pointed to patients scattered across the grounds. He kept his head down, his notebook in his hand, and Grace reminded herself not to let her gaze follow him too often.

Elizabeth and Nell had stuck by her the entire day, explaining that their duties—Nell's in the laundry and Elizabeth's in the kitchen—had been excused so that Grace could be shown around the asylum and grounds.

"Ye've got perfect freedom here, as long as ye be'ave," Nell had explained. "There's nae even locks on the bedroom doors."

"As long as you behave," Elizabeth had added archly, raising an eyebrow at Nell, who had smiled wickedly.

The warmth she'd accrued from the sun in their afternoon walk was escaping her skin now, but Grace could still feel the benefits from it, as if her body had remembered in that short afternoon what it was to be alive.

The presence of the other girls had its own effect, and Grace felt a smile tugging at her mouth as she remembered Nell unabashedly laying claim to Elizabeth's dessert that evening as they ate together in the women's ward. "On account of ye 'aving the wrong color eyes," she'd mock whispered to Grace, clearly meaning for Elizabeth to overhear. "String didn't know *that*, did 'e?"

Her comment had caused Elizabeth a diatribe of objection to String having any gender at all, to which Grace had listened with half an ear while devouring her dish of strawberries, which Nell had later informed her came fresh from the asylum's gardens.

Her hands lay crossed on her belly now, no longer in protection of an unseen presence but in remembrance. Grace closed her eyes not against the world but in an effort to trap it in the moment, so that she could know fully how lucky she was to have come to this place where the kindness of strangers deemed unsuitable for society had filled her day more fully than any ever spent with the higher echelons.

There had been friends in Boston, girls her own age who were approved for her to spend leisure time with. Walks in gardens and timid conversations that only touched on respectable topics had been all that were allowed them. Grace knew that the horrid truths of her nighttime hours would only seem like garish nightmares to these half-formed shadows of their own mothers who parroted manners and giggled behind their hands when boys' names were mentioned.

That she could tell Elizabeth and Nell the truth of her existence without hesitation if she were allowed to speak, Grace knew without a doubt. Their lives were like her own, flavored with the misery of the past, which made the safety of the present all the more sweet. The bonds grown out of shared suffering were strong indeed, and though forged only that afternoon, Grace felt a closeness to them that had never existed with the well-bred friends handpicked in her former life.

It was easy to shut the doors of her mind on the faces of the past. Grace had done so without hesitation and thrown away the key. But Alice's voice slipped through the keyhole, echoing into her dreams and bringing with it the image of her little sister's face, still full with the baby fat of youth and wide, innocent eyes.

"Grace." Even her name sounded sweeter in those high, childish tones. "Grace, you haven't eaten your strawberries," Alice said, her small pink lips stained with the redness of her own dessert.

In her dream, Grace lifted her eyes from the pattern of the lace covering on the dining room table, her stomach turning in revulsion at the red fruit in front of her. "I can't," she said weakly, her fingertips barely strong enough to push the china away from her as the nausea swept her body.

"Mother," Alice said, her thin blond brows creased with worry. "Why does Grace not eat her breakfast anymore?"

"Grace is not feeling well," their mother said, a permanent line in between her brows darkening as she rose to stand beside her oldest daughter. "Perhaps you had best go to your tutor alone this morning, Alice. Grace and I need to talk."

"We did talk." Grace seethed, her words tasting like the vomit she tried so hard to keep down. "I told you and told you and YOU WILL NOT LISTEN." The rage she'd held on to in reality burst forth in her dream, and Alice's small face collapsed in tears as Grace grabbed her fork and drove it through her mother's hand. Mother's blood flowed and her hand turned to a man's, the silver tines of the fork exposing bone and gristle while Heedson yowled in pain, and Alice's cheeks hollowed out, the ends of her lovely hair splitting while she shoved handfuls of it into her mouth in an imitation of Cracked Pat.

"You wouldn't listen," Grace cried out, sitting up in her bed and trying to stop the words before they seeped through the walls and betrayed her to her neighbors.

Though she knew she could share parts of her story if she chose, her slate was small and no words were big enough to encompass her past. Grace wiped at her mouth, almost wanting to spit to rid the aftertaste of the nightmare and the memories that had rushed at her unbidden. It seemed safer to lock it away and leave everything behind along with her last name in the murky darkness of a Boston asylum.

And it would be so easy if not for Alice, whose sweet face had greeted her every morning and whose tiny fingers had once wound through Grace's own. The very fingers that might that moment be pressed to red-rimmed eyes as she mourned for a sister dead at the hands of whatever lies her parents had fed her to cover the trail of the ones before.

Grace flung back her covers, all sleep stolen at the thought of Alice mourning for a death that hadn't happened. Lies had covered her home for so long that Grace had accepted them as a matter of course, as ever-present as the smell of drink on Mother's breath and strange perfume on Father's coat. She'd been born and bred on them, and now she'd turned the tables, using all the tricks and trumperies she'd learned by watching to deliver herself from their web.

But her escape meant a shield was removed from her little sister. Alice had been born too late to foster anything other than resentment for a ruined figure from their mother and grumblings about another wedding to pay for from their father, but those words had never found her delicate ears. Grace hovered near her always, drawing the angry glares herself, and suggesting outdoor activities when the barely restrained arguments seeped through closed doors.

Grace reached through the decorative iron grille on her widow to trace her fingertips along the glass, now cool with the night air. She wondered if Alice sat at her own window, or if Falsteed thought of her behind his bars.

"Miss Madeleine Baxter," Grace said softly to herself, remembering the false name Falsteed had told her to write to Reed under. A smile formed as a mockingbird sang on the lawn, echoing the gibberish of the inmates he'd encountered that day.

"I wouldn't be surprised if Miss Madeleine Baxter has a little sister," she said.

Falsteed—

I hardly know what to call you. Mister? Doctor? Friend? Fiend?

Dr. Thornhollow has told me of your past, but how can I find fault with your deeds when without them our paths would never have crossed? If you are mad then I owe my life to a madman, and he is no less dear to me for his actions. Truly evil people do exist, this I know, but I do not count you among them. Instead, I choose to see you as a good person who has done bad things, and who among us cannot be dubbed so?

Somehow you smelled out the dark origins of my incarceration. Perhaps you also smelled mixed with my own scent a lighter one. So much time was spent holding this one close to me that I would not be surprised to learn that her smell clung to my skin, even in the darkness.

As we are, after all, one flesh.

She is my sister, a small, lovely creature who I shielded daily from the secrets in our shared home. That the pall of our parents' lies should descend upon her now, I can hardly bear. I know what it is to live in that house. Even before the worst, life there was bearable only because I had her to coddle and protect. She must have some comfort, for she is surrounded by anger and deception. I recognize the danger in correspondence, but fear more the results should I not take some action.

Though she sheds her childhood now, once there was an imaginary friend she held dear, who she claimed would meet her in the gardens and leave small presents on a certain rock. That I was the bearer of these, you no doubt realize, and I would be that again. A carefully worded letter from the same friend need not be associated with me. If Reed would endeavor to be the bearer, I can tell him of a hole in the fence surrounding the house, long hidden by ivy. If ever I find myself in a position to repay both you and Reed, it will be done tenfold.

Of my new life I will say little and of Thornhollow even less. You know the deal that was struck in order to facilitate my escape, and I fear you disapprove. What then would you think if I were to tell you that I have already proven myself not only useful but also a keen student of this dark enterprise into the criminal mind? I would say that the work is distasteful, but only because that is what you want to hear. In truth I find myself looking forward to the next opportunity to sharpen my skills and must remind myself that in order for that to happen, someone must die. If it was darkness you feared I would turn to while in his employ, fear not. The darkness has long lived inside me, sown if not by my nature then by nurture.

Grace's pen faltered as she lingered over the closing. How was she to end a letter written in the sunshine to a man who would receive it in darkness with the death of another still on his breath? She settled for a simple, *Always,* and left off signing it altogether.

Even though she was confident that Reed would spirit the letter to Falsteed and it would be destroyed soon after, Grace did not put her name to it. The enclosed letter needed to be written with even greater care, worded so vaguely that curious adults would spot only child's play.

Dearest Alice—

I hope this letter has found you well. You may think it odd to receive a letter from someone you thought no longer existed, but I assure you that imaginary friends never cease to be, even when we have outlived our usefulness. Much like real people, we look for the right time to make ourselves known.

If you would like to leave a message here for me, the fairies will spirit it away during the night. But remember—fairies can only come when good girls are asleep, so do not watch for them. They shall not come if you do.

Do not let them tell you I am gone, for I am always here.

Fair Lily

Grace signed the name of her sister's imaginary friend with a relish, using the same loopy scrawl she'd employed when they were younger. Her fingers trailed over the paper, reluctant to fold up and enclose it with Falsteed's so quickly. That Alice's small fingers might touch the same place as hers sometime soon left a happiness in Grace's heart so fragile she refused to examine it more closely.

Falsteed might deem it too dangerous for her to contact Alice. Reed might refuse the delivery. Rain and sun might ruin the letter before her sister happened upon it. But there was still a chance that she would receive it and find solace from the same hand that had given it so many times before, though she would not know the source. Grace pressed the letter to her heart before folding it, hoping that somehow her unspoken emotions would seep into the paper and flow back out to Alice, even if it was the only reunion the two could ever know.

SEVENTEEN

"We got our man. Or rather, *they* were competent enough to. And it was a woman, after all. So ignore my first statement." Thornhollow sat on the arm of a chair in his office, staring moodily at the floor by his feet.

"You don't seem particularly happy about it," Grace said, welcoming the freedom to speak after another day of feigned inability. Having Nell beside her made talking unnecessary and walking with Elizabeth usually consisted of companionable silence, both enjoyable in their own ways. But Grace's voice grew in power every day as she discovered the joys of speaking her mind, and she never missed an evening in Thornhollow's office to share her opinions.

"I'm not," Thornhollow admitted. "How can I teach you anything without a more complex crime than a jealous wife?"

"Careful what you wish for," Grace said, thinking of her words to Falsteed in her letter. "That opportunity means someone's death."

"Yes, yes," he said. "But we didn't even get to use the blackboard."

"What would you write on it if we had?" Grace asked, carefully handling him as if he were Alice in a fit of pique.

"Oh, the basics," he said, lackadaisically rising from his seat, approaching the board, and drawing a neat line down the center of it. "I suppose we can have a lesson even if there is no object at the moment." On the left-hand side of the board he wrote *Planned*; on the other, *Impulsive*.

"A killer may be able to remove evidence from a crime scene, hide the murder weapon, clean up spilled blood, and take any number of steps necessary to cover their tracks. Yet even by doing this they are giving us clues as to who they are—or rather, who they were."

"What do you mean by that? Who they *were*? Aren't we more interested in who they *are*?" Grace asked.

"We are, all of us, the sum total of our life experience, Grace. Everything that happened to you as a child, from the geography of your birthplace to the social status of your family, even the order of your birth, can be read in your actions today." Thornhollow tossed the chalk from hand to hand as he warmed up to his topic.

"If I told you we had a victim who had been stabbed multiple times and there was little blood on the scene or under the body, what would you learn from that?"

Grace closed her eyes, picturing a faceless body in a dark street, cold hands lying still on the cobblestones that remained clean despite the fact there should be blood spreading. "The body was moved," she said, opening her eyes.

"Very good," Thornhollow said. "But what else?"

"I . . ." She pictured the scene again but could see no more.

"Let me rephrase the question—what does the fact that our fictitious body was moved tell you about the killer?"

Grace again imagined the clean street beneath the hand, so different from the bricks reddening with blood under the man whose wife had killed him. That killer had been in a rage, her passions driving her to murder, and the panic that followed her action chasing her from the scene, unable to hide anything about her identity as she fled.

"They knew they had to protect themselves," Grace said slowly. "For someone to move a body indicates a clear head at the time of the crime."

"Yes, because the crime itself had been . . ." He pointed at the board, eyebrows raised as he silently asked her to finish his sentence.

"Planned," Grace said.

"And the very fact that it was planned speaks volumes of our killer," Thornhollow continued. "Years of talking with killers has not only been for conversational purposes, I assure you—although in one or two cases it really was quite pleasant. In speaking with other researchers like myself we've all discovered certain patterns that arise so consistently it is hard to explain away."

The chalk flashed out words in a column on the left side of the board as he went on. "An organized killer is usually intelligent, has a skilled job, is socially competent—indeed, most of their acquaintances deny it could be them based on how *normal* they are."

"Yet these are all things in their present," Grace said. "What of your claim that the past has defined them?"

"It has. As I said, certain themes arise when experiences are compiled. And I can tell you with some certainty that a killer who plans and executes their crime with control of their emotions is an older sibling or only child whose father had a stable job throughout their childhood."

"And how does that help you catch them?"

"In so many ways, Grace. The simple fact of identifying whether the crime was planned or impulsive informs us that we are looking for an intelligent person with a steady job—and by the way, since our fake killer dumped the body it also tells us he is probably familiar with that area. These seemingly small facts narrow the populace of an entire city down to a neighborhood."

"And then you can use the assumption that they are an only child to narrow it down still further?"

Thornhollow clapped his hands together, producing a cloud of chalk dust. "Exactly. Much of what we do can be described as exactly that—a narrowing of the possibilities."

"Until we are down to one," Grace said.

"Yes. And that process begins with deciding whether our killer is a planner or impulsive. The meticulous nature of the planner can be misleading. If you have a killer who, say, drains the blood from all their victims, or removes the left hand consistently, the untrained want to say they are insane. But the definition of insanity—an inability to use rational thought—immediately precludes that they must, in fact, be sane."

"Not an easy thing for the average person to accept," Grace said. "Most would want to believe that a fellow human being would have to be out of their mind to do such a thing."

"But they're not. Far from it, in fact. Simply using the words *sane* and *insane* is a way for the population to draw a safe line through humanity, and then place themselves squarely on the side of the healthy."

Grace's hands went to her temples, where her scars shined brightly. Thornhollow had taken the wrappings off a few days earlier, and the nakedness of her skin against the air had been a relief as well as a shock when she glanced in the mirror. The scars were a price she was willing to pay, but the evidence of the payment had set her back when she first saw them.

"They will fade," Thornhollow had said quietly.

But she knew she would always carry them, and her fingers

traced the thin webbing of smooth skin on her temples that would forever mark her as one on the wrong side of that line.

"So are we really that different? The healthy and the ill?" Grace asked.

"I would argue there is no difference at all," Thornhollow said. "To me the insane are simply people who have chosen not to participate in the world in the same manner as the majority, and there are days I wonder if they've got the right of it."

"You make it sound as if hardly anyone is insane with a definition as narrow as that."

"Quite the opposite; my definition is too broad. I think we're all quite mad. Some of us are just more discreet about it."

"Surely there is such a thing as true insanity?"

"There is," Thornhollow said reluctantly, "but I would argue those cases are much fewer than most suspect. These walls exist for a reason, but there is no cause for there to be so many rooms inside."

"Nell doesn't belong here," Grace said, almost to herself.

"Certainly not," Thornhollow agreed. "There's nothing wrong with the girl mentally. Physically . . . well, perhaps she hasn't told you."

"Elizabeth said she's a syphilitic."

"That's correct." The doctor nodded. "Which means she receives mercury baths on a regular basis, but that's something a physician could administer as easily as asylum staff. The true reason for her being admitted here is that she is a young woman who takes an active interest in men and feels no shame in it. The world can't understand this behavior; therefore the girl must be insane."

"And Elizabeth? She believes a string dangles from nowhere beside her ear and whispers things to her."

"Highly unlikely. Janey told me that she sees little Lizzie hovering in doorways often. I think she's highly attuned to detail, much like yourself. She gleans information from people, then picks up some like any busybody. But in her mind she attributes it all to String." Thornhollow shrugged. "Then again, I could be completely wrong. Who's to say String isn't real?"

"I can hardly agree with that," Grace said. "I like her quite well, but there's clearly something wrong with—"

"With her brain?" Thornhollow interrupted. "What would you say, then, if I told you that I've dissected hundreds of brains—of both the sane and insane—and found no difference whatsoever in them?"

"None?"

"My brain, and yours, Elizabeth's, Heedson's, even our mutual friend Falsteed's would all look the same if we ever had the opportunity of comparing them. It's one of the reasons why I have no use whatsoever for phrenology."

Grace stifled a yawn. "I'm afraid I'll have to ask you to explain what phrenology is, Doctor."

"No, no. Don't let me keep you up. I tend to go on once I've got my teeth in a subject, and sometimes I forget that my audience may not be as keen as I am on the matter of dissecting brains."

Grace glanced at the clock. "Explain phrenology, and then I'll take myself to bed. I don't mind being kept up when it's the only time I am allowed to be myself."

"Very well." Thornhollow returned to the board and drew a caricature of a human head, dividing it into uneven sections with a few slashes of the chalk. "The idea behind phrenology is that the brain is divided into certain parts, each part with a specific purpose. Within these parts are smaller areas that control certain functions that determine your personality." He made smaller crosshatch marks within the sections.

"So, for example, in a particularly brave person the part of the brain that handles courage would be overdeveloped. That section would be larger than others, pressing against the skull and reshaping it to create a subtle bump there. The theory is that a person trained in phrenology—as I am—would be able to feel the bumps and ridges of a person's skull and intimate from them what their characteristics are."

"That's utterly ridiculous," Grace said. "I'd sooner ask Elizabeth's string."

"And get a more accurate reading," Thornhollow agreed.

"Yet you are trained in this pseudoscience. Why?"

"Because there are those who swear by it. I've gained access to a few killers for some stolen moments of questions by offering my services as a phrenologist to law enforcement. Although the vast majority of the people whose skulls I'm brought in to read are thoroughly innocent and utterly terrified of being proved otherwise."

"And what do you do then?"

"Gather information from them, once they're calm enough to provide it. Analyze the facts, starting with the first and largest step—the one I've taught you tonight. As with our made-up killer who planned his crime and dumped the body somewhere familiar to him, I use the crime to paint a portrait of the killer. When faced with an accused innocent, the best possible defense is to find the guilty." Thornhollow wheeled back to the board, pointing at the series of words he'd written. "That one who . . . I spelled *sibling* wrong."

Grace smothered a smile with her hand.

"It's all very well for you," Thornhollow said irritably as he wiped the offending word away with his sleeve. "You don't have to be concerned about your intellect slipping."

"I very much doubt yours is slipping," Grace said as he flung himself into a wing chair. "You are simply overtired, as am I."

Thornhollow tented his hands over his eyes. "That I am. I can't serve my new patients if I don't know anything about them, but their histories make for long and occasionally disturbing reading. What about yourself? How are you finding your new residence?"

Grace thought for a moment, aware that she could never verbalize the feeling of safety that enveloped her as she slept, the ease of companionship she found even among those who could only stare blankly. "I am content," she said.

"Ah, contentment," Thornhollow said. "A wholly underrated feeling." His suddenly blank gaze was drawn back to the floor. "Go to bed, Grace. I'll wake you if there's a murder."

EIGHTEEN

There was no murder. Not that night, or any of the following. Days stretched into weeks, the fine webbing of skin that knit itself into scar tissue on Grace's temples softening into a smoothness that her fingers sought out for comfort or while in thought. As a child she had sucked her thumb, and the habit had been hard to break. Her mother had scolded her about ruining the shape of her mouth, but the threats of the future had been nothing against the terror of the present, and young Grace had found solace in the action while harsh words crept down the hallway from her parents' room.

In truth, she could easily resort to sucking her thumb again, Grace thought while helping Nell in the garden. No one in the asylum would care at all, shape of her mouth be damned. But touching the smooth flesh of her scars brought its own kind of comfort, and the movement itself became an involuntary action when she was deep in thought. The doctor had noticed during their weekly lessons and hadn't discouraged it.

"The movement may help you recover information," he'd said, the third time her hands had gone to her temples the night before.

"What?" Grace jerked her hands down, distracted. The chalkboard had been cloudy with words: new theories vied for space against old ones, with Thornhollow's opinions sprinkled liberally between them.

"Touching your scars," he explained. "If you perform an action while learning something, re-creating the action may help you recall it later."

Her fingers went to them again as she worked beside Nell, heedless of the dirt on her hands. Visually she could recall scenes in intricate detail, but to catalog theories and counterarguments as to their usefulness was a different animal altogether, and she wanted to tame it.

"Sometimes I can't keep me 'ands off meself, either, though I'm not usually 'avin' a go at me own 'ead," Nell said, playfully bumping hips with Grace.

Grace pushed back gently, winning a smile from the Irish girl. "You've gone an' muddied up that nice skin of yours," Nell chided, licking her own thumb and rubbing Grace's face clean. "Don't want a pretty lass like ye lookin' like a field hand when your doctor comes around."

Grace grimaced at Nell and shook her head, yanking at a weed with more force than necessary.

"Dinna worry yerself about it," Nell said, shaking off the wordless chiding. "Anybody that's been around the two of ye fer more than five minutes knows there's nothing between yer bodies. It's yer own minds that ye each find so fascinatin', odd as that is."

Even though there was truth to what the other girl said, Grace still wore a frown as she worked next to Nell, the early autumn weather bringing a sheen of sweat to her forehead. It was true that she and the doctor had learned each other's minds thoroughly, each complementing the other's weaknesses with their own strengths. But their efforts were for nothing if she never got the chance to apply everything she'd learned. Grace dug her boot heel into the ground against a stubborn weed as she told herself yet again that her wish for relief from boredom through the death of a stranger was the most selfish of sins.

Yet it was there, and she couldn't deny it. She itched to put herself to use on something more complicated than punching bread dough with Elizabeth or harvesting alongside Nell.

"There now, ye've gone and yanked up me leeks, ye mad thing." Nell salvaged the vegetable from the pile of refuse mounting behind them, but her touch was gentle as she pushed Grace's shoulder. "No 'arm done. We'll stick 'im back in the ground and no one the wiser."

Nell replanted the leek, but the smile slipped from her face when she straightened up, and her hands went to her back. Grace had seen her friend struggle before in small moments when she thought no one would notice, as the disease that had brought her to the asylum began to ravage her joints. The two girls sat beside the vegetable plot to rest, gazing out over the lake and the group of patients dotting the shore, watched over by two nurses.

Nell jerked her chin in their direction. "Janey says second Tuesdays is always the worst of the lot. That's when they make sure the outer wings get their proper exercise." The Irish girl shook her head, her usual good humor abandoning her. "You and me, we's lucky to be as good off as we are. Up 'ere I mean," she added, tapping her own forehead. "Janey says those outer wings . . . it ain't worth the pay, some days."

Elizabeth and Nell had explained to Grace that the asylum staff mostly lived within the walls where they worked. All of the employees roomed near the center of the building, with the quietest and most calm patients living in the wings nearest them. As the bricks stretched, so too did the tenants' tenuous hold on sanity, with the most violent and deranged patients farther from the offices.

But even they were treated with respect, Grace knew. She'd seen them on their outings, the staff doing their best to keep the wanderers from walking into the lake, the indignant from arguing among themselves, and the truly violent from harming anyone. One screamer had dug a trench under a bush and had to be removed by a team of male attendants, still clutching at the roots as he was dragged away. His echoing laments had traveled uphill to Grace's room, reminding her of the spider girl in Boston.

Sheer chance had landed that poor creature into Heedson's hands and the darkness of the cellar. Here, she might've had the chance to recover her voice and share her name. Here she might have even found what little bit of peace was possible for one so far gone. Instead, fate had put her into the darkness, and Thornhollow's hand had made the arrangement permanent.

Thoughts of the black cellar in Boston drove Grace's hand to her pocket to run her finger reassuringly over the edge of the envelope secreted there. The letter had come for her that morning, delivered by Janey at breakfast in the women's ward while Elizabeth and Nell were arguing over whether String slept while Elizabeth did, or stayed awake all night. Grace had glanced at the handwriting quickly, even though she knew it could have only come from one person. Irregular letters, spelled out as if unsure as to their proper form, made her heart swell with affection as she imagined Reed struggling over their making, his brow furrowed in concentration as he addressed it to "Grace, in the care of Dr. Thornhollow."

Nell rested her head on Grace's shoulder, her dark hair fanning into Grace's lap. Grace stroked it absently, the silky smoothness of it as comforting as her scars. "Ah, it's a blessing to have someone play with yer hair," Nell said, her eyelids suddenly heavy. "It brings something like a calmness."

Grace wanted to ask her friend how badly she hurt, but the weight of her own lie kept her silent. She offered the only comfort she could, with her hands. Nell's fingers twined with her own to quiet them, their dirt-stained fingers still within each other.

"Don't let wee Lizzie know 'ow bad I'm gettin'," she said, lifting her head so that Grace could see the seriousness in her usually sparkling eyes. "That one likes nothin' more than ter worry."

Grace held a finger next to her own ear and cocked an eyebrow.

"What's that, then? Ye're thinkin' String might know? I tol' 'er that if I ever 'eard about String sayin' a word about me I'd sneak inta 'er room one night with the shears. I may not be able ter see it, but I know where 'er ears are, sure enough."

Grace laughed aloud, the song ringing out in the cool evening air and taking both girls by surprise. She clapped a hand over her mouth, eyes staring wide at Nell.

"Seems like yer noisemaker isn't entirely broken, then, is it?"

Mortified, Grace could only shake her head from side to side.

"One day soon enough I'll 'ear yer voice," Nell said, rising wearily to her feet. "Until tha' day I'd not mind listenin' to that laugh every now and then." She held out a hand to Grace, and they crossed the lawn together, following the groups of patients and scattered nurses toward the asylum.

"Did ye know there's an alligator in the front fountain?" Nell said, the usual playfulness back in her voice.

Grace rolled her eyes.

"Aye, but there is," Nell insisted, her eyes large with pretend innocence. "One of the nurses went for a visit to some of 'is family down in Florida, brought back the wee beastie. I suppose it seemed like a good idea at the time, but 'avin' an alligator in your own 'ome was a bit taxin' in reality. So he brought it 'ere, and it lives in the fountain."

Some of the patients walking near them caught Nell's words and shied away from the marble fountain as they neared it, one or two moaning and leaning against their nurses, who shot Nell dark looks.

"Oh, the toils of a prophetess in 'er 'omeland," Nell said when she noticed. "But what better place for such a beastie than 'ere, I ask you?"

They were about to pass the fountain in question, and even though Grace knew better than to believe her fanciful friend's tale, she found herself pulling her skirts away from the rim as they passed.

"Oh, Grace! Grace! It's got me!" Nell's hand was suddenly pulled from her own and there was a gigantic splash, followed by a cascade of cold water that drenched Grace's dress. She gasped as more spray followed, covering her skin with goose bumps. Nell's flailing wasn't the least bit alarming, as she was smiling merrily while she did it, gleefully sending waves of water in Grace's direction.

"I tol' ya there was a beastie in 'ere," she yelled, throwing herself backward and bringing Janey to the edge of the fountain.

"Going on about the gator again, is she?" Janey asked Grace, arms crossed in front of her. Grace nodded, fighting the smile that wanted to spread across her face. "I haven't the heart to tell her it died years before she came here."

"But there was one, once?" Dr. Thornhollow arrived just in time to catch a glimpse of Nell's face as she came up for air and mimed being pulled under again.

"Sure enough, sir," Janey said. "Just because the insane tell the tales doesn't make them false."

"Excellent point," he said before beckoning to Nell when she surfaced again. "You'll be hours drying out. The soaking won't do your bones any good tonight."

Nell jerked her skirts unnecessarily high as she climbed out of the fountain, exhibiting an expanse of pale leg. "I've got an idea about what would do me bones good, if I can pry ye away from yer books for an hour."

"Nell," Janey said, taking her by the arm as she cleared the edge of the fountain. "That's no way to be speaking to the young doctor."

"There are a myriad of reasons why that won't be happening, Nell, all of them quite good," Thornhollow said. "And while I have to credit your showmanship, I still say that you'll regret your swim once the cold penetrates."

"Aye, well," Nell said, slinging a wet sheet of black hair out of her face, "I live in an insane asylum. May as well jump in the fountain, I say."

"And yet another lesson for you, Grace," the doctor said, guiding her by the elbow away from the asylum doors and down the path to a waiting carriage. "By our standards a person who flings themselves in a fountain isn't sane, yet Nell says she's already deemed insane, so what more damage can be done by giving in to the temptation?"

"Therefore using reason and proving herself to be, in fact, sane," Grace said.

"Very good."

"I haven't eaten yet," Grace reminded him, knowing well enough what the carriage meant for their evening.

"Not a concern. You won't be hungry soon."

NINETEEN

The girl lay staring at the sky, her gaze missing the first sparks of the stars in the dying daylight. Grace fought the urge to shift away from the warm bodies pressing on both sides of her, only too aware of how different this scene was from her first outing with the doctor. On that night, her facade had been under the scrutiny of only a select few and the heavens had poured as they worked on the blood-soaked cobblestones.

Here rain didn't fall; blood did not flow. There was only the softest of breezes from the river, carrying with it the moist smell of a night just ready to begin. The last rays of the sun were drying the wet folds of her dress and Grace bit the inside of her cheek as someone trod on her foot.

"Pardon me," the man said, glancing at her. She remained blank, staring straight ahead as he took in her scars and the doctor's black valise clamped tightly in her hands. The sight of a mental patient was just as entertaining as the dead, and he elbowed the person next to him, whispering something. The white moon of another curious face filled her peripheral vision, but Grace remained unmoved, her attention focused solely on the girl and Thornhollow as he knelt beside her.

"Step back, now. C'mon, step back." The policemen walked in a widening circle around the body trying to move the crowd away. Grace's spine stiffened as she recognized Davey. His eyes met hers and she willed herself to show no reaction as he approached.

"You're all right," he said quietly, reaching for her elbow, then pulling away as he thought better of it. Instead, he gestured for her to move closer, separating her from the crowd. "Can't do the doctor much good from back here, can you?"

Grace stepped forward, letting a long exhalation escape silently as she left the press of other bodies behind.

"Look here—why's she get to go in front?" the man who had stepped on her foot protested.

"What do you think this is? An exhibition?" Davey shot back. "This here's a murder scene and that girl is the doctor's assistant."

"What good is a doctor on a murder scene? Seems to me she's already dead."

Grace left their argument behind her, their words sliding away as she lost interest in all but the girl, whose blank stare was so like her own. Thornhollow glanced up as she moved closer, his eyes glazed with concentration as he feverishly cataloged all he could in the moments allowed him.

"Ah, there's your girl," the heavyset policeman said as he joined them, having successfully threatened the onlookers enough that they kept a distance. "Almost makes a murder worth it, seeing her pretty face. Shame about the scars, though."

Thornhollow rose, and she caught the slightest whisper of his words as he leaned into her. "Watch the crowd."

"Hardly a shame," Thornhollow countered George in his next breath. "The surgery made her violent fits much less common, although admittedly, less predictable. Just yesterday she chased a squirrel across the front lawn, caught him too. The nurse told me she spent hours picking all the hairs from Grace's teeth."

"You don't mean to say she ate it?" Davey asked.

"That's the tale. I wasn't there to see it, but one of the patients told me the doomed thing was still trying to climb out as she was chewing."

George backed away from Grace. "Might want to keep your distance, in that case, Davey. No face is pretty enough to outweigh having something chewed off."

Davey hovered nearby, nonetheless. "There's a fella over there not too happy about the girl, uh . . . Grace, getting to come up close for a good look. I'll just stay near."

"She knows no difference, either way," Thornhollow said, looking at Davey shrewdly. "If the gentleman in the crowd were to bother her past her point of endurance, Grace would handle it. Now, if I could direct both your attentions to the girl on the ground and not the one standing, that would be most beneficial."

Grace's eyes wandered over the crowd that had gathered in a loose circle around them, the girl's body on unwitting display as her death provided the night's entertainment. People pressed against one another three deep, the ones in front informing those in back what was going on. Eyes bounced off her own as Grace took in each face, each reaction as they noticed her scars.

The three men conversed in low tones, their words suddenly scattered by the shrill piercing of a train whistle. Several people in the crowd jumped, hands going to their ears.

"Some vagrant's done it," someone shouted. "Probably hopped the next train out too. Never catch the bastard once he's on the rails." The man broke to the front of the crowd. "You'd best be watching the tracks, coppers."

George rounded on him, hand dropped threateningly to his billy club. "You let me decide what I best be doing."

"Make way," Davey shouted, parting the crowd on the opposite side of the circle. "Coroner's wagon is here. Make way, all of you. Show's over."

Thornhollow took his valise from Grace, and she followed him to the carriage. "Back to the asylum. We've seen all we need here," he said to the driver, who nodded.

"It seems vultures of all types follow the dead, don't they?" Thornhollow asked Grace as they watched the crowd gather around the coroner's wagon.

"Vultures don't have such heavy feet," Grace said, rubbing her toes through her buttoned boots. "I'd have been trampled by them if Davey hadn't noticed me. Why did you ask me to watch the crowd?"

"Yes, I think Davey has taken notice of you, to say the least," the doctor said, lurching forward as the carriage moved into motion. "As for my request, I believe our killer is a planner and an intelligent one at that. Some of that ilk return to the scene of the crime. They rather enjoy watching the police bumble about, not knowing the person they seek is a stone's throw away. Now, quickly, tell me what you gathered while it's fresh in your mind."

"The body wasn't moved," Grace said. "The grass around her was crushed as if there had been a struggle."

"I noticed that as well. However, we don't know how many people passed close to the body even before the city's finest could be called. Judging by the crowd, a good many. We can't be sure she wasn't killed elsewhere."

"If she were moved it's a much more complex picture," Grace went on. "There's a railway nearby, a river, a road, even a footpath leading out of the park. The killer could've used any number of means."

"Very true. What else?"

"Her clothes were . . ." Grace fumbled for words, unsure how to continue. She pictured the girl, her skirts a confused pile of twisted fabric. "She was in a disarray. As if she were a doll in the hands of a child who is too young to dress it properly."

"Or someone who didn't know how to handle women's clothes," Thornhollow added.

"A man, then?"

"Most definitely. But continue."

Grace closed her eyes, bringing the picture to full light under the darkness of her lids. "She had no clear marks of violence on her arms or wrists, indicating that she didn't fight off her attacker. So she knew him well enough to not believe she was in any danger, or in the least, trusted him.

"There were pine needles in her hair, yet her face and hands were quite clean, as were her fingernails. She was hygienic by nature so the needles tell us that she was . . . was on her back for a period of time, most likely in the park as that's the only place I see pines nearby."

Grace's brow furrowed in concentration, her eyes screwing even more tightly closed. "If she was moved, she was not dumped or tossed carelessly aside. She was arranged almost comfortably. Ankles crossed, hands folded across her abdomen. Her eyes were left open. I can almost believe a few people walked past her thinking it was simply a girl relaxing in the grass at the end of the day. All in all, she was very lifelike."

"Lifelike, indeed. What does this say?"

Grace opened her eyes, unsure past the details she could recite from the picture in her head. "That the killer had remorse? He wishes she weren't dead?"

"Maybe. But I'm afraid that's too simple for this scenario. Your earlier comment strikes much closer to the truth."

"I said she was clean," Grace said, ticking her fingers with each point. "That she was laid out with her comfort in mind, and that she was dressed awkwardly."

"'As if she were a doll' were your exact words," Thornhollow repeated, raising his voice to contend with the clatter as they passed over the stone bridge toward home.

"A doll," Grace echoed, picturing male hands fumbling with the delicate buttons of the girl's skirt, clumsiness and nerves botching the job. Yet even in his haste he'd covered her. "He's not familiar with women, but there's a degree of respect at work. He could've tossed her aside, left her naked for everyone to see, but he didn't."

"All true," Thornhollow agreed. "You've seen almost everything."

"With the glaring exception of how she died," Grace pointed out. "No bruising, no bullet, no blood. She wasn't strangled, shot, or stabbed."

"None of those things. Which is what makes this so much more interesting than our last outing."

"And?" Grace prodded.

"Ether," the doctor said, his face eerily lit by the gaslights of the asylum as they pulled into the drive. "It has a distinctively sweet smell, and she was rank with it. A strong dose would paralyze her lungs and she would float off to her death, much like a deep sleep during which one simply stops breathing."

"You make it sound almost desirable."

"It would be, honestly, in comparison to some. But what's important here is not how you or I—or even she—wishes to die, but how the killer wanted her to die."

"Quietly," Grace said. "No marks. No blood."

"He can almost pretend she's alive," Thornhollow said. "Yet she can't berate or condescend. She can't even ignore him."

"No," Grace said. "All she can do is lie there."

"An ideal situation for our man," Thornhollow said, his hand reaching for the carriage door. He handed her down, and Grace pushed the river rock of her voice back down into her belly, to be shared with no one else.

"One last thought, that I'd have you think on later—as I will. As you said, the girl's clothes were mussed. If she's a doll, he hasn't familiarized himself with feminine wardrobe enough to dress her well. He also missed quite a few buttons, which makes me think he was in a haste and flustered. Yet to kill with ether shows planning at work. He intended to asphyxiate someone—maybe even her specifically—yet once it was carried out, his nerves got the best of him.

"And while the ether would kill our victim quietly, it doesn't do so quickly. Ether has to be absorbed into the lungs, its effects weakening the body but still allowing for movement until a high dosage has been inhaled to render immobility. The girl was taken by surprise, but her killer would have to hold her quite still for a period of time while she struggled. He'll be a large man, maybe even remarkably so."

"I saw no one like that in the crowd," Grace said. "I'm sorry, Doctor, it won't be so easy as that."

They climbed the stone steps together, listening to the crunch of the gravel as the driver took the carriage and horse back to the stables. Thornhollow dropped his hand to the front doors but halted Grace with a look before opening them.

"This was likely a first kill, Grace, and a somewhat botched one at that. Whatever his goal, I don't think it was achieved tonight. And even if it was, this won't be the last girl we find stinking of ether."

"And why is that, Doctor?" Grace asked, giving her voice rein in the safety of the shadows.

"Because a killer who plans this kind of ritual never stops at one."

TWENTY

"It's a special day when I get to work on a fine head of hair like yours," Mrs. Beem said as she dug her fingers into Grace's scalp, massaging soap through her hair. "This is as nice of a mane as I could find down on the plaza, I tell you."

"I wouldn't go on bragging about yours," Miss Chancey called from another chair, where Nell hung over a large sink, hair dripping. "My Irish lassie is as nice looking as any. I pile these black curls up on her head and she'll look good as any queen."

"Oh, aye," Nell said proudly. "This 'ead o' 'air is the pride o' Ireland, and I'll drape the braid over me tombstone when I go."

"Now there's a morbid picture." Elizabeth tutted as she waited her turn, tugging somewhat nervously on her own hair. "You'll be careful, won't you?" she asked for the third time. "String gets nervous around the clippers."

"That's only natural, dear," Mrs. Beem said. "How many times have I done your hair and never once cut String?"

Grace peeked out of one eye while the rinse water rushed over her head to see Elizabeth was only slightly mollified. She was the only one of the three not utterly thrilled when the town hairdressers came up to the asylum for a monthly treat, trimming and styling the female patients' hair. Grace relaxed under Mrs. Beem's brush and comb, giving in to the ebb and flow. She closed her eyes and saw the girl from the night before, ankles primly crossed though her mussed skirts indicated some violence had been done.

"Our killer was unsuccessful," Thornhollow had informed Grace that morning as he joined her on a morning walk around the grounds.

"On the contrary. His victim is dead," Grace had said, pitching her voice low and keeping her face blank even though they walked alone.

Thornhollow cleared his throat. "What I mean to say is that he was unsuccessful in his attempt to rape her. I visited the coroner this morning to see if anything more could be learned. The ether had mostly evaporated at that point so he disagreed with me on cause of death, but I hold to my conclusion. Ether is highly combustible, very tricky to mix. Only the most skilled surgeons and doctors would have access to the knowledge. Given that there are only twenty or so doctors in the city, it greatly narrows our window of suspicion." He swiped at a clump of grass with his walking stick.

"You seem almost disappointed."

"It's too easy," he complained. "This afternoon we'll go into the city. I'll pose as an uncle searching for medicine to mollify his niece's sick headaches. You'll meet me in the offices shortly after my arrival. If our killer fits the mold for intelligent killers, he'll be socially capable with men, at least—as he'd have to be in order to get through medical school and hold a practice. But if he's incapable of touching a woman who isn't unconscious, with women he'll be quite awkward."

"It does seem simple," Grace had agreed. "Why involve yourself at all if the ether so clearly indicates a medical man as the culprit? Can't the police deduce that themselves?"

"One would think," Thornhollow said, a muscle in his jaw ticking. "But George's report at the station identified the smell as alcohol. He claims the girl drank herself into a stupor in the park, *got herself roughed up*—his words, not mine—and then expired in a coma. The death of a migrant kitchen worker is less than interesting to the police in a city such as this. Their police force isn't large enough to investigate too deeply anything that isn't potentially lucrative."

"Lucrative?"

"Certainly. Expired liquor licenses, tax evasion . . . anything that actually brings revenue to the city you'll see carried out to the letter of the law. Digging into a murder with few clues—again, their words, not mine—requires time, something policemen want to be paid for."

"But not you," Grace said, stopping to rest under a maple near the banks of the pond, its wide leaves red with the arrival of fall.

"No. I do it for the experience. The science of the matter."

Grace had been silent for a moment, watching the ripples of the pond as fish fed on the early morning insects. "What was her name?"

"I'm sorry?"

"You said she was a kitchen worker, so she must have been identified."

"Ah, yes. Uh . . ." Thornhollow's brow creased as he tried to recall a fact less imperative to him than others. "Anka. Anka Baran. She was Polish. Something we'll want to keep in mind as we move forward. Assuming we don't catch our man today we need to make note that there may be some racial motivation. Perhaps a dislike of immigrants."

"I don't think so," Grace argued. "There was nothing to show hatred. The method he used to kill, it's almost as if he specifically did not want to hurt her."

"A very good point. I'll amend it to add that perhaps he only wanted to hurt her in a very specific way and did not have the time. Or was physically incapable. Either way, we'll know soon enough. I imagine we'll be face-to-face with him within a few hours."

Grace remembered Thornhollow's prediction as Mrs. Beem's comb passed near her scar, the feeling of the teeth fading as it touched the numb skin there, then reappearing as it trailed down her cheek.

"Hold still now. No jumping when I work around your face. Don't want to mar you any more, do we?"

The last delicate clips were done, her hair dried and curled, Mrs. Beem's fingers expertly twisting a pile of curls complete with pins holding a few in place to hide the damage at her temples.

"All right, Miss Chancey," Mrs. Beem said. "Take a look. Doesn't my pretty quiet one look as good or better than any of the fancy ladies that walk the shops down below?"

"Better," Miss Chancey said around a mouthful of pins as she worked with Nell's heavy hair. "With those scars covered she'd pass for normal easy as the rest of us."

Grace glanced in the mirror and silently agreed. She was ready to go to work.

"You're turning into a regular criminal," Thornhollow teased when Grace produced the hairpins she'd lifted from Mrs. Beem's sink stand.

"A planner, for sure," Grace agreed, looking at herself in the mirror of his office. "I knew you'd have all the details right when finding me a dress. It's fashionably cut so that I don't look out of place, but not too distinctive of a print so as to attract undue attention. You've matched the hat, but completely forgotten that I'd need pins to hold it in place. Unfamiliar with women's garments, indeed."

"Perhaps I've taught you a little too well," he said, holding out his arm for her as they went to the carriage.

Ned was waiting for them, happy to drive the carriage two days in a row, his bright smile almost bringing an answering one to Grace's face. Thornhollow produced a list of addresses once they were moving, the clattering of the horse's hooves hiding their conversation from Ned.

"I made inquiry and came up with a little over twenty doctors in the city. We'll try to visit them all today while your hair is twisted into this unnatural shape. Doesn't that hurt?"

"Hasn't anyone ever told you that beauty is pain?" Grace asked.

"I'm much more familiar with the latter."

"Yes, it does hurt a little. By the end of the day there'll be no farce involved as we try to procure headache medicine."

Thornhollow shook his head. "I'll never understand."

Grace pulled a hand mirror from her purse and inspected her reflection. "Yet women do these things in order to appeal to men."

"I didn't say it wasn't appealing. I said I don't understand it."

"Yes, well . . ." Grace put a hand to her unmoving hair, and the pins digging into her scalp. "Sometimes the actions of the sane make no sense."

"Amen."

They clattered to a stop on a busy side street, and Thornhollow handed her down from the carriage. "Our experiment today is two-fold, Grace. As I explained before, I'll go into each practice a few minutes before you, to judge the doctor's social ability with his own sex."

"And I come along after in the guise of your niece, to see if his demeanor changes around females."

"Yes. And your free time is to be exactly that. Free. Go about town; you'll find money in your purse. Shop. Buy things. Do whatever it is you want, but be Grace Mae, not the broken girl who lives on the hill."

Grace's face fell, her eyes carrying a shadow that had lifted during their conversation. "I don't ever want to be Grace Mae again, Dr. Thornhollow. I don't want pretty things in shopwindows, and I don't want to playact at being carefree. I am that broken girl. She has a purpose, at least, and it's hidden in the identity of the man whose address is somewhere on your slip of paper."

He crumpled the paper in his fist. "Try. For my sake. Your whole life can't be wrapped up in the endings of others." He turned his back on her, and she went the opposite direction, assuming the false smile that he wanted to prove true.

Even though she'd tossed his words aside the moment he'd said them, the effect lasted. She caught the reflection of her pretended happiness in a window that she passed, looking every inch like a privileged girl enjoying a beautiful day. But she knew she had never been that, even before the scars on her temples had set her apart from others. Playacting was something she had perfected long before meeting Dr. Thornhollow, and at least the darkness that haunted her now was one she had the power to end.

She entered the doctor's office to find Thornhollow in deep conversation with a bored-looking man who brightened up the moment she walked in. "Any luck, Uncle?" she asked.

"Not so much," he said ruefully. "Doctor Maggill here was just saying how he's about to close for lunch and doesn't have a moment to help us."

"Nonsense, nonsense," Maggill said as he approached Grace. "I can certainly postpone something as pedestrian as lunch to help a lovely young creature such as yourself." He beckoned for Grace to sit on a stool, but she shook her head.

"No, Doctor, I wouldn't dream of interrupting your daily routine. We can return later, can't we, Uncle?"

"Of course," Thornhollow agreed, putting his hat back on and taking Grace by the arm. "Back in an hour, Doctor?"

"Lovely, and you can make it half an hour," he said, smiling, showing too clearly that he'd already had lunch and some of it was still located in his teeth. "I hate to think of you suffering for one second longer than absolutely necessary."

"That was certainly not our man," Thornhollow declared, once they were back in the carriage. "Though I'd like to give him a sound drubbing anyway. Not interested in treating a girl he's never seen until he likes the sight of her." He shook his head, talking only to himself. "A disgrace to the Hippocratic oath."

Grace rapped his knee with her knuckles as they slid to a halt once again. "Our next stop, Doctor."

"I'm going to lose my faith in humanity before the day is over, Grace, mark my words," he said as they descended to the street.

So it continued in office after office, until the dirt of the streets covered Grace's boots and her plea of a headache was no longer a lie. They played their parts, each dissecting the man they spoke with the second they saw him and comparing notes as the carriage took them to their next destination. Not once did they find a doctor who was noticeably flustered by Grace, and Thornhollow's patience stretched as thin as her smile.

"Dammit," he bellowed, tossing the paper on the floor of the carriage as they headed toward home. "A whole day spent trying to prove our theory and all I have for it is twelve doses of medicine I don't need."

"I do," Grace said, hands to her temples.

"I'm sorry for shouting," he apologized. "I've had such a day in town it's a lovely relief to return to the asylum."

"It is," she agreed, pulling pins free and letting her hair tumble loose, scars on display as the wet air from the lake filled her lungs. "It truly is."

TWENTY-ONE

Grace's letters were waiting on her nightstand when she went to bed. The pages had been soaked through by Nell's would-be alligator attack, and Grace had been terrified that they would fall apart in her hands if she didn't let them dry thoroughly. The pages fluttered in the night breeze as she reached for them, her heart leaping at the sight of her younger sister's handwriting.

> *Fair Lily—*
>
> *The breeze brought me your letter. I don't know that I would've gone looking for it otherwise, it has been so long since we played. I am glad you came back.*
>
> *Do you remember my sister, Grace? She has died. Mother and*

Father say that a sickness killed her on a boat when she went on a trip. I miss her. She would always play with me and tell me everything would be all right, though it looks like she was wrong.

Father tries to comfort me. He even let me sit on his lap the other day, although Mother said I'm much too big to be doing that sort of thing now. Mother put my hair up in curls to try to cheer me up, but when Father said I looked very pretty she got angry and pulled it all out again. It hurt and I had to cry, and Mother didn't let me come down to dinner and I don't know why.

I miss Grace and I miss you.

Write back—

Alice

Grace's fingers shook as she refolded Alice's letter, placed it under her pillow, and turned to Falsteed's.

Dearest Grace—

From one asylum to another, greetings. Enclosed you will find a letter that Reed retrieved for you. I gave it a good sniff before entrusting it to him. Your sister has the smell of innocence about her still, and the whiff of purity that came from your presence may indeed have been due to your close proximity to her. But I choose to believe otherwise.

You say I am a good person who has done bad things. You are a good person who has had bad things done to her, which is a different *situation altogether. Do not sell yourself so short in assuming that the darkness inside you cannot be overcome, or that your only path to redemption lies with the footsteps of Thornhollow. There is more to you than beauty. There is more to you than strength. There is more to you than intelligence. You are a whole person, and I would have you treat yourself as such.*

Falsteed

Grace's sob took her by surprise as her tears fell on Falsteed's declaration that Alice remained innocent. "Thank God," she said quietly to herself as a night rain began to fall outside. "Thank God."

Grace slammed her hands over her mouth before she realized that the screams that had awoken her were not her own. Pulse racing, she listened with the rest of the wing's inhabitants to see if it would happen again. And it did. A piercing wail that floated up through the floorboards, its maker unrecognizable in her grief. Footsteps shuffled in rooms all around her and doors creaked open, hushed voices seeking answers as lamps were lit.

"What's happened?"

"Who is it?"

"Where's it coming from?"

Grace lay still in her bed, willing her heart to a steady rhythm before joining them.

"It's comin' from down under me own room. Luck o' the Irish, my arse," Nell's voice joined the throng and Grace slipped through her door to see a cluster of familiar faces gathered together.

"Under your room?" a tall woman named Rebecca said. "That'd be the widow Jacobs."

Another shriek reached the group, trailing off into a series of racking sobs that made Grace's throat ache.

"That old loon?" Nell said. "Christ, she's a case, sure enough. Best get used to it, lassies. We'll be up the rest o' the night."

"Nell," Elizabeth chided. "That's no way to speak."

"I can't help me accent."

"You know what I mean," Elizabeth bit back, more harshly than usual, her hand clamped firmly in the thin air beside her hair. "Something's gone horribly wrong."

"Oh, really?" Nell asked. "And what does String know about it?"

Elizabeth twisted her hand furtively, uncomfortable under the hungry stares of the others. "It's not my place to say."

"You do know, then?" Rebecca asked, raising her oil lamp higher and peering at Elizabeth.

Elizabeth's eyes bounced from one face to another, and Grace felt a stab of pity. She tugged on Nell's elbow just as the door at the end of the hallway opened. Janey's hair was down and loose, her eyes still heavy with sleep.

"All right, ladies, back to bed, back to bed," she said, her voice still carrying authority even though she was wearing a nightgown.

"Nothing to get upset about."

"Somebody who sleeps in the room under me own doesn't think so," Nell disagreed, arms crossed in front of her. "She was verra upset indeed."

"Is it Mrs. Jacobs?" Rebecca asked.

Elizabeth only fretted at the air beside her ear, fingers entwined in something invisible.

Janey looked at the circle of faces and sighed. "All right then, if it'll get you back in your beds. Her daughter's died, and the police have just been to tell her."

"And her just a wee lass," Nell said, real sadness in her voice. "Tha's a terrible thing to hear."

"She's not," Rebecca said. "Her daughter's a full-grown woman, same as me. I've seen her when she comes to visit. Unless there's more than the one?"

"Mad or not, yer dense as can be," Nell said. "'Ave ye not 'eard the woman speaking of 'er lass like she's just a bairn? Goes on about 'ow she cries all the night till 'er mum brings 'er a drink."

"Ladies," Janey said, her voice bringing a halt to the argument. "Mrs. Jacobs has just the one daughter, if I must say so to end this ridiculousness."

"She walks on 'er own two legs and still cries for 'er mum in the night?" Nell said incredulously. "Sounds like she'd be better off in 'ere with the likes of us."

"Except she's dead," Elizabeth reminded her. "And Mrs. Jacobs chooses to think of her as a child because it's easier than recognizing the adult she's become."

The group hushed, all faces turned to Elizabeth, who blanched under the attention.

"How did you know that?" Janey asked.

Elizabeth only shook her head, hands clenching tighter to the air near her hair.

"Oy there, String," Nell called, peeling apart Elizabeth's hands. "Perhaps ye tell me where to find some buried treasure? Or the cure for the pox? Somethin' useful for once, ye invisible bastard."

"You dare!" Elizabeth gasped, flashing her teeth at Nell, who backed off. "You keep a civil tongue in your head when addressing String, Nell O'Kelly, or I'll . . . I'll . . ."

"You'll what?" Rebecca asked.

"I'll spit in your tea," Elizabeth said, stamping one tiny foot as she said it.

The other girls burst into laughter, and Grace bit down on her tongue to keep from joining them. Janey tried hard to control her face but her lips were twitching. Even Elizabeth's angry pout changed into a hesitant smile.

"Aye, she's a vicious one, our Lizzie," Nell said. "Tell String I'm sorry and not to get 'imself in a tangle over it."

"String is neither male nor female," Elizabeth said.

"I don't care one way or the other," Rebecca said, looking sternly at Janey. "All I want to know is if String is right?"

Janey looked from each face to the next, all eyes now latched on her in the orange glow from the lamps. "Fine then," she said, tossing her hands in the air. "Yes, the widow Jacobs's daughter is an adult, but Mrs. Jacobs has found it easier to pretend she was still a little one, rather than an adult who chose to . . . to . . ."

"Are ye sayin' she's a whore?" Nell asked, drawing out the last word lasciviously.

"*Was* a whore," Elizabeth corrected yet again. "She's dead."

Janey nodded. "Dead indeed. And the knowledge of that has sent the poor woman into a fit. Now you know, and I want all your legs moving back to your rooms. And don't you be telling the other staff I said a word to you. They'd have my hide for sharing stories that aren't my own."

Grace wandered back to her bed, listening to Elizabeth and Nell's good-natured bickering as she went. She'd not known Mrs. Jacobs well, but the few times they had met she'd been reminded of Mrs. Clay. They shared a respectful bearing, a way of holding themselves that communicated a power restrained. Now Mrs. Jacobs was broken, for whether her daughter was child or whore, she was lost forever. Grace's thoughts strayed to Boston and Mrs. Clay, Reed and Falsteed, the deplorable Nurse Croomes and Dr. Heedson, whose straying hand she'd so gladly impaled.

Her consciousness trailed down into the darkness of sleep, where even that blackness could not compare with the hues of her past.

"Is she going to be all right?" Grace asked, in an attempt to distract Thornhollow from the blackboard.

"Who?" he asked, tearing his eyes away from his own handwriting reluctantly.

"Mrs. Jacobs," she reminded him. "I was asking how she's handling her grief?"

"Not well," he said, slumping in the chair beside hers and tenting his hands over his eyes. "The ferocity of her emotions is tearing apart her mind. Sometimes I think we'd all be best suited by not caring for others at all."

"A bleak picture," Grace said. "I dislike most people as much as you, but the few that I care for I hold very dear. If not for those who care for us, we'd never make it through the worst. I'd not have survived Boston without Falsteed and Mrs. Clay. Likewise I'll do my best to steer my sister through mourning my own death, false though it may be."

A long silence greeted her words as Thornhollow slowly pulled his hands away from his face. "You have a sister?"

"Yes," Grace said hesitantly, realizing her blunder.

"Older or younger?"

"Younger. She's ten years old."

"And she remains at home?"

"Yes," Grace answered, nerves making her voice thready. "Why do you ask?"

"And how exactly are you offering comfort to her, if you are—as you say yourself—supposedly dead?"

Grace stiffened in her chair, braced for the argument. "I wrote to Falsteed and enclosed a letter to her written by an imaginary friend. Reed placed it for me and retrieved her response, sending it to me here."

"You did what?" Each word was succinctly bitten off, each syllable a vibrant slash in the charged air between them. Thornhollow's brow was dark, his eyes snapping in a way she'd never seen.

"I wrote to Falsteed," she repeated, matching him tone for tone. "He gave me an alias to use. Reed handles all our correspondence. I'm sure the hospital staff in Boston believes he has a lover named Madeleine Baxter, nothing more."

Thornhollow rose from the chair, pacing the room with an influx of energy and anger. "And this same Madeleine Baxter happens to enclose letters to the younger sister of a female inmate who supposedly died under my blade? What if a busybody decides to go through Reed's letters, or his wife somehow gets wind that he receives missives from a female at his workplace? I didn't deliver you from that pit only for you to allow sentiment to drive us both back into it!"

"Sentiment, Doctor!" Grace exploded, rising up from her chair to meet him in her fury. "My little sister lives in a more refined pit, but a viper's nest nonetheless. You truly think I would leave her abandoned to that horror simply to save my own skin?"

"Your own skin?" he bellowed back, not cowed in the least by her display of temper. "What of mine? What of my career? How would it appear if it were discovered that I colluded in the disappearance of an attractive young woman and reappeared with her elsewhere as my dutiful assistant?"

"Am I to be a kept woman, then?" Grace yelled, not caring that his office walls may not hold her voice. "Not for what's between my legs but my ears? Here to hop to your beck and call when you need a plaything for your night's adventures, no less of a doll for your own purposes than our killer's victims are to him?"

"Enough!" Thornhollow roared. "I'll not be spoken to like this when I've risked everything on your behalf. Your father is a powerful man, Grace Mae. You don't realize what could happen to me if he should uncover our ruse."

"No, Doctor," Grace allowed, her tone suddenly cold. "But I know exactly what would happen to me." She turned her back to him and left the office with all the disdain her mother's training had instilled in her, head held high.

TWENTY-TWO

Their argument did not sit well with Grace. She searched for solitude under a willow by the lake, aware that her emotions were running high and might find vent through her tongue if she kept company with her friends. It would be a double betrayal of her pact with Thornhollow, wrecking not only the work they'd put in to covering their tracks in Boston but the lives they'd built in Ohio as well.

It was a Sunday, and so the grounds were brimming with people. Though the mad themselves may be a nuisance, the beautiful ponds, rolling green hills, and fragrant orchards of the asylum grounds were open to the public, and they often came. Grace sat quietly in her shaded spot, aware that her plain homespun marked her as an inmate for those too far away to see her scars. The sane had the assurance of the staff that only the meek and mild were allowed free to roam among them, but they stayed to the paths nonetheless.

"Can my Sally have some tea?" a high-pitched voice questioned, and Grace turned her head toward the noise.

A young mother came around the bend, pushing a pram from which a low coo emanated. A small girl trotted beside her, gold curls bouncing, a doll in her hands. "Momma," she said again, tugging on her mother's skirts. "Sally is thirsty."

Grace's heart plummeted, and her lungs ceased working for a moment as the sun lit up the little girl's golden hair. Her fingers clenched on Alice's letter, crushing a corner.

"Sally will have to wait a moment, dear," the mother said, bending over the pram to adjust the baby's blanket. "We'll head back home after this turn; Brother needs his nap."

"Brother always needs something," the little girl said, pulling a face.

"Babies are work, sweetheart," the mother said, looking up from the pram. "Excuse me, I—"

She broke off, her words lost at the sight of Grace kneeling next to the little girl, hands brimming with lake water.

The girl looked at Grace suspiciously, then down at the water dripping from her hands. "For my Sally?"

Grace nodded, her gaze devouring every detail of the child's face and comparing it to Alice, measuring the bones of their cheeks and the curls of their hair in her mind. They were not twins by any means, nor could they be confused for sisters. But the spark in this little girl's eyes matched the one in Alice's, a testament to the spirit inside that had just begun to know itself. The girl dipped the doll's porcelain mouth in Grace's hands, unconcerned with the scrutiny.

"Better," the little girl declared, then peered at Grace closely. "You've got a chip in you," she said, cool fingers reaching up to touch Grace's scars. "You're broken just like my Sally."

"Mary!" the mother chided, and her small hands dropped from Grace's temples. "I'm sorry," the mother said, pushing the pram off the path over to them. "I hope she's not bothering you, and she didn't mean any offense about your . . . about . . . that."

Grace waved off the apology and smiled at the mother, not missing the fact that this woman was only a few years older than herself. Her clothes were fine, the pram expensive, the spark in little Mary's eyes evident in her own. She wore the trappings of what Grace's life should have been, and Grace felt the hollow echo of disappointment for the first time since coming to the asylum.

The mother looked back at Grace, taking her measure, gaze resting briefly on her scars. She glanced around furtively. "Am I allowed to talk to you?"

Grace shrugged, unsure.

"Why wouldn't you be?" Mary asked, her little hand slipping into Grace's and sending a streak of warmth through her heart. "She's a nice lady. And she's pretty except for being cracked."

The mother's mouth fought against a laugh at Mary's unintended joke, but it erupted when she saw that Grace was smiling. "Except for being cracked . . . ," she repeated. "Oh, Mary, what am I going to do with you?"

"Why should you do anything with me?" Mary asked, now swinging Grace's arm with her own.

The mother glanced around once more. "Would you . . . would you like to see my baby?" she asked. Grace nodded, leaning over the pram as the mother pushed the cover back.

"Hello there," the mother said to her baby. "Hello, my beautiful boy."

Grace watched his tiny hands come up against the rays of the sun, face squished in irritation. She shaded his eyes with her hand, eyes drinking in the sight of him.

"He's just six months," the mother said. "Healthy as a horse. Watch his hands. If he gets ahold of you, your fingers will be in his mouth."

A tiny fist reached up, latching on to Grace's pinkie with a strength she hadn't expected, his skin as soft as velvet. A breath escaped her in a rush as he pulled her down to him, and Mary squeezed her other palm.

"He's not so great," Mary assured her. "Smells something awful."

"Mary," the mother chided her again.

Grace disentangled herself from the baby, pulling the pram cover back and over to shut out the sun. Mary tugged on her hand and when Grace leaned down to her, she found the little girl bounding into her for a hug. The pressure of the little body against her own brought back a wave of memories, and she fought to keep her balance as Mary leaned into her.

"We best be going, Mary," her mother said, and Grace pushed herself to her feet, hastily wiping tears from her eyes.

"'Bye, lady," Mary said, waving to Grace as they walked away. "I hope I see you again."

"Me too," Grace said once they were out of earshot. Her fingers played with a frayed corner of Alice's letter, her eyes still on Mary's golden crown of hair. "I'll not stop writing."

"Grace? Grace?" Her name sailed over the green hills, calling her out of her reverie and resurrecting the blank eyes the asylum staff expected to see. Letter shoved safely in the folds of her dress, she stood and waved to gain Janey's attention.

The nurse spotted her and crossed the space between them, hair flying loose from the tightly coiled bun she usually wore. "There you are. Someone is wishing to speak with you."

Grace's stomach rolled. She'd thought Thornhollow would give her more time to collect herself before tracking her down. Janey groaned in irritation as the ends of her hair whipped around her face. "The wind today," she complained, beckoning Grace to come out from under the shelter of the willow branches. "It'll pull my hair whichever way it pleases, comb and brush notwithstanding. And you with a gentleman come to see you and your own head a sight indeed."

Grace's head jerked up at Janey's words, confusion in her glance.

"It's a policeman, name of Davey," Janey explained. "Said he wanted to speak with Dr. Thornhollow but nobody could find him. So then he asked for you and wouldn't leave until we produced you. I don't know what it is you and the doctor are up to, but if it brings the like of him around here every now and then I don't think I dislike it."

Grace smiled to herself, aware that Janey was madly trying to tame her hair for more reasons than one as they came around to the front of the asylum. Davey was waiting on the gravel path beside his mount, his hat in his hands so that it wouldn't be blown from his head.

"Here she is, Officer," Janey said, voice brighter than usual.

"Thank you, miss," Davey said, hands turning the brim of his hat in a circle as he spoke, eyes everywhere except the women's faces. "I appreciate you finding her for me."

"It's no problem, no problem," Janey said quickly, then looked back and forth between the two of them. "Well, I'll just be out of your way, then, let you go about your business."

Davey waited until Janey had gone into the asylum. He

approached Grace cautiously, hands still buried in his hat and his eyes never quite able to settle on her own.

"Thank you for . . . for seeing me, I suppose," he began slowly. "I have something to say to the doctor, but he don't seem to be here and I got to say this thing before I lose the nerve to get it out."

Grace raised an eyebrow to invite him to continue, breaking the usual dead stare she reserved for strangers.

"You see, when you're a new man on the job you're supposed to learn from the ones above you. But George . . . don't get me wrong, he knows his trade. He can handle the drunks and the men going after their wives and the other way around better than any of 'em. But that girl, the other night, the one who . . . well, you're well enough aware of what I'm saying, I suppose. Anyway, he's got it in his head that she was just a drunkard, and he don't want to hear nothing about what the doctor thinks, though I tell you right now if it was drink on her breath, it wasn't no spirit I've ever smelled before, and I've had my nose in a few." He chuckled, then glanced back at her. "Sorry, ma'am, if I shouldn't be saying so."

Grace shrugged.

Davey ran one hand through his hair, tapping his hat against his hip with the other. "What I'm here for is to say that I was on late shift the other night when we found a whor—when we got a call about a woman who had died in her bed. That bed being located above a brothel, if you take my meaning. She was dead as a doornail and laid out the same way, with her eyes open and looking every second like she'd sit up and tell us to pay up or get out of her room." He laughed again, then blushed when he realized what he'd said.

"Anyways, the room had that same smell about it. I tried to say as much to George, but there ain't nobody too interested in a dead woman of ill repute who drunk herself to death. And that's how it went down in the books. Drunk herself into the dark, and I couldn't quite bring myself to let that stand so I came here to tell the doctor what I seen, and find you instead.

"Which, I think . . ." He trailed off again, nerves back into his voice now that he'd lost momentum. "If you don't mind my saying so, I think that you've got your own way about you, talking or not. Soon as I knew the doctor couldn't be had I said I wanted that Grace girl, because I feel that telling you is as good as telling him, and that I done what I came to do."

Color flushed his whole face, rising up through his neck and filling every pore straight to his hairline. Davey cleared his throat and jammed his hat onto his head.

"And I . . . I wish you a good evening," he said, bowing awkwardly and jumping onto his horse, the back of his neck as red as the sunset.

TWENTY-THREE

"Dr. Thornhollow, I—" Grace burst into his office, only to stop cold two steps later. "Doctor, are you drunk?"

"Thoroughly." He mock toasted her with a tumbler from his armchair, which he'd moved to squarely face the blackboard. "And this time there's no deceit in it. It appears you get to see all my worst traits today, Grace."

She closed the office door behind her, latching it for both their sakes. "Doctor," she said slowly. "Davey was here and he—"

"Yes, I heard Janey knocking. She said there was a policeman here but as I've found them so totally unhelpful I wasn't inclined to spare any of my time." He threw back what was left of his drink and pointed the empty glass at the blackboard. "On the other hand, since my theory has completely collapsed, I suppose that

187

may have been a mistake."

Grace pulled a chair over next to his, their argument forgotten for the moment. "You were confident in the hypothesis before our trip to town," she reminded him. "Did the failure of our visits to the doctors' offices truly constitute a complete collapse?"

"Yes," Thornhollow said. "The ether indicates a medical man, for sure. But that's not criminal psychology at work, Grace, that's a fact any bullheaded policeman could wrap his head around."

He nodded toward the board again, where their handwriting intersected each other's, weaving a web of notes in which to capture the killer's personality. "But our work, the beauty of conjecture we spun here, has failed us. I had hoped to catch our man so easily, but it was presumptuous." He leaned forward, elbows propped on his knees, bloodshot eyes darting over the board. "I've missed something, or built the entire thing on a false cornerstone. Regardless, our house of cards has fallen."

"Then we shall pick up the deck and reshuffle," Grace said. "If the ether points to a doctor, then we still have a narrowed list of suspects. Perhaps he is smart enough not to kill in his own area. He could be a country practitioner who travels here to make his kills anonymously."

"Kill, singular," Thornhollow said. "We have just the one body. For all we know it's as that idiot at the murder scene said, some railroad bum stopped off here to dabble a bit in his dark fantasies."

"A railroad bum with ether in his pocket?" Grace asked. "You're drowning in self-pity along with spirits, Thornhollow. And besides, if you'd bothered to answer the knock on your door, you'd know that there's been another victim."

"What? When?"

"Mrs. Jacobs's daughter," she answered. "The other policemen were content to write it off as an unhappy woman finding her end in a bottle, but Davey said the room smelled of ether and that she had been positioned in the same manner."

"Eyes open? Ankles crossed? Hands folded over her abdomen?" Thornhollow's questions came quickly as the dull sheen over his eyes evaporated.

"Yes to all."

He was on his feet in a moment, his path winding a circuitous route around her chair. "If this is true, it's a wonderful occurrence."

"Mrs. Jacobs might disagree."

"Emotions aside," he went on, waving his hands at the inefficacy of her thoughts. "Don't you see? This may put our suppositions back on track, Grace. Our killer failed in his first attempt to be intimate with his victim, perhaps too hurried by the fear of being caught or too flustered in the moment of his first kill. But he learned from his error and tried a different approach. Any struggles or cries in a brothel would hardly be out of place, and he would be free to entertain himself as he saw fit after the fact."

"But the exposure," Grace argued. "Anyone could see him go up to the woman's room. Why would he take the risk?"

"Perhaps he's confident that the police would not recognize the smell of ether, chalking up her death to drink. Which, it seems, they were quick to do if not for the observations of young Davey. And," Thornhollow added, "as much as it would satisfy my ego to believe wholeheartedly that Mrs. Jacobs's daughter is indeed our second victim, I can't properly ascertain that."

"Nonsense. Davey said that—"

"I think Davey would happily say just about anything in order to see you again, Grace."

"He asked for *you*, Dr. Thornhollow."

"Knowing full well that by finding me, he would be led to you." The doctor held up his hand to stem her next flow of words. "I'm not saying Davey is a liar, only that he might have preemptively jumped to a conclusion that helps fulfill his own whim."

"Then you'll have to see the body yourself, I suppose," Grace said, only slightly mollified. "She's been moved by now, I'm sure, but maybe you can determine whether ether was at work in her death."

"'Moved' is putting it mildly," Thornhollow said, approaching the blackboard. "She's already in the ground."

"That was fast work."

Thornhollow shrugged as he reached for the chalk. "She's a whore with a mother in the insane asylum. Who would go to the funeral?"

"No one, I suppose."

"If—and I stress the *if*—Davey is correct that she was the second victim of our killer, we could have learned much from the scene. All those clues are now lost to us, sadly."

"Unless someone saw who the girl took into her room last," Grace said.

Thornhollow made a notation on the blackboard. "It's a possibility. Although I'm sure there's plenty of traffic, and anonymity is the key to the game played in those walls."

"It's still more than we had a few hours ago," she insisted. "A simple visit and a few questions could be the answer."

Thornhollow turned to her, face pale. "You're not suggesting we visit a brothel?"

Grace felt a bit of warmth in her cheeks as she spoke. "I don't see a way around it. We can't blanch at an unpleasantness when it could remove a hurdle."

"An unpleasantness," the doctor huffed, returning his attention to the board. Grace watched him write, the slanted cursive sentences he listed on the board ending with more question marks than periods.

"I didn't know you had a sister," he said suddenly, a tenseness in his shoulders.

"I didn't think it was worth mentioning," Grace said, her voice unsteady at the first allusion to their heated words of that morning.

"I met a little girl today, on the grounds, and a . . . a baby," she said, her mouth barely able to pronounce the last word. "In some ways the girl was like Alice; the set of her mouth, the curl of her hair. But mostly it was the light I saw inside, the innocence and joy of life. Doctor, I hope you realize that I wouldn't have written to Falsteed if I had any concerns—"

"It's all very well, Grace. I can't fault you for making emotional connections with other humans."

Grace toyed with the glass he'd abandoned on the desk, and the only sound in the office was the scratch of chalk against slate.

"You do realize the danger your sister is in?"

The question was asked quietly, though the weight of it tore a hole through her heart.

"Yes," Grace said, the single word spoken aloud more horrible than anything she'd ever heard in the asylum. "I had thought that when the temptation was removed he would no longer . . ." Her throat closed on her words, and the tears that filled her eyes drowned all thought.

She put her hands over her eyes, the sobs that she choked down racking her body. Cool fingers closed around her wrists and the doctor knelt in front of her. "Grace," he said quietly. "The fault does not lie with you. It never did. You are not a temptation but simply a target for another's black sin."

"I wish it were not so," she cried, tears flowing freely now. "If

I had somehow invited his actions, made him feel . . . what he felt, then going away would bring it to an end. Alice would have nothing to fear, and no one need ever know."

Thornhollow removed his hands from her own, fishing in his pocket for a handkerchief. When he spoke again his voice was matter-of-fact. "Has there been any indication in your letters that his actions have transferred to her?"

"No." Grace shook her head, taking the offered handkerchief to dab her eyes. "Merely the beginnings, mirrored exactly as they were with me. She has some time yet."

Thornhollow sighed heavily. "That's a relief, at least."

"Doctor," Grace asked. "What are we going to do?"

"I don't know," he said. "I simply do not know."

But his eyes were on the blackboard.

TWENTY-FOUR

His indecision was replaced with action by nightfall. An urgent knocking at Grace's door interrupted her dressing for bed, and Janey's irritated countenance in the hallway did not bode well.

"Why he can't just leave you alone for the time being, I don't know. We can't all keep that man's hours."

Grace twisted her hair into a simple knot as they descended the stairs together, the nurse's steps still heavy with her anger. "I tell you, it's not right, Grace. Sometimes I think he forgets that you're a patient too, you know. He may need your assistance from time to time, but you need your sleep. A few more interruptions in your schedule and I may see fit to say so."

Grace listened mildly as they crossed to the large front doors, which stood open, letting in the cold air. Thornhollow's carriage waited outside, Ned at the ready.

Janey took off her own wrap, draping it over Grace's shoulders with a frown still on her face. "I'm quite serious, Grace. You're my charge as well as his, and if I think his activities are interfering with your best interests, I'll speak up."

Grace grasped the nurse's hand in a flood of affection, squeezing to communicate her thanks. Janey looked at her, a sigh hitching deep in her chest. "You'd be devastated if I put a stop to it, though, wouldn't you? Your eyes are brightest before you step into that carriage, Grace, though the darkest circles are on your face the next morning."

Janey impulsively pulled her into a hug, and Grace's back stiffened. "Sorry. I get too close to you girls for my own good. Go on, then," she said, giving Grace a playful push out the door. "Go do your work."

The nurse watched as the carriage clattered off into the night, shaking her head, arms close around herself for warmth. "Those two," she muttered. "There are days I think we've incarcerated the wrong one."

Grace's question as to their destination died on her lips as she closed the carriage door behind her to find they were not alone.

"Mrs. Jacobs will be joining us," Thornhollow said, arm wrapped around an awkwardly long package as they bumped their way across the river. "It's not the usual activity that takes us out tonight, as you'll see."

"It's dark, Doctor," Mrs. Jacobs said, her face pressed directly against the glass. "My Mellie, she don't like the dark. Cries something awful and calls for me in the night."

"So you've said."

"I can hear her. She's thirsty." Her hand joined her face against the glass, leaving a murky condensation trail behind it. "She needs a drink, Doctor. I can't rest till she's had it."

"Of course not," he said. "And no one would expect you to."

Grace kept her eyes rooted on the grieving mother, whose mouth worked constantly, teeth tearing her lips to shreds. Tears leaked from her eyes, finding well-worn tracks within the wrinkles of her cheeks. If Janey had been upset about Grace's health, she would've been apoplectic over Mrs. Jacobs. Her eyes were sunk so deeply they were only black pits in her face, and the circles under them were nearly as dark.

Grace nudged Thornhollow's foot with her own, nodding toward the package he carried with a raised eyebrow.

"You'll see," he mouthed.

The carriage rocked to a halt and Ned opened the door with a lantern in hand, his face betraying no curiosity or irritation at the late hour or oddness of their destination. When Grace alighted from the carriage her heart skipped a beat at the sight of the headstones, row after row standing bleak and immovable in the dark, naked tree branches shifting wildly above them in the wind.

"Apologies," Thornhollow said. "Perhaps it would've been best to warn you." Grace shook her head, a blank mask back in place as she followed Ned, who seemed to know more about their duties that night than she did. They made their way to a freshly dug grave, the wind whipping Janey's wrap around Grace's shoulders as she hunched defensively against it.

"You've got to keep them out of the beds of your toenails," Ned told her solemnly. "Once they're under 'em, there's no getting 'em out."

Grace nodded as if she understood.

Thornhollow's words carried on the wind, his voice so gentle she could hardly believe it was the same man who had yelled at her that morning.

"Come now, Margaret," he was saying, hand outstretched. "She's waiting."

"Mellie?" The name, filled with hope, fluttered through the night, torn away by the wind.

Ned wordlessly took the oblong package from Thornhollow as they approached, the doctor still holding on to the widow's arm to offer support. A sharp intake of breath came from the woman as she saw the fresh grave, and Grace moved to her other side to help keep her on her feet.

"They come and told me she was gone," Mrs. Jacobs said, her

eyes flat in the moonlight. "But I didn't believe them. How can it be so when I still hear her calling for a drink?"

"You hear her now?" Thornhollow asked.

"Aye, Doctor," she said, absently wiping at her face. "She's thirsty down there. It's the long sleep she's gone to, and she'll be needing a good drink if the Lord expects her to rest easy."

"Then she shall have it." With a nod from Thornhollow, Ned began to unwrap the package, while the doctor motioned for Grace to follow him into the deeper shadows of a vast maple.

"Despite what you may think, I didn't spend the entire day drinking in my office. Mrs. Jacobs has refused rest as long as she can hear her daughter calling for her. Shortly after you and I had words this morning, I made a trip to town with specifications for an instrument to remedy that situation."

Grace watched as Ned produced a long auger, taller than he was, alongside a slender reed. "And what is my role this evening, Doctor? You do not need my eyes or ears for this."

"No," he admitted. "I asked for you to come along so that you might have a full picture of myself, as a person. Today I said things that I shouldn't have, and I apologize. Too often I forget that you are a patient as well as my protégé, and I spoke to you in a manner I would never take with someone under my care. I wish to regain your trust, and this is a first step toward earning that back, by showing you that I do care for others, though I often fail to show it."

Grace nodded that she understood and they returned to the graveside in silence, where Mrs. Jacobs had fallen to her knees, fingers trailing through the loose dirt.

"We'll need you to step back, Margaret," Thornhollow said, and Grace gently took the older woman by the shoulders when she showed no sign of moving.

"Ready then, Doctor?" Ned asked, auger in hand. "Should be easy going, with this so recently moved. Also, the squirrel said so."

"Helpful creature," Thornhollow said, and the two men went to work, each taking turns twisting the narrow auger into the ground near the headstone. It slid into the earth easily, and Grace shuddered as she watched it sink farther, each twist bringing it nearer to their goal.

"They digging her up, then?" Mrs. Jacobs said into Grace's shoulder. "The doctor thinks she's not dead after all, doesn't he?"

Grace eyed the small pile of earth growing next to the stone where the men deposited the dirt the auger brought up and shook her head. Their task was much more exacting than a disinterment, a job that required precision and not the blunt instrument of a shovel.

A light rain began, the cold turning each drop into an icy needle. Grace shivered and drew Mrs. Jacobs closer for her own comfort as well as the other woman's. Thornhollow and Ned paused for a moment, the easy turning of the auger at an end.

"We've struck it, then," the doctor said, eyes meeting Ned's.

"I had the point made sharp, so a few good pulls ought to punch through. Are you up for it?"

Ned's gray head went up and down, and they twisted together, the sharp tip straining against the pine box six feet below for only a few moments before forcing itself downward.

"Stop!" Thornhollow yelled, and Grace shuddered to think what the tool might bring up on its sharp tip if they'd gone even a few inches too far. They pulled hand over hand, each exertion bringing more silver into the light. Dirt slid off the coiled edges and finally at the tip, splinters from the coffin.

The doctor nodded, tossing the auger aside. "Ned, if you would hand me the reed?"

It slid into the hole easily, and Mrs. Jacobs's soft mewling eased as she began to understand. Thornhollow rose from his knees beside the grave, went to the carriage, and returned with a canteen.

"Madam," he said solemnly to Mrs. Jacobs. "I believe your daughter is thirsty."

The older woman disentangled herself from Grace, took the canteen from Dr. Thornhollow, and crawled to the gravestone. Thornhollow offered Grace his hand, and she rose, watching as Mrs. Jacobs whispered something into the reed, her words disappearing into the coffin below, followed by a long, cool drink of water.

Her sobs followed, long and heavy. "I can't hear her no more,

Doctor," she said. "That's all she needed. A drink, and her mother to give it to her."

Ned removed his hat and leaned on the auger, his voice surprising them all as it rang out low and strong, mixing with the moan of the wind as the storm rolled in.

> *O say can you see by the dawn's early light,*
> *What so proudly we hailed at the twilight's last gleaming,*
> *Whose broad stripes and bright stars through the perilous fight,*
> *O'er the ramparts we watched, were so gallantly streaming?*

Thornhollow let go of Grace's arm and covered his heart with his hand, his baritone joining with Ned's thrumming bass.

> *And the rockets' red glare, the bombs bursting in air,*
> *Gave proof through the night that our flag was still there;*
> *O say does that star-spangled banner yet wave,*
> *O'er the land of the free and the home of the brave?*

Grace's throat itched to join them, but it was not only subterfuge that kept her mouth firmly shut. Emotions had welled close to the surface, and she thought her heart had never felt so full as it did standing next to the defiled grave of a whore while lunatics sang the national anthem.

Four sets of muddy footprints crisscrossed the black-and-white floor of the atrium, the doctor having convinced Ned to come inside for tea upon their return. The rain had unleashed on them, though Mrs. Jacobs had remained unperturbed, even when the closest of lightning strikes set Grace's arm hairs on end. Ned was soaked through, and though he normally wouldn't leave the stables, the doctor's offer of a warm drink had brought him inside long enough to slug it down, then venture back out into the night. Thornhollow rested near the fireplace in his office, face dejectedly in his hands though he himself had proclaimed the night a success.

"It was a good thing you did tonight," Grace said, once they were alone.

He waved off her praise. "It was no miracle. All I did was listen to the woman and give her what she was asking for."

"When no one else would."

"Mmmmm," was the only response Grace got, and she saw that his eyes had wandered to the blackboard again.

"Not still in a foul mood about our killer, are you?"

"I'm in a foul mood about our lack of a killer," he said. "You've listened to me lecture long enough to know that a person who attacks with a method as specific as this doesn't stop. It will happen again, and me too dense to see to the heart of it and stop him in time."

Grace eyed the board. "It's as if something inside of him has been unleashed; he won't restrain willingly. But, I'm curious—why start in the first place?"

"A lethal mixture of any number of things. Judging by his attitude toward women, he deals with an overbearing mother. Add his failures with wom—"

"No, Doctor," Grace interrupted. "I mean, why start *now*? If he is a medical man, he will have had schooling, so he can't be terribly young. Yet the sloppiness from Anka Baran's murder indicates she was his first victim."

Intrigued, Thornhollow leaned forward. "Yes, and most killers tend to seek out victims within their own age range. I'd say the Polish girl—"

"Anka," Grace said her name.

"—was in her late twenties at least. From seeing Mrs. Jacobs's daughter when she visited here I'd say she was a comparable age, though her lifestyle may have added a few years to her face."

Thornhollow tapped his fingers on his knees, eyes roaming the board as if trying to find a place to fit their new puzzle piece though he didn't even know the shape of it yet. "A good question, Grace. Why now? The answer may shed light on the portrait of our man."

"As would visiting Mellie Jacobs's place of work," Grace said.

His fingers stopped drumming, and he shuddered. "I need not tell you how much I dread it. I doubt the employees will understand where my interests lie. I'll be in for some rather awkward explaining, I'm sure."

"I could do the talking," Grace said. "I'll cover my scars. No one will know I'm a mental patient."

Thornhollow shook his head. "As I said before, sometimes even I forget that you are one. I'm not sure it would be wise to expose you to—"

"I am hardly naive," she said, cutting him short.

"I know that," the doctor said, hands returning to his face as he rubbed his forehead. "But I can hardly defend taking a young woman who is under my care into a . . . a . . ."

"Whorehouse."

"Yes, fine. Into a whorehouse. Really, Grace—how would that look?"

"Then you need not accompany me," she said.

"I wouldn't let you go in there alone under any circumstances."

"You won't have to," Grace said. "I have an idea."

TWENTY-FIVE

"Ye want me to do what now?" Nell asked, her black eyebrows almost meeting her hairline.

"Shhh." Thornhollow shushed her with one finger to his lips, his eyes shooting to the doorway.

Grace watched from her chair, the midmorning light slanting through the office windows. Nell's voice had carried, but no one came to inspect her outburst. Grace relaxed, one hand reaching over to cover her friend's.

"I know that this is highly irregular," Thornhollow went on, his voice pitched low.

"'Ighly irregular is me daily life, Doctor. Bein' asked if I want to go for a stroll down to the whorehouse with a mute lassie alongside me by a man who's supposed to be the next Jaysus Christ is flat cockamamie."

"I'm hardly Jesus Christ," Thornhollow said, already looking exhausted by their conversation.

"Janey says ye are," Nell shot back. "A peculiar brand of savior, but a saint for the crazies nonetheless, she says. Ye can't do no wrong in 'er eyes, now that Mrs. Jacobs sleeps the night through."

"My canonization aside, you need to know that I wouldn't ask you to expose yourself to that kind of environment without good reason."

Nell rolled her eyes. "I've exposed meself to worse, as ye well know. Ye say that I may be able to 'elp catch the fellow tha's done in Mrs. Jacobs's daughter, then I'm in. Takin' Grace 'ere with me makes me feel a bit odd, but if ye say tha's the way of it, then tha's the way of it."

"I need Grace's eyes and ears. Her memory is impeccable and she may see things that you miss."

Nell shifted uncomfortably. "Aye, well, I'm a little worried about 'er seeing things tha' per'aps she'd rather miss."

"Grace is unflappable in any situation, Nell. Trust me on that count."

Nell reached over and squeezed Grace's hand. "In tha' case, go put on yer pretty dress, lassie. We're going to the whorehouse."

Grace tucked her slate and chalk under one arm, lacing the other with Nell's as they strolled casually down the hill.

"Now, don' you be tellin' Janey or even Lizzie, but this 'ere isn't exactly the first time I've wandered off the grounds," Nell said. "They make it nice an' easy. No fences, or the like. If you look like ye know what yer doin' ye can walk off fer a few hours and come back in time for dinner, none the wiser."

Grace nodded as they turned the corner, wandering into a copse of trees that hid a footpath. Nell said it would lead down to a shallow patch in the river, and from there town was only a stone's throw away. The girls unlaced their boots at the bank, and Grace sucked in her breath as she stepped into the cold water.

"Aye," Nell agreed, wobbling on one leg as she pulled off her stocking. "It's gettin' to the time of year I won't be makin' me trips till she freezes over. Charlie's family, they sends him some money once in a while. Ever' now an' then I sneak down here and we splits a bottle or two of somethin' 'ere in the woods."

Nell crossed after Grace, and they yanked their boots back on quickly, Grace's toes curling against the cold. Grace felt the other girl's eyes on her as they emerged from the riverbank and made their way into town.

"If I don't remember all the questions I'm supposed to be askin', you be sure an' give me a nudge. The doctor, 'e's done me a good turn or two that no one knows nothin' about, and I doubt I'm the only one in that place who can say so."

Grace nodded, patting her slate reassuringly as they passed

a house where a mother sat in a rocking chair on the front porch, children playing at her feet. She nodded in greeting and both girls nodded back, Grace's scars hidden under her curls.

Nell giggled into her hand. "Playing at bein' respectable always gets a rise outta me. Though once we find our way into the whore-house I 'spose that game is up." Nell hesitated in her step at the next crossroads. "I don't exactly know where we're goin'."

Grace walked confidently on, her memory of the first night with Dr. Thornhollow seared into her mind. The buildings around them deteriorated slightly as they moved on, their presence gaining more attention as their clothes marked them as people who didn't belong on the wrong side of town. But the establishment they were headed to still held a front of respectability, advertising only alcohol for sale and not women as well.

Nell steered Grace down an alley once she spotted it. "Ye may know the place well enough ter find it, but I don' think walkin' in by the front door is the wisest thing. Ye don' want to be mistaken for a workin' girl. Thornhollow would have me hide."

They approached from the back, where a couple of women wrapped in threadbare cloaks were sharing a smoke on the balcony. Nell hailed them from the side street.

"Oy, there! We was wonderin' if we might 'ave a word?"

"With who?" one woman asked, flicking ash from her cigarette.

"Uh . . ." Nell's voice lost some of its confidence. "We come about Mellie Jacobs."

"Poor Mellie," the other woman said, tugging her shawl tighter. "Didn't no one even let us know about the funeral. So's I don't know a soul was there when they stuck her in the ground."

"Don't be wasting your pity, Sarah," the woman with the cigarette said. "Ain't nobody going to our funerals, neither. Feel sorry for yourself and for me. At least we're alive to know it."

"I'll go t' both yer funerals if ye spare me a damn moment," Nell shouted up.

"There's an offer." Sarah cackled. "Come on up, the both of you. Birdie and me's got some time before we go back to work."

Nell and Grace climbed the wooden stairs, stepping carefully over one that was broken, and joined the women on the balcony. Birdie offered a puff of her cigarette to Nell, who took a drag gratefully.

"So you knew Mellie?" Sarah asked.

"Nay . . . ," Nell said, exhaling smoke. "We know 'er mother."

"Ah . . . so you're from up on the hill, are you?" Birdie said, taking the cigarette back from Nell. She nodded toward Grace. "Is that why you don't do any talking?"

"Aye, she's crazy as a loon, that one," Nell said.

"And what about you?" Sarah asked. "You don't seem to have nothing wrong with you. And a pretty face like yours, you could make good money down here with us. Lots of men be willing to pay a bit extra to toss a crazy girl."

"They'd pay with more than money," Birdie said shrewdly, looking Nell up and down. "She's got the pox."

Nell's smile froze on her face. "How'd you know?"

"It's in the way you walked up them steps, stiff like it hurts in your joints, though you're too young to have the arthritis. And it's cool today, surely, but you're buttoned up to your neck, covering every inch you can." She flicked her cigarette again. "How far's it spread?"

Grace watched her friend's normal confidence fall away, replaced by a stony wall of indifference. "Far enough tha' I don't care to say."

"You got one blooming, here," Birdie said, touching the side of her own mouth.

Nell's hand went to her face reflexively. "I don't."

"You do." Birdie nodded. "I see the way you've got your lips clenched a bit to hide it, but there's a lump there sure enough. It'll be leaking before long and that'll be the end of your face."

Sarah smacked her friend's shoulder. "That's enough, Birdie. No need to scare the girl. If she's up to the asylum, she knows about her condition, more so than the town whores."

"Whores may not know a lot," Birdie said, eyes still on Nell's face. "But I know the pox. Mellie had it too, you know."

Grace nudged Nell, anxious to tear her friend's mind away from her own troubles. "Did she?" Nell asked, taking the cue.

"She'd just had the first sores, down here." Birdie pointed at her crotch. "But Mrs. Teekler, if she knows one of the girls has got a spot, they're out on the street. She makes a good business off us, and she only wants one kind of thing erupting down here on River Street."

"If you're sick, you're out of a job," Sarah agreed. "And Mellie knew it well enough to take herself to her room with a bottle when her time was up."

"Is tha' what happened, then?" Nell asked, enough of a question in her voice to make the other two women look at each other uneasily.

"That's what we was told," Sarah said. "And around here you both do as you're told and believe what you're told."

"Or at least put on a good show of it," Birdie said, pitching her cigarette into the street below. "But Teekler's downstairs balancing the books and there ain't no one to hear what I say but the robins and you two loons."

Sarah laughed again, shaking her head at her friend's cleverness.

"So you don't think she drank herself to death?" Nell pressed.

"Oh, I wouldn't say that exactly," Birdie said. "She wouldn't be the first of us to make her way out, but Mellie wasn't the type. And besides, she wasn't entirely sure that it *was* the pox. Women in our line of work can get all kinds of things go wrong down there without it necessarily being the end of the line. She had a bit of money saved up and told me she was having a man come and take a look at her."

Grace's fingers tightened on her slate, the brittle edges cutting into her fingers.

"He must not've had good news for her," Sarah said.

Birdie shrugged. "I can't say for sure. All's I know is that's the last thing she said to me after Teekler took her off of shift."

"So she wasn't seeing any customers?" Nell asked.

"No," Birdie said. "Once you've got a spot on you you're not a working girl no more. Not here, anyway. Teekler even made her pay for her room the last few days she was here without earning money, as if she thinks she's running a hotel or some kind of rot." Birdie spit over the side of the railing. "The last bit of her money went to that doctor man, trying to prove she wasn't going to spread the pox to every last john who paid good money for a go at her."

"Do you know who the doctor was?" Nell asked, responding to the pressure on her elbow from Grace's fingers.

Birdie looked at Sarah, who shook her head. "No. She would've brought him up the back stairs just like you are here, quiet like. Teekler don't allow us to have a man here who she isn't getting money from."

"Why not go see him in his office, then?"

Grace silently thanked her friend for being so quick.

"Maybe the doctor don't like it being known he treats whores, thinking it might hurt his more respectable business," Sarah said.

"Or maybe he offered to take payment in something other than money," Birdie added. "Some men don't mind taking their chances, if they're desperate enough."

A shout from downstairs made all four women jump. "You'd best be going," Sarah said, urging them toward the stairs. "I don't know that Teekler would care for us talking to two girls from the street, but it's hard to say and life's tough enough as it is."

Nell and Grace picked their way down the steps as Grace scratched at her slate, turning to face the prostitutes before they went back inside. Grace held it high so that they could see her two words, written large.

BE CAREFUL

"So me and Grace, we think it was some doctor that done ol' Mellie Jacobs in," Nell said, leaning closer to Lizzie to whisper. The three girls sprawled on Grace's bed, one lantern shared conspiratorially between them, burning low.

Lizzie's blue eyes were wide. "Is this true?"

Grace nodded, slate set aside when she was among friends.

"But why would he do such a thing? Mellie Jacobs never hurt a fly, I'm sure."

"It's easy enough to figure, isn't it?" Nell said. "'E's got a burning but the candle wax has gone soft."

"Nell!" Lizzie objected.

"What? Oh, 'ere's another one. 'E'd like to start a fire, but the wick won't stand."

"I'll go back to my room, I will," Lizzie said. "I'm not disobeying Janey just to listen to you make lewd remarks."

Nell laughed. "I'm bein' lewd, sure, but tha' don't make me wrong."

"Do you think that's what it is, Grace?" Lizzie asked. "He's angry that he's unable to . . . to . . ."

"Get a cockstand," Nell put in, and Lizzie threw Grace's pillow in Nell's face.

Grace pulled the lantern off the bedside table in time to keep it from falling to the floor as Nell tweaked Lizzie's long braid. "Ye go ahead and doubt wha' I'm sayin' if you like, me friend," Nell said. "If you want a better reason, maybe String knows what drives a man to killin'."

"It doesn't work that way," Lizzie said. "String only hears what goes on in the people around me, and then only those that let their thoughts flow free. I couldn't tell you what President Harrison had for dinner or anything like that."

"And who cares, anyway? I'm more interested in wha' I'm having," Nell said. "I almost forgot to tell you lassies, wha' with the excitin' trip to the whorehouse—we been invited to Janey's for Thanksgiving dinner."

Lizzie clapped her hands together. "Have we really? What a treat! But, poor Grace, you look confused."

Grace was indeed quite lost, as her eyes went back and forth between her friends.

"Sometimes for special occasions, certain staff members can take well-behaved patients off grounds," Lizzie explained.

"An' the rest of us go along illegally," Nell interrupted.

"Nonsense." Lizzie shushed her. "You've been to Janey's before. We went last Halloween, remember? The girl from the third floor went too . . . what was her name?"

"Sophia," Nell said. "She were a nice enough lassie till Janey's mum brought the jack-o'-lantern out."

"I never did understand it," Lizzie said.

"I had seeds in me hair fer days," Nell said. "And we near burned the 'ouse down. But Janey said she assured 'er mum that Grace won't be throwin' nothin'."

"And it's Thanksgiving anyway," Lizzie said. "So there won't be any jack-o'-lanterns."

Nell narrowed her eyes at Grace. "Ye don't 'ave anythin' against turkeys, do ye?"

The three girls burst into laughter, heedless of the dark and the wind outside.

TWENTY-SIX

Sundays brought fewer people as the air found its teeth, the bite of cold chasing them away from the grounds and into the warmth of their homes. A few brave souls still traversed the paths, their desire for fresh air before winter bringing them out despite the colder temperatures. Mary and her mother were among them, though the baby was left behind to rest more comfortably with his father. By an unspoken agreement Grace had been under the willow every Sunday since they met, and when their paths crossed she would look to the mother for permission before holding out a hand to Mary.

The girl always flew to her, the weight of her little body bringing a bittersweet happiness. This was not her sister but a stand-in for Grace's affections, the mother a walking reminder of what Grace's life should have been. She looked to the little family for a glimmer of what life was like beyond the brick walls she now called home, and while she knew they offered her safety, they also denied her a life like theirs.

One Sunday they did not come, and Grace's fingers curled around Alice's most recent letter, the tips of them nearly blue with the cold. The pages had become fewer and far between, and though Grace continued to write to Falsteed and Alice, she often received no reply from her little sister. Reed weighed her pages with stones, but the fingers of the wind could reach into any crevice, and Grace knew that many of her well-intended letters were read by no one. She pored over the one in her hands as the wind whipped at the pages, until she heard someone coming along the path.

Grace came to her feet, a smile of greeting in place for Mary and her mother, but it soon disappeared when a fellow inmate rounded the corner, his loping gait stalling when he spotted her.

"Hello, hello," he called. "Cold day. You must have the wandering bug, like me." He left the path, his feet eating the distance between them as Grace tried to widen it by backing away. But the lake was behind her, and she could only retreat so far.

"Don't be afraid," he said. "Patrick's never hurt anybody. Patrick don't hurt people."

She motioned at him to go away, Alice's letter fluttering in her hands. He ignored her, eyes drawn to the paper.

"What have you got? What is it?" He came closer and Grace dodged to the side, ready to run for the asylum. He snagged her wrist and bent it, plucking the letter from her numb hand in an instant.

"From a lover? Is it? From a man?" His eyes roamed the pages, and Grace felt her panic dissolving into rage as he followed a line with one huge finger, mouth moving with the words.

She ran at him, but he moved quickly, holding the pages above his head and dancing out of the way as she grabbed for them.

"She wants it back, yes she does. She wants it," he sang. Grace tore at his arm but he lifted her whole frame, swinging her in the air easily. She kicked at his shin and he yelled, dropping her near the base of the willow. Grace grabbed a broken branch from the ground, whirling to stab at him with the sharp point. He sidestepped her lunge, laughing as he tore one of the pages in half, lifting the shreds to the wind.

Grace screamed, the sound tearing through the cold air and following the ripped pages as they blew out over the lake. She went after him again, no feint in her stab as she drove at him. Footsteps were running down the path but she ignored them, her entire being bent on getting what was left of Alice's letter back even if it meant impaling her tormentor. Strong hands grabbed her before she could do it, and she was wrestled to the ground, her stick tossed out of her reach.

"Patrick!" a male nurse yelled as he squared off against the patient. "What do you think you're doing?"

"Me?" he asked, hands in the air where the single page still fluttered. He curled it up quickly, popping it into his mouth. "I ain't doib nuffin."

Thornhollow had flipped the blackboard to the clean side on more than one occasion. But two new murders had brought nothing more compelling than a son anxious to inherit sooner than nature intended and an inconveniently pregnant girl whose lover had turned himself in at the station only hours later.

"There's nothing here," the doctor bemoaned, as he flipped the board back to the doll killer. "There's no real work involved in finding any of these people, especially when they're boring enough to turn themselves in. It's a fairly bleak time when I find my protégé attacking people with sticks a welcome diversion."

Grace didn't comment from her seat by the fire, her feet tucked under a blanket. Patrick had been disciplined for taunting her, and Janey had gravely informed Grace she'd had to make a note in her file about possible violent tendencies, but nothing stung like the loss of Alice's letter.

Thornhollow sighed when she didn't answer, his eyes drawn back to the board. "Yes, I believe the winter may be dulling us all. But this man . . ." His voice wavered, almost verging on admiration. "This man I'd like to meet."

"It seems unlikely," Grace said. "Even if we count Mellie as his work, it's been weeks."

"I know it," the doctor mused, eyes roaming the board. "And why would that be? We've only spotted two of his victims, and them somewhat close together. There's not enough to establish a pattern."

"There's not much of a pattern when our killer has stopped killing," Grace said.

"He can't have stopped," Thornhollow said over his shoulder. "I've told you. A man like that doesn't indulge in a passion and then move on."

"What if it's exactly that? What if he has, in fact, moved on?"

"It's possible," the doctor acknowledged. "But I've been keeping tabs on the medical men, and they're all still in practice. None of them have died, either. I'd have noticed."

"You've had an eye on them all this time, even when we saw them face-to-face and you were sure our theory was wrong?"

"Off," Thornhollow corrected, a finger in the air. "Our theory is *off*, not wrong. I may have made a mistake or two in guessing how our man would react to you, Grace, but that doesn't unravel all the threads."

"Well then," Grace said, joining him by the board. "Let me review. We're looking for someone familiar with ether who is strong enough to hold a girl against her will long enough for it to act. He may be healthy physically but he's unable to be intimate with a woman, possibly connected to the idea that he had an overbearing mother. He's intelligent but socially awkward, perhaps mostly with women."

She thought a moment, hands on her hips. "I'm sorry, Doctor, but we could be talking about you."

"I'm offended. You've never met my mother," he said. "One other thing makes me unfit for the profile, but we need not get into that."

Grace rolled her eyes but let the comment pass. "Our visit to the brothel only solidified the idea that a doctor is at work here. And if, as you say, none of the locals have moved practice or died, I suppose this leaves us with nothing more than to wait. And watch, although it sounds as if you're doing that rather thoroughly."

"And not just the local medicals, Grace," Thornhollow said, his eyes not meeting hers. "I have some news from Boston."

Grace's knees were suddenly weak, her vision fuzzy on the edges. "Is it Alice?" Her voice barely made it past her lips, her treacherous throat closing on itself.

"No, nothing like that. Grace, please sit down." His hands were on her shoulders, and she leaned into him gratefully, all her strength sapped at the mere mention of her birthplace. Thornhollow set her back in the chair by the fire and returned with a glass of amber liquid.

"Is it that bad?" Grace asked, taking the drink and sniffing it cautiously.

"No danger has come to your sister, I know that is your main concern," he said, standing in front of her to gauge her reactions to his words. "After I learned that you were in correspondence with Falsteed, I began to take the Boston papers. I agree that Heedson's mouth is forever shut to protect his own skin and that both Falsteed and Reed are more than trustworthy. However, the efficacy of a secret is strained thin the more people who are drawn into it, and I thought it best to stay apprised of news in Boston."

"If not for Alice I'd be happy to never hear of that place again," Grace said, taking a drink. It burned a path down her throat and heated her belly, bringing a false relaxation in its wake that was welcome nonetheless.

"I quite agree," Thornhollow continued. "But both our pasts are anchored there. Your father is a highly prominent man. Heedson, as the head of a major medical facility, does merit mention from time to time in the papers, and I thought it best to be aware of their movements. If Heedson were to suddenly be replaced, your father to travel unexpectedly, any indication that their normal lives were disrupted could indicate that tongues may have loosened and our secret was a secret no more."

"And?" Grace's hands went to her scars, fingers massaging the smooth skin there for the comfort it brought.

"And there's no reason to think either of us is in any danger."

Relief swelled along with exasperation as Grace swallowed another mouthful of her drink. "Really, Doctor. I know that you're not terribly good with people, but you need to learn how to deliver news so as not to needlessly—"

"Your father is coming here, Grace."

"What?" Her grip on the glass loosened, and it wobbled along with her quickened heartbeat. "You said there was no danger."

"And there is not," Thornhollow insisted, dropping to his knees in front of her chair. "Grace, I assure you if I thought for one second that man suspected you were alive, I'd put us both on a ship and damn what people would say."

"Then why would he come here, if not because he was following us?"

"Unfortunately, like most disagreeable things in the world the answer is *politics*. Your father is campaigning for the presidential ticket. You've seen for yourself that the grounds are open to the public, and the formal ballroom falls under the same banner. The asylum offers work for half the town, and a lovely place for the rich to gather so that the employed ones can serve them. It seems that when I brought you to the only place that could offer safety, I never considered that it's in a river-and-railroad town in a swing state before an election year."

Grace laughed bitterly, her breath tinted with alcohol. "So that's it? He's coming here to stump for the party? Lord." She threw back the last of the drink and handed the glass to Thornhollow.

"It's the worst of luck, I admit."

"Yet, I'm not entirely surprised," Grace said, her eyes on the fire. "Have we not both learned by now that fate is cruel?" She fell silent for a moment, words lost in the flames.

"Fate may be cruel, but it does occasionally play fairly. The superintendent has been insisting on throwing a formal dinner to honor my employment here and introduce me to key citizens. I've put it off but was able to convince him to make your father's visit a dual event. As one of the two guests of honor I'll be able keep an eye on your father throughout the evening, and you, of course, will be nowhere near the ballroom."

"I may seek out Ned's company," she said.

"Nonsense. The guest carriages, horses, and drivers will be in and out of the stables. You'd be more visible there than sitting quietly in your room."

She opened her mouth to argue, but he held up a hand. "However, I understand that being closed away would only tax your nerves. I thought fresh air would be best and the company of friends." He reached into his vest pocket, pulling out a small iron key. "The west turret. Take Lizzie and Nell to the roof and treat it as an adventure."

"An adventure," she repeated, turning the key in her fingers.

"One in which you can keep an eye on the comings and goings of the guests," Thornhollow said. "I thought a degree of control might make you feel more secure."

"It will," she agreed. "Thank you."

"Oh, you're quite welcome," he said. "Meanwhile I'll be taking a meal with a man I detest, surrounded by people who want to make small talk and wear evening clothes. I may end the night as a patient and not an employee."

"If so, I assure you that you'll be under the most excellent care."

"Watch yer step now, Lizzie, there's a bit o' ice here on the flagstones, and we don't want String takin' a tumble."

Grace firmly tied Lizzie's hat under her chin while Lizzie supposedly held String out of the way. Once Grace was finished, she took the other girl in hand and they picked their way down the steps to meet Nell on the gravel roundabout. The fountain stood silent, its gurgling voice frozen by the frigid air.

"Come on, then," Nell called, practically dancing in front of them down the path. "Janey said if we're late she'll never be able ter talk 'er mum into bringin' the crazies 'ome again."

Lizzie shivered and cuddled close to Grace as they walked, hand cupped protectively near her ear. "String doesn't like to be whipped about," she explained as they crossed the footbridge. "Janey's mother's place is just at the base of the hill, though."

Their feet punched through the snow behind them as they left the path for a side trail into the woods. Nell passed in front of them to hold back branches for the other girls to duck under.

"I promise I'm na leadin' ya into the woods to murder ya, dear

Grace," she said. "Janey's mum likes 'er peace and quiet, and she's got it, sure enough."

They arrived at the step of a cabin with merrily lit windows, bare branches interlacing thickly above it to create a canopy even without leaves. Nell shooed a chicken off the stoop with her boot and then knocked.

"Hello, girls," Janey said, opening the door with a smile. Grace couldn't help but smile in return, seeing her stoic nurse in an apron with a dab of flour on one cheek. Her eyes were bright, her cheeks flushed with the heat from the kitchen. Janey bustled them inside and hung their coats near the fire as they stomped the snow from their boots.

"I hope it wasn't too cold of a walk," she said. "I didn't want to bother poor Ned to rig up the horses just to drive a little ways. Besides, I thought it nicer to just have us girls. Don't you think so, Mother?"

"Of course," agreed an old woman, wrapped in blankets even though she sat by the fire. "And one I haven't met yet in the mix. Come here, dear, let me see you," she said, motioning to Grace.

Grace glanced at Janey, who nodded, and she knelt by the woman's rocker, leaning closer when she noticed the cataract covering one eye. A hand full of bones bent by age, but skin still soft, brushed against her cheeks. "A pretty girl, my Janey said as much. She also says you're not inclined to speech?"

Grace shook her head, and Nell answered for her. "She dinna talk much, no, but our Grace can play charades with the best of 'em. I can't say there's once tha' I didn't know wha' she was sayin', though 'er mouth never made a word."

The hand patted her head, as if in blessing. "Ah well, there's days when Janey's up the hill for work on a stretch that I don't speak to a soul myself. It leads to an understanding of your own self."

"I run me mouth plenty, Mrs. Wilcox, and I think I know's meself pretty well," Nell objected.

"And the rest of us do too, whether we want to or not," Lizzie said.

"My Irish lassie has returned," Mrs. Wilcox said, turning her good eye to Nell. "And how many hearts have you broken since I saw you last?"

"I've had me teeth in a few," Nell said, leaning low over the old woman to hug her. "But I don' remember 'em complainin' much."

"And, Elizabeth, don't think you'll be helping set the table when you could share news," Mrs. Wilcox scolded, motioning Lizzie over to the fire. "You let Janey see to things and come tell an old woman what String has to say."

Lizzie blushed and sat at Mrs. Wilcox's feet, but her tongue soon loosened as she reiterated news from the asylum, confirming tales that Janey had brought home from work. Every now and then she'd fall silent and turn her head to consult String on a detail, but even

Nell let it pass without comment as they relaxed to the sound of Janey setting the table behind them.

"All right then, girls, give Mother a hand and let's eat a meal together like civilized women."

And they did. Grace hadn't had such good food since her family table, though the faces around this one were so different. There were no stilted conversations and awkward pauses, no guarded looks or hidden kicks to urge silence. Words flew back and forth, bandied about in the warmth from the fireplace as if they'd grown in the air. Grace could not speak, but she wallowed in the conversation, laughing at Nell's frequent interruptions and Elizabeth's constant attempts to get her under control. Janey didn't object when her mother instructed her to pour some wine, though Grace covered her own glass with her hand.

"A teetotaler, are you?" Mrs. Wilcox asked. Grace shook her head but wouldn't move her hand. The little drink she'd taken in Thornhollow's office had gone to her head immediately. The company of her friends and the vivacity of the moment had her voice aching to speak already; a drink could easily throw the door open.

"Ye can feel free to pour me 'er bit," Nell said, passing her already empty cup back to Janey.

"Don't you get drunk now, Nell," Elizabeth warned. "Janey wouldn't hear the end of it if we came back to the asylum sheets to the wind."

"It takes more than a dram of wine to get an Irish lassie lit, ye wee Englishwoman," Nell said. "Even Charlie says 'e's not seen the likes of me for putting away the drink, and 'e's seen a few hardwood floors up close."

"And who is Charlie?" Mrs. Wilcox asked.

"'E's a poor drunkard up the hill," Nell said. "'Is family put 'im away for loving the bottle."

"He also did say he was drinking them because Jesus was trapped in the bottoms," Janey put in.

"If I were Jaysus, that's where I'd go," Nell said, tipping her glass again.

"Is Charlie a special friend of yours, then?"

"Och, no. A girl like meself can only get so close to a lad, if ye take me meaning." Her tongue slipped out of the side of her mouth to touch the sore there, and in the firelight, Grace could make out the shadow of another blooming under the skin next to it.

Janey patted Nell's arm, and Elizabeth's face grew grim as she tilted her head to the right. Nell refilled her own glass and looked around the table.

"I've never told ye girls how I got the pox, 'ave I?"

"I imagine you got it the same way anyone else does, and there's no terrible shame in it," Mrs. Wilcox said.

"Aye, there was no shame. Not on me own part, anyways. But the boy who got me with it, ye see, 'e was me mother's boss's son, and their name was gold back in Pennsylvania. And there weren't no one who was going to speak up for the washerwoman's daughter, least of all 'im."

"Would no one help you?" Janey asked.

"I went to me ma, straigh'aways when I knew somethin' was wrong. She was right sore wi' me. Said she didna leave Ireland behind to raise a whore in America. I'm the last of ten bairns, and I think she was wore out with the rearin' of us all. She tol' me I made me own bed and I was to lie innit. Said the mercury treatments was so expensive they may as well be made on the moon."

"Couldn't the boy in question afford it?" Mrs. Wilcox asked.

"'E could afford it well enough, no doubt. But when I went to 'im 'e said I didna catch it from 'im but from a stable boy or vagrant— 'one of yer own kind' was 'ow 'e put it. I knew well enough it was from 'im, as I'd not been with anyone else and 'e was my first. And 'e knew it too. I could see the fear in 'is eyes as to 'is own welfare and still 'e tossed me out o' the 'ouse, landed on my rear in the back garden I did, gave me a jolt straight up to me skull."

Grace was utterly still, as were the other women, lost in the lull of Nell's voice as she spoke, her own eyes staring into nothing.

"'E was me only chance of savin' meself, and I well knew it. Me mum and da 'ad turned me out, and there I was with scraped knees and the pox roarin' in me blood. I knew 'twas all up, but damned if I was lettin' the likes of James Cavendish get the better o' me. I knew the fam'ly, knew all their 'ouses from years of 'elpin' me mum cart their dirty sheets 'ome, never knowing I was to leave a blood spot on one someday meself.

"So I found me way into the bedrooms of all 'is menfolk. One by one they all 'ad me, each unbeknownst to the other and me makin' noises like it's me first toss each time. Them so proud of themselves, so 'appy to have a young, pretty thing moanin' underneath 'em, the whole time I'm givin' back to them what their own relation delivered unto me. From 'is cousins and uncles and grandfather, right down to the youngest brother, who only got but a minute or two of pleasure from it, I 'ad 'em all. And their pride will keep 'em from the doctor, and their sores will keep 'em from their wives, and their cocks will rot right off and they'll be wiped from the face o' the earth. And it's Nell O'Kelly that's done it to 'em."

"Amen," Mrs. Wilcox said, raising a glass.

"Amen," Elizabeth confirmed, raising hers for her first drink of the night.

"Amen to that," Janey said, tapping her glass alongside Grace's, who raised her water and met Nell's eyes, coldly nodding in agreement before tossing back what was left of her drink, warm now from the fire. It slid into her belly but barely touched her throat, parched with the need to comfort her friend.

TWENTY-SEVEN

"The kitchens are a wreck, I've never seen the like," Elizabeth complained a week later over dinner. "All this fuss over one man." She clucked her tongue and looked at her own plate regretfully.

The kitchen had been holding back on the patients' dinner the whole week, reserving the best of everything for the upcoming party. Grace stared at her plain bread, dry chicken with no gravy, and rather small carrot. Still, she hadn't had to fight anyone for it like in Boston. She concentrated on eating, her fingers rubbing the key to the west turret through the folds of her skirts for comfort.

"Aye, I'm none too happy meself," Nell said. "I been down in the root cellars findin' the best potatoes, as if I grew them for this

Mr. Mae in the first place. Which I didna, and I've 'alf a mind to tell 'im so."

Grace grabbed her friend's wrist and shook her head violently.

"Oy, now, feisty lass." Nell pulled away from her. "I'll not be misbehavin'. Come tomorrow night I plan to make meself scarce, unless they try to put us all to work. Not that they'd let me in the kitchens, anyway." Her hand went to the trail of sores that worked its way from the corner of her mouth, marring her once porcelain complexion.

"They've hired out the work," Elizabeth said, mouth tight as if she found it offensive. "The insane aren't good enough to prepare Senator Mae's food, I suppose."

The sound of her father's name in her friends' mouths made Grace's stomach clench shut, her hands form fists. His impending arrival had weighed heavy on her mind, causing nightmares that interfered with her sleep. Their dark fingers dug for purchase into the daylight hours, where sudden movements caused her to jump and she found herself wishing there was a lock on her bedroom door after all.

"There's nothing to fear, physically," Thornhollow had repeated that morning. "Your father believes you are dead. He has no knowledge of me or our connection. There's no reason for him to suspect a thing. You'll be safe with Nell and Lizzie. The only thing that could go wrong would be if I happen to punch him in the jaw."

Grace smiled to herself as she remembered Thornhollow's words, his own tension showing through the joke. The trio of girls left the dining hall, shooed out early by attendants who needed to put everything in order early, in case the senator could be enticed into a tour of the asylum. This sort of hospitality was exactly what Grace feared. Even if he were kept to the public areas, his presence was a stain she'd be able to sense long after he'd gone.

Janey met them in the hallway, eyes alight. "Girls, you'll never guess—I've been invited to the reception this evening. The dinner is only for a few of the politicals in town of course, and our own doctors, but the superintendent said the head ward nurses could come to the reception, if we've got the proper clothing for the thing." She fell in beside them, her happiness at the thought overwhelming the fact that she was an employee and they patients. "I half think he assumed we'd not have the right wardrobe, but Mother always insisted I keep the church dress for church only, and I suppose if it's good enough for God, it's good enough for Senator Mae."

Grace squeezed her eyes shut, fingers on her temples. Elizabeth's hands were on her shoulders instantly. "Are you all right, Grace? Is it a headache?"

Grace nodded and Janey herded them all into Grace's room, her excitement about the dinner overwhelmed by concern for her patient as she leaned Grace back on her bed. "Is it the dinner? So many strangers being here? Sometimes I know that can send you quiet ones over the edge. But don't you worry none. The super said that he'll be happy to show off the common places, but nobody's to see your private rooms. He said you're not to be paraded about for their entertainment, fancy-pants politician or not."

Grace kept her eyes closed, fingertips on her scars. That Janey had guessed somewhat correctly left her nerves more frayed than soothed. If the night was to pass uneventfully, she had to get herself under control. Weights settled on both ends of the bed as her friends nestled in with her.

"We'll stay with 'er, Janey," Nell said, one hand rubbing Grace's foot. "You go put on yer pretty things. Have a night without thinkin' o' the mad, fer once."

Janey remained in the doorway, hands working each other in her indecision. "I don't much like leaving with Grace being in a state, though."

"She's in less of a state than you," Elizabeth said. "Go on ahead."

"All right," Janey agreed. "If it helps her, you girls have my permission to bring your pallet here into her room tonight, sleep all together if there's some comfort in it."

"That's a wonderful idea," Elizabeth said. "Thank you, Janey."

After the door shut behind their nurse, Nell let out a giggle. "As if we 'aven't already done tha' a time or two before."

"Except now we have permission," Lizzie said. "Which means we don't have to get up with the cock crow so that no one knows any different."

"Oh, I dinna," Nell said. "I don't mind wakin' up with a co—"

"Enough out of you!" Lizzie shushed Nell's comment to focus on Grace. "What's wrong, love? Is it really the guests or . . . Grace? What is that?"

Grace held up the little iron key, a small smile on her face.

The stairs to the turret were thin, the plaster brushing both Grace's shoulders as she pushed cobwebs out of their path. Even though her calves were beginning to burn, each step took her upward and away from the guests who had begun to arrive, their unfamiliar voices lifting through the floorboards to the patients.

"I don't believe many people come this way," Elizabeth said, coughing politely as dust filled her nose.

"Nae, only the crazies who fancy a toss, I'd say." Nell's voice carried from the rear.

"Do patients really do that?" Elizabeth asked over her shoulder.

"There's a few, fer sure. Charlie said 'e's had 'alf the female ward, though I'd wager 'e does a bit o' exaggeratin'."

Grace reached the end of the stairs, handed the lamp down to Elizabeth, and put the key into the lock on the trapdoor. It turned easily, and Grace swung the door out into the cold night air with a gentle push. Disrupted snow fell on their upturned faces and Elizabeth sputtered. Grace gratefully took in the clean air and the openness surrounding her as she climbed onto the roof.

The west turret looked down over the gravel roundabout, just filling with carriages from town. Grace gave them a glance before reaching down to help Lizzie climb up. She put a hand down for Nell, but the Irish girl shook her head.

"Thank ye kindly, Grace, but I got a fresh rash on me hands just this evenin'. We don't want you ter get your lovely face all spoilt like me own, now do we?" Her words were light but her mouth twisted with the effort involved in keeping it that way.

"Come along and see," Elizabeth called from the railing. "It's a sight . . . oh, Grace, I don't know how you got the key, but I'm so glad."

"Ye don't know? Me money's on Dr. Thornhollow. If Grace told 'im to cut off 'is own leg because she fancied it, I think 'e'd saw through bone then an' there."

Grace pinched Nell lightly on the forearm and her friend yelped. "All's I'm sayin' is that 'e would. I'm not inferrin' anythin'."

"Keep your voice down," Lizzie hissed as they joined her. "There's people getting out of their carriages. Our fun is over if they spot three madwomen on the roof, and Janey's place at the reception gone for sure."

The dying winter light left a rosy tint to the snow, and the gas lamps that bordered the winding road to town had all been lit for the occasion. The flames danced, drawing the young women's eyes down to the bridge and the first lights being lit in the homes across it. Grace's nerves quieted a bit at the sight before her, the naked branches of the trees no less beautiful for being without leaves.

Elizabeth laced arms with the other two, leaning ever so slightly over the railing. "If you're very quiet, I bet we can hear the river from here," she whispered.

"Tha's just String pullin' a fast one on ye," Nell said. "We're sixty feet up if we're a foot. Ye can't hear the river, but I bet we might hear an interestin' thing or two, nonetheless. I see a fancy carriage comin' up the bend now, supposin' that's the senator?"

Grace's heart sank in her chest, her body quivering at the thought. Elizabeth pulled her closer, eyes full of concern. "Are you all right, Grace?" she asked, then tilted her head to the right, brows pulled tighter.

Grace nodded that she was fine but disentangled herself from Lizzie to lean both hands against the railing, pulling in deep lungfuls of air. It wasn't her father who alighted from the carriage but a businessman from town and his garishly overdressed wife. Nell leaned forward as they passed under them toward the portico.

"I think I just seen more o' that woman's cleavage than 'er own 'usband."

"Oh, look, another one," Elizabeth exclaimed as more wheels came crunching up the drive, hooves ringing as they circled behind the asylum to the stables. "Poor Ned. He'll have more than his fair share of work tonight."

"Och, 'e'll love it," Nell argued. "'E'll be able to tell us the name and 'eritage of every new 'orsie 'e meets tonight. 'E's probably the 'appiest insane person fer miles."

The carriages kept coming, people piling out of them. The drivers gathered on the back of the grounds, the bobbing heads of their lit cigarettes wafting the smell of tobacco to the girls to mingle with the voices of their bosses.

"Now that one's nicely dressed," Elizabeth said, nudging Nell to bring her attention to a woman in blue.

"Not bad, not bad," Nell agreed. "And lookie 'ere, the super's going to come down the steps to bring 'er in. Goodness me, in the upper crusts tha's the same as announcin' ye want to give 'er a go." She fanned herself in a mock fit.

"As if you'd mind for a man to hand you down from a carriage," Elizabeth said.

"What's 'e doin' with 'is 'ands after that?"

Elizabeth sighed. "Now, let's test their manners," she said. "All the women have come in with their husbands, except for the lady in blue."

"She didn't 'ave to wait for no 'elp."

"No, and here's a little old lady, come alone."

"And a gentleman come to see to 'er, right away," Nell said, slapping the railing. "Ye can say what ye like about the insane asylum, but—look 'ere, Grace, that's yer Dr. Thornhollow 'elpin' 'er. Ooooh and don't 'e just look nice as can be. My, my . . ."

"Yes, he does look handsome," Elizabeth agreed.

"Cover yer ears, lassies, then hit the boards." Nell said, a split second before putting her fingers in her mouth and letting out a wolf whistle. Grace dropped to the roof, dragging Elizabeth down next to her. Nell fell in pile of skirts, red-faced with laughter.

"Nell!" Elizabeth gasped. "What were you thinking?"

"I was thinkin' it's a lovely night, and 'e's a good-lookin' man who don't 'ave no one to tell 'im so. So I did, and damned if 'e didna look straight up 'ere as if 'e knew there'd be someone in the turret."

Elizabeth peeped over the edge. "Do you suppose he's still looking?"

"It doesna matter, Lizzie. 'E knows we're 'ere, and I imagine it's all for wee Grace's sake, so let's stop worryin' about the rules and 'ave the fun of it."

They went back down the stairs single file to retrieve chairs, making their way back up awkwardly, chair legs bumping each other in the shoulder blades. Once settled, Nell produced two cigarettes, lit them off the lamp, and offered one to them.

"I could never," Elizabeth said, waving it away.

"Ye could," Nell said, jabbing it back at her friend. "I begged two off of Charlie so's ye wouldn't have to share me own, so ye damn well better take a suck or I'll set String afire."

Elizabeth took a reluctant pull, coughed out a plume of smoke, and handed it off to Grace with a grimace. "It's the devil's own weed," she complained.

"Aye, the devil gets all the credit," Nell agreed. "Go on then, Grace, ye don' use yer mouth for nothin' else."

Grace took a puff, drawing the smoke into her lungs and back out in a rush that left her eyes watering. She handed it back to Lizzie, shaking her head.

"Amateurs," Nell said, sucking in and releasing smoke through her nose.

The cigarette made the round again, Nell coaching the other two as the moon rose higher and their laughter grew louder. Grace allowed herself to be lulled, to follow their voices and stories to a place where she didn't fear the arrival of her father. Lost in each other's words, they didn't even hear the party breaking up until the first carriages were brought around to the front, wheels crunching in the gravel.

"Already?" Elizabeth asked, rising from her chair to watch the guests depart.

"Ye've got no sense of time," Nell said, pointing at the moon. "It's two in the mornin' at least. Or 'ave ye never seen the sky this late?"

"Does it matter?" Elizabeth said, at the railing. "Here they go."

"Aye," Nell said as she and Grace joined their friend. "And the rich stagger 'ome just the same as the poor."

They emptied out slowly, women leaning on men and vice versa, drivers helping everyone into their carriages. Grace stood watching solemnly. Her father had been under her feet for hours and her friends had drawn her thoughts elsewhere. Now that he was leaving she felt a perverse need to see him, to revel in the knowledge that he had truly been so near and she'd been unaffected. The bricks had not crumbled; the air was not poisoned. She could continue to be Grace of the asylum on the hill and let Grace Mae truly be a ghost.

She went to the railing with triumph in her step, leaning into Elizabeth as they watched the revelers leave. Her father's booming voice sailed through the night air to her, the laughter he used in public so different from the low chuckle she'd heard in the dark. He emerged from under the portico, his shadow stretching as if it would engulf everything below her, leaving Grace in her turret surrounded by his darkness. His heavy step seemed to reverberate, the rhythm of her nightmares carried through the bricks to shake the boards beneath her feet. Her knees quivered and she dropped slightly, clinging to the rail but forcing her eyes on him as he turned to speak to the superintendent, his hand emerging from his coat sleeve as they shook. His teeth flashed, bright white against the pink of his lips, and Grace's stomach revolted at the sight, clenching down on her paltry supper as she bent over, gagging.

"Grace." Elizabeth gripped her arm. "Grace, what's wrong?"

Grace didn't respond, eyes still focused on her father as he climbed into a carriage and was lost from sight.

"The smoke get to yer stomach?" Nell asked.

Grace shook her head, eyes glistening with unshed tears. Next to her, Elizabeth's face went pale, her own knees buckling, and the two went down together.

"Yer a fine pair," Nell said, slumping to the ground with them. "One cigarette 'tween the two of ye, and yer both the color o' the sea."

Grace wrapped an arm around Elizabeth, her own strength returning. She squeezed her friend, who smiled delicately, though her face was still ashen.

"I'm all right," Elizabeth said weakly. "It's the cold getting the best of me. I lost my breath there for a minute."

"Yer fine to climb down?" Nell asked, holding the light in one hand, the trapdoor propped open on her knee.

"Yes," Elizabeth said, rising to her feet. "Can we leave the chairs, though? Maybe we'll come up again another time?"

"Oh, aye. It's gone so well. Grace is pukin' an' yer faintin'. Let's do it again tomorrow."

The three crept down to their hall with the light extinguished, hands on one another's shoulders as Nell led the way in the dark.

Moonlight streamed in through the high windows at the end of the hall, lighting their faces as they stopped at Grace's door.

"Good night, Grace," Elizabeth said, her hand on Grace's shoulder still. "Feel better."

"Aye, feel better." Nell suddenly pulled her into a hug, crushing Grace to her. "I love ye, I'll tell ye that. Like a sister. Even though me own 'aven't much use fer me. Yer my real fam'ly, the both of you." She pulled Lizzie in with her other arm. "Yer the best two women in the world, mad as hatters. And I'd take ye both over the lot of 'em that was 'ere tonight, money and all."

"I love you too, Nell," Lizzie said, tears flowing silvery streaks in the moonlight.

Grace could only move her head up and down as she leaned into both of them, tears streaming over her cheeks and down her closed throat.

The faces came back that night, the proximity of her father drawing them up from her subconscious. Even before his sins drew him to the ultimate depravity, he'd destroyed those around Grace, her young memory registering every occurrence though she'd not understand until later. Her nanny, the young sweet face that had become thin and wan almost overnight, the bruises around her throat not quite covered by a raised collar. The replacement, a girl with a simper, had lasted only three months before Mother sent her away with cash and a growing waistline.

The servants had always bustled away from him, exchanging glances with one another that Grace had been unable to interpret, but he hadn't limited himself to easy prey. Some of the faces Grace was forced to look upon as she lay in her room had styled hair, ears that dripped jewelry as their mouths tried to form a smile though the lipstick was smeared. Her father's lust recognized no boundaries as his power grew, and Grace's memory rattled off names from her childhood along with the faces she'd forced herself to forget.

His face waited for last, filling her mind, though she dug her palms into her eye sockets to block the vision. He was impeccable, dark mustache trimmed daily, hat slightly cocked over one eye as he surveyed those around him, the smile never touching his eyes.

"Stop," Grace said, her lips moving against her wrists as she railed at her own mind. "Please, stop."

But the words brought another vision, one that she'd banished for fear of becoming truly mad. She heard his voice as it had been hours before, rolling confidently through the blackness of the night to fill her ears, but in her memory it was only her name he said, over and over again.

"No more!" Grace gasped, forcing her hands out of her eyes and to her scars, where the smooth skin brought solace, the only safeguard in place to keep him from ever seeing her again.

"I'm dead," she reminded herself, breath coming more easily as

245

she steered her brain elsewhere, to the hollows and planes of Thornhollow's face as he cut her in Boston. "He believes me dead. Thank you, oh, thank you," she said, her voice trailing off into sleep, though her mind lingered on Thornhollow's face a little longer.

TWENTY-EIGHT

Ned's screams were wordless as he stormed into the
entrance hall with the morning light, his terror filling the
atrium and roaring up the stairs. Thornhollow reached
him first, taking the ax from his hands and trying to discern what
had happened. Patients lined the staircases and staff poured from
their rooms as Ned led the doctor out the front door.

Grace was pulling on her shift when she saw the figures streaming
toward the pond, the sane outrunning the mad by only a few steps.
She flew outside, her bare feet numbed in the first few moments as
she tore down to the lakeside behind the others. Thornhollow tried
to stop her as she broke through the crowd, grabbing her roughly
around the waist.

"Grace, Grace, wait," he said into her ear. "You don't need to see
this."

She shrieked and wrested out of his grip, cold terror pushing up through her belly as she forced her way to the front to see a perfectly chopped hole in the lake's ice, and Nell's black braid lying beside it.

Grief made her truly mad. It took two male attendants to force her inside the padded cell, Thornhollow bellowing at them to be careful as she fell in a pile on the soft floor. She was screaming, hadn't stopped since she saw Nell's braid, carefully cut off and laid on her self-fashioned tombstone, as she'd threatened so long ago. Grace's voice ripped, wordless, through her mouth, and she clawed at the leather padding.

All her rage burned through her fingertips as she tore away. She thought of her father, taking a meal in the only place she had ever known safety. His name, used in ignorance on the innocent lips of her friends, pouring bile over her soul with every pronunciation. And Nell. Poor Nell with the pox eating her beautiful face, the damnation brought upon her by the lust of another. Anka Baran and Mellie Jacobs, lying deceptively peaceful as their killer pawed their bodies. And Grace, unable to stop any of it.

There were no words for the language she was speaking and so Grace only screamed, tearing into the walls, kicking and biting at the leather until it split, spilling horsehair and feathers into the air. Her flailing sent them ever higher, her sanity stretching thin as she gave vent to all that was within.

She ripped and tore and screamed until the thin tissue of her throat was as shredded as the walls of her cell, her eyes swollen and throbbing with no tears left to shed. Grace collapsed, the last feathers drifting down to land on her dry, cracked lips, her exhalations too small to disrupt them again. Strength gone, she could only lie quivering, her emotions spent and body exhausted.

The rectangular viewing screen slid open with a metallic screech.

"Grace." Thornhollow's voice was low and calm, the same tone she'd heard him use with the most difficult of patients. "Grace, I'm coming in to get you."

She couldn't object. Her exhaustion ran so deep she could not raise a finger. The door opened and he scooped her into his arms, her hands and feet trailing as if she were dead as he carried her down the hall to his office, where Janey waited. He set her in a chair by the fireplace, and Janey sponged her face clean, cool water erasing hot tear tracks.

"I know, Grace," Janey said, her own face puffy. "It's a hard thing to reconcile yourself to, but Nell went out her way. She wasn't going to let that boy's sickness have the last word."

"Yes," Thornhollow added, settling into the chair next to Grace's. "Nell said the mercury made her feel worse than the disease. She'd stopped taking the treatment weeks ago, and I thought it was best to let her determine her own course of action."

Grace looked at him coldly, no words necessary for the thought in her eyes.

"It was the right choice," Janey said, pulling feathers and horse-hair from Grace's clothes. "The pox would spread anyway, Grace. All the mercury could do was slow the spread, and Nell hadn't felt well in months."

Grace shifted her stare to Janey, who met it without flinching.

"Yes, I knew she stopped taking the mercury baths," Janey said. "What's the use of treating you like people if we don't let you make your own decisions?"

Grace closed her eyes, the truth of Janey's words striking home. She nodded, forgiveness in her eyes when she opened them again. She put a finger next to her ear and raised an eyebrow.

"Elizabeth is taking things rather well, which, I have to say, I'm surprised," Thornhollow said. "The girl is made of sterner stuff than I imagined."

"It's true," Janey said, running her fingers through Grace's hair to tame it. "When I went to her room to tell her the news she was sitting quiet by the window, watching the crowd. I think she knew without me saying what had happened, for she was crying all silent and proper, sitting there looking down on the lake."

Janey's voice hitched as fresh tears fell and she pulled Grace's hair up out of her face, tying it back with a ribbon. "There," she said, wiping her face quickly. "And now I've got to go and see to the other

women. Nell's gone out the way she'd want; has the whole place in
an uproar."

"Grace," Thornhollow said after Janey shut the office door behind
her. "I'm very sorry about Nell. I want you to know that I didn't have
any idea she would . . ."

Grace shook her head, absolving him. Nell had staged her own
triumph and left the audience wishing she were still with them.
Grace put her hand on her throat and looked at the doctor.

"No, I don't doubt you'll have it back, but it will be a few days at
least," Thornhollow said, glad to have the subject changed. "You've
done some damage to yourself."

She rose on unsteady legs, pushing away his assistance as she
walked to the blackboard. She flipped their notes on the doll killer
to the back, bringing the fresh side to face her. Chalk in hand, she
wrote her question.

AM I MAD?

"No," Thornhollow answered from his chair. "You've had an
extremely taxing few days. Your tormentor was under your roof,
your close friend took her own life, and you've been denied the use
of your voice by a lie that must hang over you for as long as you
remain here. Emotions were tearing you apart and they came out
the only way they could. Grief is by nature the most violent of them

all. The ancients tore their hair and rent their clothing to express it. Now we keep the dead body in our homes, shaking people's hands as they pass by to view it and trying to stop ourselves from crying because it's not socially acceptable. Tell me—which of these mourning practices is least sane?"

Grace's mouth turned up slightly, grateful for his words. But there was no feeling alongside it; all of her convictions had flown out of her in the padded room. She could not avenge the dead, or protect her sister, or even stop her own mind from reliving her horrors. Her fingers trailed upon the chalk letters she'd made, leaving a white film on her fingertips.

"You are not mad, Grace," Thornhollow said, watching her movements. "I assure you."

She found the chalk and wrote again, the only thing she knew.

THEN I AM NOTHING.

"For God's sake, man! Do you not think I know a suicide when I see one?" Thornhollow's voice brought Grace from his office, where she'd been dozing by the fire. George and Davey stood in the atrium, holding their wet hats in their hands.

"It's not my place to say what you know or don't know," George said. "I was told to come ask a few questions about a girl that's gone missing up here at the madhouse. And from what I heard, there's a screaming fella running around with an ax mixed into this story as well. That don't sound much like a suicide to me, though I'm just a policeman, not a doctor."

"I thought it was you," Davey said, going to Grace as she stepped into the hall. "When I heard there was a girl gone, I . . ."

Grace stared at him as his sentence evaporated, his words hitting nothing. The concern she'd seen in his eyes before, the tiny attentions that he'd bestowed upon her meant nothing now. They could only be absorbed by her blankness.

"You'd best step away from her," Thornhollow said, intervening between the two smoothly and taking Grace by the hand. "The girl in question was a good friend of hers, and Grace has had . . . a spell."

Davey looked at her again, but she didn't meet his eyes. "I'm sorry to hear that."

"Gentlemen," Thornhollow said. "I can assure you that Nell committed suicide."

"How so?" George pushed. "And where's the man with the ax being held?"

"He is *held* nowhere," the doctor answered. "He is a docile resident of the asylum who merely found the instrument Nell used to chop through the ice in order to throw herself into the lake. Now if you would please go."

"I don't believe we will," George said. "I'd like to see this Nell girl's room and talk with the ax man myself. And if you want to keep having access to all our crime scenes, I suggest you let us into yours."

Thornhollow heaved a sigh, his grip tight on Grace's wrist. "I will be with you every step of the way."

George mocked a bow. "But of course. I wouldn't dream of trying to solve a crime without your assistance, *Doctor*."

They climbed the steps together, Davey pausing to allow Grace to pass in front of him on the landing. She walked by without acknowledging him, leading the men to Nell's room among the whispers of the girls who gathered in the hall. Thornhollow let go of her arm when they entered the room.

"As you can see, Nell has laid out all of her personal belongings very carefully," he said, indicating her desk. "She didn't own much but what she had is here—hair ribbons placed with precision alongside one another, what clothes she had freshly laundered and folded."

Grace slipped away mentally; the room where her good friend had quietly prepared for her death became simply another room. The ribbons that she'd seen adorning Nell's black curls transformed into evidence easily, her emotional attachment to them vacuumed away by the cold, clinical evaluative stance she had used so often by Thornhollow's side. Her breath came more easily, her pain sinking into the coldness that grew inside her.

Thornhollow walked the men through Nell's room, but they

insisted on seeing Ned, whose face still bore signs of tear tracks. The musty smell of the stable enveloped them as Ned talked, his hands telling the story as well as his mouth, but Grace heard little and felt less. Thornhollow was more than capable of convincing the police that Ned was innocent, and she let her mind drift to a place where facts held sway and emotion meant nothing. A place where she could never be hurt again.

She ignored the knock when it came, well aware of who it would be in the middle of the night. Janey cracked the door and slid inside Grace's room. "Grace," she hissed. "The doctor needs you."

Grace rolled onto her side, presenting her back to Janey. "Grace." The nurse's hands shook her. "The doctor said to tell you that . . ." She paused, the oddness of the words catching on her tongue. "He said to tell you that he's found another doll."

A spark of interest ignited in her belly, but what good would come of looking at another dead girl, eyes wide with questions Grace could not answer? She shoved Janey's hands aside and shook her head, burrowing deeper into the pillow.

"All right," Janey said with a sigh. "I'll tell him you're not coming. I said before that I'd take your part if I felt it was too much. But I can't help but think it might do you some good. You're not one for talking, but I always see a purpose in you, Grace. I haven't seen a trace of anything in you at all these past few days."

Janey left, but Grace remained motionless in her bed. In the days since Nell's death, the bleak winter had wrapped itself around the asylum, seeming to fill even Grace's head. Everything inside of her was gray, all of her actions meaningless. Letters written to Alice were taken by the wind; long conjectures with Thornhollow produced nothing more concrete than chalk on slate. She was a madwoman in truth, with no direction and no hope.

There was a timid scratching at her door. Grace ignored it but the door creaked open slightly and Elizabeth appeared, long braids hanging out from under a sleeping cap. She crept inside, crawling into bed with Grace without being invited. The girl's hand wound into Grace's unbound hair and she nestled in beside her.

"String said you needed me," she said, tucking the comforter around both of them. Grace slipped off to sleep, lulled by Elizabeth's hands moving through her hair.

"It was a mistake," Thornhollow informed her the next day in his office.

"In your opinion," Grace said. "I didn't want to look at a dead girl."

He strolled around her as she sat, deep in thought. "How are you feeling, Grace? Lonely? Hollow?"

"Useless," she said, eyes not meeting his own.

He slapped his hands together. "Exactly what I'm trying to remedy. Your eyes could've gleaned much last night, Grace."

"As could your own. More than mine."

"I learned things, yes," he said. "But you know yourself the million tiny details that assault you in these situations, any one of them holding the key to our killer. What if that one thing avoids me but you catch it?"

"I don't know, Doctor," Grace said, head in her hands, fingers finding her scars.

"I do know," he said. "You complement me, Grace. I work better with you by my side. My mind can be sharply focused while you capture the larger canvas."

Grace worked at her scars, the soft skin numb to the touch but pleasant to the fingertips. "I wasn't only mourning for Nell when they locked me away, Doctor. These girls we see, their helplessness is so evident. The ether strips them more completely than he does. They don't even fight. All they can do is lie there, and be posed and pawed as he pleases."

"I understand," Thornhollow said. "I haven't had a chance to talk to you since . . ." He trailed off, searching for the right words. "I met your father."

"Yes," she said, her throat threatening to close still farther. "I saw him, from the turret."

"He's an arrogant ass," Thornhollow said, slamming his hand

257

down on the chair arm. "I'd have disliked him even if I'd never met you."

"Was it difficult?"

"The entire thing was difficult," Thornhollow said, drawn back into his own sufferings. "There were people who needed to be met and talked to, a ridiculous amount of food to eat. And there were—"

"Women?" Grace asked, thinking of the lady in blue.

"A few," he said. "Though they were less of a problem than usual. Your father is a magnetic man."

"Yes," she agreed.

"It's easy to see that he's accustomed to getting his way."

"Father doesn't lose. Ever."

Thornhollow cleared his throat. "Grace, I can't help but wonder if you see yourself in these helpless girls. Our inability to catch their killer combined with the arrival of your father has intensified the connection."

"No." Grace shook her head, voice aching with use. "You've drawn too many lines, looked too deeply when it's really quite simple."

"How so?"

"I don't see myself, Dr. Thornhollow. I see Anka. I see Mellie. I see exactly who they are and what's been done to them. It's what I can't see that I couldn't face last night—the man who had them to their last breath and at his mercy until their darkness fell."

She went to the blackboard, spinning their notes to the front.

"I can't see him, Doctor. And neither can you. Both our minds have touched every detail, turned it to see if we've missed something, and then examined it again. And yet we've found nothing, come no nearer than we were the night we saw the crowd forming around Anka. I can't bear it."

"Then perhaps I'm wrong," Thornhollow said. "Taking you out last night would've done nothing to gratify your need to avenge them."

"But you said you learned things?"

"And I did." Thornhollow rose to join her at the board. "The girl had been dead for some time, her body only discovered when a farmer went to cut a Christmas tree for his family. She was frozen solid and had been laid out at the coroner's to thaw when I saw her last night. It was definitely our man—arms laid across the chest, ankles crossed, eyes open."

"Why would he kill again now?" Grace asked, drawn in despite herself. "It's been months."

"And why out in the country this time?" Thornhollow shot a question back. "The first two girls were in town, which carries much more risk and implies that he's comfortable in that environment and therefore a city dweller. Except now we get a girl out in the woods, and it makes me wonder if your earlier thought about him being a country doctor might be right."

"When was she killed?" Grace asked, standing back to look at the board. "If we can establish a timeline, it could answer any number of things."

"Wouldn't a timeline be lovely?" Thornhollow said, his gaze roaming over their notes. "But no, sadly, last night's victim won't help in that respect. As I said, frozen solid. She was a kitchen girl in one of the larger country estates, unhappy in her position. She'd been talking of returning home, so no one thought anything of it when she went missing. With the temperatures we've been having she could've died weeks ago, or within the last two days. It's impossible to tell." He slapped his leg. "And with her discovery in the middle of nowhere under a foot of snow, it makes me wonder if there's a whole bevy of corpses out there, just waiting for the spring thaw to announce that they've died."

"That's really quite horrible," Grace said, closing her eyes against the picture he'd drawn.

"It's true," Thornhollow insisted. "This discovery throws off everything we thought we knew."

"You're certainly not putting together a compelling argument to make me want to return to this," Grace said, pointing to the board. "This is its own kind of madness."

"I know it," the doctor agreed, returning to his chair. "And all to see my own pet theories proven, to capture criminals in order to vindicate this new science."

"This is where we're different, Doctor," Grace said quietly, her fingers tracing their chalk notes. "We both look upon things that no one should see and yet we do not flinch. I see the blood and think of the person it's leaving while your mind is only on the one who spilled it. My thoughts are on the people and yours the puzzle."

"And that is exactly why I need you."

TWENTY-NINE

The late-evening sunlight slanted in through the windows of the women's dining hall, illuminating every dust mote and bringing a false sense of warmth to the room. Elizabeth pulled her wrap closer around her and leaned over the table toward Grace.

"Would you like a game of checkers before dinner?"

Grace nodded, grateful to find something to do other than wait for the announcement that food was ready. Though the winter daylight hours were so few, she was hard-pressed to fill them. Lizzie went to a cupboard and drew out the game board.

"This set is missing a few of the red ones, as Mrs. Neckard ate three when she lost last week to Miss Payne. But I'd like a game all the same. I was getting pretty good, if I may say so. Nell and I, we used to play a lot but . . ."

Elizabeth's voice faded out as it often did whenever their lost friend was mentioned. "Sorry, Grace. I knew her for so long. It's hard when all the little things are still there but she's not."

Grace understood too well. Nell's room had held all her things, the bed neatly made, hair ribbons laid out in flat rows on her stand. Yet Nell was gone, her body never recovered, while her room looked as if it awaited her return any moment.

"I'll be black, if you don't mind," Elizabeth said, unfolding the board. "I think you're quick enough to play minus three pieces and still beat me."

Grace smiled and began lining up her checkers as other women filtered into the dining hall. She moved a piece forward and Elizabeth hovered over the board, tip of her tongue sticking out as she concentrated.

"Janey is worried about you," Lizzie said as she made her move. "Said she doesn't know whether she should knock on your door the next time Thornhollow sends for you, or tell him to go pound sand."

Grace only shrugged and made her next move. She hadn't decided herself what she would do.

"I don't know what to think about it, myself," Elizabeth said, squinting at the board. "But having a purpose does seem to make the time go faster, am I right? Our checker game is making dinner come closer every second, and we're not sitting here thinking about how hungry we are. We're thinking about checkers. Or at least I am."

Grace ignored the tremor in her hand as she made her next move, thinking that having a purpose was exactly what she needed.

Grace was in the carriage the next time she was summoned. Her blank stare sliding over her features the moment she exited, Thornhollow handing her down like royalty to a macabre parade. Davey's eyes glanced off hers and back again as she and Thornhollow made their joint assessment of another murder that hardly required their presence, another lover's quarrel ended badly.

"Honestly," Thornhollow huffed as the carriage door swung shut behind him. "Why do people bother to fall in love? I've never seen it bring anything but pain."

"You hardly spend time in places that happy couples frequent," Grace reminded him, burying her hands in her wrap to warm them.

"Mmmmm . . ." He looked out the window, thoughts following the same scattered path as the blowing snow. "How is Lizzie holding up? It's been two months. I worry that she's not eating enough."

"I watch her at dinner. She eats enough to keep her going," Grace said. "I think she's all right, but she has her dark days. When Joanna moved into Nell's room it was difficult."

The new girl had arrived along with a blizzard that trapped them all indoors for a week, her presence reminding them that Nell would never come back. Janey had divvied Nell's hair ribbons among Grace,

Elizabeth, and Rebecca, keeping one for herself. Nell's clothes had been taken to the poorhouse after being boiled, the sheets stripped and the bed made ready for the next unfortunate, who turned out to be a scratcher.

"Keep your eyes on that one, girls," Janey had warned Grace and Lizzie as she swept past them one day, bloodied furrows on her forearms. "I don't want any of you peaceful ones ripped to shreds."

Joanna had ended up in leather mitts that prevented her from hurting others, but she vented her frustrations by pounding them against the wall hard enough to send plaster trickling down onto Grace's pillow.

"And how are you? I can't help but notice you aren't yourself lately."

"I'm fine," Grace said a little too quickly. "You'll not need to put me back in the padded room."

"I wasn't inferring that I would," Thornhollow said. "Or that it would be necessary. Quite the opposite, actually. You seem to have little room for your emotions these days."

"That's the pot calling the kettle black if I ever heard it," Grace said irritably. They fell quiet as the carriage rattled over the brick streets of town and Grace bit her lip. "I'm sorry, Doctor. I didn't mean to snap. The new girl has made our floor a little less welcoming. I don't think I've slept the night through since she arrived."

"Mmmmm . . . ," the doctor said again, his gaze riveted on the blank pane of the window. "Grace, would you like to meet my sister?"

"I . . ." Grace tried to make out his face in the darkness of the carriage. "I didn't know you had a sister."

"Oddly enough," he said. "Like all other humans, I was born from a mother and like many of my kind I'm not the only person she gave birth to. In short, yes, I have a sister. Would you like to meet her?"

"Yes, I think I would," Grace said. "Why are you asking me?"

"Because it's winter, and it brings a person down. You and I both have had some harsh strokes played against us lately. I've taken to long walks despite the cold. A change of scenery can do wonders for the mood, and it occurred to me the other day that you might benefit from that as well. This thought came along with a letter from my sister saying that we should spend some time together."

"That you 'should spend some time together'? It hardly sounds like she's looking forward to it."

"I assure you neither one of us is," Thornhollow said as they rattled onto the gravel driveway toward home. "But my sister doesn't respond well to rejection. I've reserved myself some rooms in town so that I can get out of the asylum for a bit myself. Of course, I can only spirit you away for one evening, but I thought you might like an opportunity to speak freely with someone other than me. Another woman, especially."

"So I can be myself?" Grace asked.

They pulled into the roundabout, the gas lamps from the portico turning each snowflake into a brilliant meteor. "You shouldn't be Grace Mae, specifically, no. If we simply present you as a girl who was removed from unfortunate circumstances and now assists me, I think that will be sufficient. I can't promise a lovely evening, but I can promise that you won't have to listen to Joanna tearing out a supporting wall. My sister arrives tomorrow evening. Will you join us?"

"Yes," Grace said slowly, her own eyes now focused on the whirling snow. "I think I will. I'll have to wash this plaster out of my hair first, though."

"You deserve it," Lizzie said as she sat on Grace's bed, watching her pin her hat on. "Whenever you put on your street clothes and cover the scars you look like such a lady, Grace."

Grace made a face as she bent to button her shoes, pointing at her friend.

"You're thinking you're not the only one who deserves it," Lizzie interpreted. "But there's something more to it than the difference between the sane and insane. You've got a high quality about you, right down to the way you walk. Me, if I left the asylum . . ." She shivered even at the thought. "I've been here too long, Grace. I may not be mad but if you dragged me out of these walls you'd think I was. I wouldn't even know how to buy a pound of flour, or refill my favorite perfume bottle anymore."

The other girl's voice drifted off sadly, her fingers toying with the ends of Nell's ribbon, the edges frayed with her endless worrying. Grace captured the fretting fingers with her own, pressing them down tight in her hand.

"You go," Lizzie said. "I'll be here when you get back."

Ned was waiting outside, the horse's breath making warm clouds around its nose. "The doctor said I was to take you to the hotel. Also to tell you the number two hundred and eight," he said, and she nodded. He handed her into the carriage, his usually calm face twisted into a grimace. Grace touched her hand to his, eyebrows raised in a question.

"I don't . . ." Ned's brow wrinkled as he concentrated, weighing each word. "Your friend, the girl that died with ice. I'm sorry about her. She had nice hair, like a pony's, but almost better." He stuck a finger into the air to clarify. "Almost."

Grace squeezed his hand, and he shut the carriage door, her thoughts straying from the evening she was supposed to enjoy to the image of Nell's braid, black against the ice. The gravel drive gave way to the bricks of town, and Grace focused on maintaining a mask of sanity, her back straight, her face resisting the slack muscles she usually adopted.

They stopped in front of a brick hotel, well lit from inside against the already failing light of the day. Ned helped her out of the carriage, then leaned over her before leaving. "Three hours," he said sternly, pointing at the stone steps. "The doctor said to be back for you in three hours. So you be here."

"I will, Ned, thank you," Grace said, so deeply fastened on to the image of a healthy young woman out for the evening that she forgot to be mute. Her eyes widened for a moment, but Ned only nodded. "Three hours," he reminded her before he drove off, and she nodded.

Grace shook off her nerves at the slip, mounting the stone steps as if she belonged there. She swept into the lobby, pulling her gloves off and cutting a quick turn to the right staircase before anyone could ask her what she was doing. Remembering Ned's broken instructions, she found room 208 and knocked. The door was flung open, and Thornhollow motioned her in without a word of greeting, his hair standing up in red spikes all over his head.

"I've stabbed myself with the tie tack twice; never have managed to tie an ascot without a little blood spilled. Janey had to do mine for the reception at the asylum, and I swear she was giggling when she left my office. I'm sorry, Grace, everything is a bit of a mess, and Adelaide hasn't arrived yet." He waved around the sitting room, where she could see at least three jackets that had been dismissed as unsuitable for dinner. "Have a seat, I'll just . . . it shouldn't be more than a minute or two," he said, running into the bedroom and slamming the door behind him.

Grace sighed, moved a jacket, and sat down only to crush a hat.

She was standing in the middle of the room, trying to punch it back into form, when there was a sharp rap at the door. She glanced up, frozen in place. From the bedroom came a muffled thump and a "Damn." She could only guess that Thornhollow was nowhere near being ready to answer the door. Another sharp rap, this one conveying impatience, sent Grace's nerves soaring, and she was reminded of Lizzie's certainty that she'd been institutionalized so long she could never function outside of it.

Her indecision was short-lived, for the door was flung open unceremoniously and a tall, dark woman soared into the room, irritation stamped firmly on her features. "Really, Brother," she was saying, "a two-line letter with an address and a room number isn't exactly inviting." She flung her wrap across a chair, words still flowing. "And not being bothered to answer the door yourself is downright rude. If Father were still alive—oh . . ." The words died on her lips when she saw Grace.

"There's one mystery solved," she said. "No wonder he's not exactly brimming with excitement at my arrival. He leave you out here to greet me? Still wrestling with the inconvenience of proper dress, is he?"

Grace knew her mouth was open and that no words were coming out. The crushed hat was still in her hands, her fingers working the brim in their anxiety. Thornhollow's sister circled her, skirts swishing as she made the inspection.

"No wonder he's mystified by his own dinner clothes. He's never been one to worry much about what is proper. But you already know that, don't you?"

Grace flushed bright red at the implication.

"You're smaller than what he usually goes in for," the woman went on. "By the cut of your dress, a little more refined as well. I'm a bit surprised, to be honest, but maybe you're simply another experiment." She finished her turn around Grace, who still stood stupefied.

The women came face-to-face, and Grace raised her eyes, locking them with Adelaide's. Even if she couldn't force words, she could wear the face she had so often presented to her mother, silent yet defiant.

"I hardly need to tell you . . ." The doctor's sister trailed off, confusion clouding her face as she met Grace's gaze. "Wait, what's this? No, you're far too intelligent. He doesn't want a challenge."

She was still trying to compute the intelligence she saw in Grace's eyes with her assumptions when the bedroom door blew open, and Thornhollow—still not finished dressing—burst out. "Adelaide," he cried, the moment he saw her. "What are you doing?"

"I was performing my usual chore of running off whatever unacceptable woman you'd attached yourself to this time, but I've come to an impasse. She's not one of your chippies, is she?"

"No," Grace said, voice suddenly found. "I'm a mental patient."

"Melancthon!" Her confusion was swept away in outrage, her nettling attitude toward Grace morphing into protection as she bodily put herself between them. "This is a new low, little brother. She's a pretty girl, but I never thought you would—"

"Adelaide!" Thornhollow bellowed, his temper flaring. "You have completely misread this entire situation, as usual assuming the worst of myself without bothering to—"

"Misread?" the woman fired back. "What conclusions should I come to with a pretty woman in your room, clothing flung everywhere, and you half-dressed?"

The doctor drew himself up to his full height in an attempt to regain composure. "I am merely struggling with my ascot."

"And no wonder, I doubt you've had to dress properly for anything since coming to this backwoods river town, pouring your prodigious talents into the mad when you could be—"

Thornhollow tore off the offending ascot, throwing it to the ground. "I did not invite you here to have my profession belittled yet again."

"You didn't invite me at all! I had to tell you I was coming in order to force you to acknowledge that you have a sister in the first place."

Grace, aware that she was not necessary to the conversation, sat down and finished reshaping the hat she'd sat on.

"Yes, and why would I want to avoid having us in the same

room?" Thornhollow asked sarcastically. "Clearly we should spend much more time together; it's so beneficial."

Adelaide's chin shot up, her nostrils flaring. "One does not maintain family bonds because they are beneficial but because they are family."

"Tell that to Grace," Thornhollow fumed. "I've had to scar her permanently and drag her across three states to deliver her from the clutches of her father."

Grace shot up from the couch, hat forgotten. "How dare you?" she shouted, her voice soaring.

"Is this true?" Adelaide asked, turning to Grace with a new softness in her eyes.

"Whether it is or not, it is not your place to announce it in front of a stranger," she said, her voice cutting. Thornhollow paled, holding up one hand in apology and dropping into a chair.

"Hardly," his sister agreed, lacing her arm with Grace's to form a unified front against her brother. "This is a lovely dinner party you've put together. I should've known better than to even come. But as it stands, I am here, and I am hungry."

The doctor had his head in his hands, eyes rooted to the floor between his feet. "I can hardly go to dinner now. I've ruined my ascot and Grace crushed my hat."

"Only the beginning of all sorts of punishment she could rightly bring down on you," Adelaide said, patting Grace's hand. "I'll see to dinner. Surely there's some decent place around that will feed us in your apartments."

Thornhollow raised his head. "They'll do that?"

"If you pay them enough, they'll do anything," his sister answered, gathering her wrap. "I shall return," she said, "and try to put right all the wrongs you've already piled onto our evening, Melancthon." The door slammed behind her as she left.

"I'm sorry, Grace," Thornhollow said, the misery in his eyes bringing instant forgiveness from her. "Adelaide's assumptions about you along with her derision of my career made me lose my temper and say things that weren't mine to say. I apologize."

Grace stood over him, one hand on her hip. "Melancthon?"

"Don't start."

THIRTY

"So then the National Woman Suffrage Association and the American Woman Suffrage Association merged to create the National American Woman Suffrage Association, which personally I think is rather a mouthful," Adelaide said as she set down her wineglass.

"I'm sure others have much shorter terms," the doctor said, sawing into his steak with more vigor than necessary.

"Such as?" Grace asked.

"There are plenty who just call us bitches, dear," Adelaide explained, and Grace's eyes went wide. She smiled and touched Grace's wrist.

"I'm sorry for my language. When you're at the front of the movement like I am you hear all manner of things and a certain coarseness creeps into your speech."

"A beautiful way of saying you've lost your manners," Thornhollow said into his half-empty wineglass.

"That's a nice criticism coming from a man who drags young women to murder sites."

"I only drag the one."

"Regardless," Grace interjected. "It's good to know that something is being done for women, and I thank you for doing it. You're free to use any language you like around me."

Adelaide shot Thornhollow a look before nodding toward Grace. "I imagine you've seen all kinds of things, as a patient."

"Yes," Grace said, her mind turning back to Boston only when she forced it to. "I couldn't quite get my mind around the fact of where I was, even a few days in. That something so horrible could happen easily, that's the true insanity."

"Well said," Adelaide agreed. "The signature of one judge and the word of a male family member and that's that." She snapped her fingers. "You're insane."

"I probably seemed it," Grace said, fingers toying with her glass stem. "I was screaming and kicking the entire way. I remember I pulled a chunk of hair right out of one orderly's scalp."

"Good for you," Adelaide said, touching her glass to Grace's.

"And I'd add, it stands as only further proof of your sanity," Thornhollow said, leaning back from the table. "You knew where you were going and what awaited you. Any mentally sound person would fight tooth and nail to prevent it."

"However, to the average person your fit only solidifies the claim," his sister said. "Believe me, dear, I work side by side with women who have been in lunatic asylums, and their stories make my toes curl. And not in a good way," she added, making Thornhollow rap the table sharply.

"I'm lucky to have your brother," Grace said quickly to avoid another family argument. "Without his intervention I doubt I would've made it another week."

"You would have," he said.

"Yes, and about that . . ." Adelaide pushed her wineglass away from her, eyeing Thornhollow over the table. "How goes this catching of criminals by studying their brains?"

Thornhollow's brow turned cloudy again, but he spoke amicably enough. "The theory behind it is sound, I truly believe that."

"I do as well," Grace added. "At the first murder we worked together your brother had the offender figured before we left the scene."

"And since then?"

Thornhollow wadded up his dinner napkin. "We've had a repeat killer we haven't had much luck with."

"Really?"

Adelaide soaked up the details as Thornhollow and Grace

filled her in on the three dolls, her mind working as quickly as her brother's.

"I don't think he's showing any particular hatred toward women," she said when they'd finished. "I've seen plenty of that, and it's a bloody business."

"I agree," Thornhollow said. "Their faces are unharmed and no particular violence done to their female anatomy."

"Were they raped?" Adelaide asked.

"Anka was not," Grace said, her memory ticking off the facts. "Mellie Jacobs was in the ground before we knew she was a victim of the same killer, and the third girl had been outside for so long that we simply don't know." Grace's eyes clouded as she realized something. "I never asked you her name."

"Janet. Jenny. Something like that. I don't know," Thornhollow said.

"A prince of the people," Adelaide huffed. "Although I'm not surprised. He's never been good with names. I didn't even have to run off the last girl who had attached herself to him. He managed that all by himself by calling her by her predecessor's name at dinner."

"That's not entirely true," Thornhollow objected, glancing at the clock. "I couldn't recall her name at all, so I chose one."

Adelaide shrugged. "Whatever the case, my job was done without a finger lifted."

"And why is it your job, exactly?" Thornhollow asked, irritation slipping back into his voice.

"Because, little brother, you're the last of the Thornhollows," Adelaide said, her eyes thinning to slits over a well-worn argument. "My last name is no good to anybody since I have to give it up or bear a bastard, which carries its own stain. Mother would die if you got a baby on a girl she didn't deem worthy, and she'll die if you don't manage to get one on anybody at all." She nodded to the clock herself. "Ticktock."

Grace's knife struck her plate with a teeth-chattering clash, her eyes wide and face pale.

"I hardly think that's the comment to lose your head over," Adelaide said, but Grace ignored her.

"Doctor," she said, her voice a barely contained whisper. "Doctor, I think I've got it."

"By God, Grace," Thornhollow said as his eyes roved over the chalkboard. "You could be right."

They were safely tucked back in his office after leaving Adelaide in a rush, anxious to get back to the asylum. Thornhollow's sister had scribbled down her Boston address quickly and placed it in Grace's hands before they left. She rubbed her fingers over the thick stationery idly, her thoughts preoccupied by the board.

"It's mystified me from the beginning," Grace said. "Why start now? Your sister's words to you over dinner made me look at it in a different light. What if he's under pressure to marry? If he's always been incompetent with women, it would be his shameful secret. To suddenly be thrust into a marriage where another will know his inability might be too painful to bear."

"That very well could be," Thornhollow said, hands on his hips. "If he doesn't want to meet with the same defeat on his wedding night, he may be attempting to practice—if you will—with these girls. His failure results in a rage. If I'm correct and there's an over-bearing mother in the picture, she may be demanding grandchildren and watching the clock as her son grows older. That helps narrow down the field, if we can assume this is no spring chicken we're try-ing to nab."

"What about the girl in the snow and the lull in killings?" Grace asked. "Are you still convinced it's a town doctor we're looking for?"

"I am." Thornhollow nodded. "Her name was Jenny, by the way. Jenny Cantor. I remembered on the way back home. And her death doesn't change my thoughts. He made his first kills in the city, where he felt safe. The kitchen girl was an opportunity—perhaps while out driving or visiting a country patient."

Grace thought for a second, piecing through Thornhollow's argu-ment in order to find any loose threads he may consider bound up.

"What if he's not an only child?"

He shook her off immediately. "No, all the evidence of his intel-ligence and planning points to an only child, or older sibling. Which, if we are to follow your line of thought, he'd have to be the only male child in order to feel the pressure of continuing the family line—which, I assure you, can be quite intense."

"What if he had an older brother who died recently?" Grace went on, ignoring his confidence. "That would explain why he suddenly has that weight to carry, and it has morphed into these horrible actions."

"I don't see it," Thornhollow said.

"What if you're wrong?" Grace insisted.

"What if *you're* wrong?" he shot back. "It's possible we're both completely off and our killer is a middle-aged mother of four who simply wants to fill her evenings with a little bloodshed."

"Now you're being ridiculous," Grace said. "I'm going to bed." She was at the office door before she turned, temper extinguished. "I wanted to thank you for dinner, and for meeting your sister. She was really quite lovely, in the end."

"Oh yes," the doctor said, slipping into the chair by the fire. "All the Thornhollows are, once you get used to us."

Grace returned to her room to find an envelope addressed to her resting on the pillow. Reed's careful handwriting sent her heart into her throat, and she tossed Adelaide's address on her nightstand to tear into the envelope. Pages fell out, one of them weather-beaten and misshapen by the elements. Grace set it aside, preferring Alice's voice to be the last she heard before falling asleep. Falsteed's letter was short, its message frightening.

> *Dearest Grace—*
>
> *I know that the long interval while you waited to hear from your sister may have seemed unbearable, but I fear what reaction the wished-for letter will bring. Reed has been as vigilant as can be expected, given the Boston winter, but I imagine many pages of your own as well as hers have been lost to the winds. I enclose the one he retrieved just yesterday with a heavy heart, questioning my judgment in sending it to you.*
>
> *The papers tell me that your father was recently under your very roof. I hope it was not too troubling for you. As to your sister, I will see what may be done, if anything. I fear my reach does not extend far beyond these walls. And yourself, as a person presumed dead, are nearly powerless. I will think, here in the darkness. You do so as well, but do it in the sunlight, where you belong.*
>
> *Falsteed*

With trembling fingers, Grace turned to the weather-beaten page, anxious to read the words, yet dreading what they would say.

> *Fair Lily—*
> *The winter must be hard on you, for I have only had the one letter*

from you since the first. I write and find my pages gone in the morning, but perhaps the fairies cannot always get to it before the snows do. The winter is not fun. I am inside always and Mother says I am too old for my toys, but when I ask to have my hair put up again she says I'm not old enough yet. I do not know if I am a lady or a child.

I miss Grace. And Father. He has left again to go talk to people. On his last trip he brought me home a pretty blue hat with velvet ribbons. He said he'll bring me something even better this time, but I'll have to do him a special favor to get it. I don't know what could be prettier than that hat. Father says it matches my eyes.

Write back if you can, as I am bored.

Alice

Grace crushed the letter in her hands, and she coiled into a ball on her bed, allowing the darkness that Falsteed had warned her against to take over.

"We must do something," Grace said, flinging Alice's letter to the table in Thornhollow's office. "I cannot stand by and let her suffer the same fate as I did."

Thornhollow picked up the letter, scanning it quickly, his expression blank. "I have been following your father's movements in the papers. His speech schedule is set and it will be a matter of weeks yet before he returns home."

"And *then* what?" Grace cried. "What will we do?"

He didn't meet her gaze, his eyes on the sleet-covered window instead. "Grace . . . I don't know what we can do. Falsteed said it himself; you're presumed dead, he's in an asylum. In my opinion you've already put too much on Reed by asking him to run your letters. What would you have him do now? Risk imprisonment by kidnapping your sister?"

"Yes," Grace said, her face a white sheet. "If that's what it takes."

"Ridiculous. As the only living child of a powerful politician there'd be a manhunt. He'd never even get her out of the city. Not to mention it would scare the poor child witless."

"Better a frightened child than a child no longer," she said. "And you forgot to number yourself among my allies."

He tossed his hands in the air, baffled. "What can I do?"

"What can you do?" Grace seethed. "Do you think I don't see the expensive cut of your clothes, or your sister's jewels? No one would care if an inconsequential family name stopped dead with a brooding doctor—who happens to drive a very expensive carriage, as well. And women don't just flock to looks, Doctor. I've been in society; I know exactly how important a good marriage—"

"All right!" He held up a hand to stop her. "I didn't teach you the power of observation just to have it turned back on me. Yes, I have money. What good can that possibly do? Shall I approach your father and ask to buy his youngest daughter?"

"Do not mock me on this subject," Grace said, eyes burning.

"I am not mocking the severity of the situation," Thornhollow said. "I'm only trying to illustrate how fully our hands are tied."

"I refuse to accept that," Grace yelled.

"Grace," Thornhollow said, the very calm of his voice sending her over the edge.

She slammed her fist onto Alice's letter. "Why am I surprised that a man who can't remember the names of dead women whose cooling bodies he stands over would take no interest in the fate of a little girl he's never seen? If she were raving mad, one of your precious insane, you'd be the first to her defense. But she's a perfectly normal girl, so her fate matters little to you!"

Thornhollow's face was stony, his voice cold when he spoke next. "My interest has always been in the science and the science only, which is why I don't remember the names of the dead. They simply do not matter to me. Your sister is not one of our victims. Her name is Alice. She is blond, like you, although her hair is naturally curly."

Grace's mouth fell open, her rage evaporated. "What?"

"She stands about four feet eleven inches, which may be taller than when you saw her last. She likes to sing and seems to have a particular affinity for 'Oh Promise Me' at the moment. As for the new hat, it is indeed quite pretty. The men I've been paying to watch your house for months even said so."

Grace gaped, her tongue searching for words. "Doctor, I . . ."

He carefully folded Alice's letter, newly stained with Grace's tears, and handed it back to her. "Alice is important to you, which makes her important to me. She will not suffer needlessly. We *will* think of something, Grace. I promise you."

Grace took the proffered letter, her hand still shaking with emotion. "I'm sorry for what I said. I had no idea—"

Thornhollow shrugged. "Once I learned you had a younger sister I knew it was only a matter of time before his affections transferred to her. Your presence shielded her for some time, but with you no longer in the house she became vulnerable."

Grace's hands went to her head. "I should never have left. I should've taken what life had dealt me so that it would never land upon her."

"Nonsense," Thornhollow said. "Actions such as your father's are driven by power, nothing else. He seeks to dominate everyone around him, and he'll use any tool in his arsenal to do so. Even if you'd stayed, Alice would have fallen victim to his need for control eventually. You being there would only result in a shared misery."

He handed her a handkerchief and she wiped her face. "These men you have watching? What can they do?"

"Little more than watch, I'm afraid," Thornhollow admitted. "But I thought having eyes there would be beneficial. If nothing else, it can bring you some comfort to know that your sister is still happy enough to sing."

Grace smiled through her tears. "It does. Thank you, Doctor."

"Am I to understand that your mother cannot be looked to for help?"

The smile vanished. "No. Our mother is a jealous woman. Once we become women we are no longer her children but competitors for his attention."

Thornhollow sighed. "All right. I will think on it. We have weeks before your father returns home. In the meantime, you're in dire need of distraction and I have just the thing."

"My mind is latched on to it rather firmly," Grace said. "I'm afraid it won't let go easily."

"Perhaps. But I considered your thought that the doctor may have had an elder sibling who died, thrusting the responsibility for the family legacy upon him. And while I still don't agree, there's no reason why you shouldn't look into it."

"How would I do that?"

"Obituaries," the doctor said, rapping his knuckles on the table. "Assuming that the possibly fictitious brother's death occurred in the months or weeks leading up to his first kill, reading the obituaries from each paper in the city from that time period might turn up something."

"And how many papers does the city have?" Grace asked, her heart sinking.

"Four. I took the liberty of visiting their offices this morning and found that their unsold copies are bought for a pittance by the fish and meat shops to wrap their wares in. I was able to find quite a few papers from the right time by wading around in their back rooms, which I can tell you was quite unpleasant. I brought the lot back here for you to go through, but they've rather taken on the smell of their last residence and I couldn't bring them into the women's wing without Janey tearing into me. You'll have to work out in Ned's stables."

"Quite all right. I wouldn't mind the walk, and if it affords me the chance to prove my point, all the better," Grace said, wiping the last of her tears away and offering the kerchief back to Thornhollow.

"You keep that," he said. "You'll want to cover your nose."

THIRTY-ONE

"**H**e wasn't lying about the smell, was he?" Elizabeth said as they pushed open the door to the stables.

A few explanatory lines on Grace's slate had been enough to lure her friend out to Ned's stable to help scan obituaries. Lazy motes of dust drifted through the air in the winter sunlight, the smell of hay not quite taking the sting out of the reeking newspapers.

"It's like a wharf in here," Lizzie said, balling her handkerchief more tightly to her nose as they ventured past the stalls. "Poor Ned."

Grace craned her neck, looking for the stable's human resident. The asylum horses nickered as they walked by, sticking their noses out for a scratch, which both girls happily gave.

"Ned," Lizzie called out. "It's Elizabeth and Grace. We're here to look over those nasty newspapers Dr. Thornhollow dumped on you."

A door at the end of the stall corridor opened, and Ned stuck his head out. "Hello there, girls. I've got mince pie on the mind today."

"Mince pie is lovely," Lizzie said, voice slightly muffled by her handkerchief. "Do you know where the doctor put the papers?"

"I've got an empty stall here to the left," he said, herding them into it. "My Helen died not so long ago and we've not replaced her." His wide eyes immediately filled with tears. "I kept her tail. The doctor said that was all of her I could have, but I've got that much, at least. I put a couple of chairs in there for you along with the stinkers."

"Thank you, Ned," Lizzie said as the girls settled in, wobbling piles of newspaper surrounding them. "We apologize for invading your space."

He shook his head. "I don't mind you girls so much. When I say the things that don't make sense you answer me anyway. It's like having green in your shirt."

"Green is my favorite color," Lizzie said.

"I'll be across the way in my quarters," Ned said. "I'll leave the door open so that the stove can heat you a little. I'm whittling today. She'll be my five hundred and sixty-seventh horse when I'm done."

"Very nice, Ned," Lizzie said. "And thanks again."

The girls looked at the papers piled around them as the steady *snick-snick* of Ned's whittling filled the air, along with his humming of "Yankee Doodle."

"I guess we should start by weeding out the pages with the

obituaries and tossing the rest," Lizzie suggested.

Grace nodded and the two girls started sifting through the piles, delicately handling pages that were moist from the humidity of their former residence. Some pages disintegrated in their hands, some had wetly adhered to one another and ruined their print. An hour later their fingers were stained black. They draped wet pages on the stalls around them to dry as they pored over readable pages that had obituaries. Elizabeth fanned a page open and pulled a face.

"Every time I think I'm accustomed to the smell I get a fresh whiff that sets me back," she said, rummaging in her pocket. "I brought the last of my mother's perfume with me. A dab under the nostrils might do the trick."

She tipped the little glass bottle onto her finger pad, then rubbed the dimple above her lips. "Here," she said, offering it to Grace. "Take a drop."

Grace waved her off, pointing to the bottle and then her friend's heart. Lizzie pulled Grace's hand toward her and put a drop of perfume on her finger. "There's nothing wrong with giving something precious from my past to someone special in the present," she said.

The delicate scent of rosewater wafted through the air, a fine, pleasant thread among the stable smells and heaviness of the molding, fishy newspapers. Grace dabbed above her lips and the rosewater filled her nostrils, reminding her of the basement in Boston, Falsteed, and Thornhollow cutting into her temples to deliver her from everything. A smile crossed her face as she rubbed her fingers together, strengthening the scent.

"It's nice, isn't it?" Lizzie asked, tucking the bottle back into her skirt pocket. "Mother gave it to me when I came here."

Grace's eyes left her own newspaper, watching her friend as she scanned hers. She touched Lizzie's knee hesitantly.

"I don't mind talking about it," Elizabeth said, looking up. "My mother didn't want to give me up, but Father insisted. Put all the blame on Mother's side of the family, which I suppose is true enough. Mother's mother had String, you see. I could always see it. Mother said I loved Grandma the most, even as an infant. I always wanted to sit in her lap and I'd swipe at String, trying to catch it.

"Grandma knew that Father wouldn't approve, so she never said a word about String in his hearing. When Mother was heavy pregnant with her second, String told Grandma that it would be born dead, with the cord about its neck. She ran over to our house, barefoot and in her nightgown, to try and save it, but it was too late. I saw my baby brother, face black as coal, and Grandma talking about String so loud she'd woke me.

"Father wouldn't have any of it, though Mother tried to tell him it was harmless. He called it witchcraft and threw Grandma out the front door. I remember he shoved her so hard her head bounced up off the rocks and String went flying. Mother was wailing and Father was screaming and the midwife was trying to keep everyone from killing one another. I put my little hand up on the window and Grandma just got up, real slow, smiled back at me, and hobbled home. I woke up in the morning with String on my shoulder and a voice in my head saying Grandma was gone. I marched downstairs and said so, and Father never looked at me the same after that."

Grace's fingers hovered on the obituaries, her eyes still on Lizzie, who tossed her old newspaper for a new one without breaking stride in her story.

"Father kept to himself on the subject until Mother was pregnant again and he didn't want me near her. She cried and cried but couldn't convince him there wasn't any harm in String. For the sake of peace she took me to the train station one day, handed me a ticket and this bottle of perfume so I could smell it and remember she loved me. Tears were streaming down her face but she let me go, my own face dry as a sunny day because String had told me all along I was meant for something different.

"If I'd known this is what String had in mind, I might've put up more of an argument," Lizzie said, holding a wet paper away from her at arm's length, nose wrinkled.

Grace laughed, reaching out to squeeze her friend's hand.

"I'm fine," Lizzie said, smiling back. "I have no shame in String. I'd rather live where String can be String and I can be me without having to pretend I'm something else."

The returned squeeze on Grace's hand was almost too much to

bear as she looked back to her newspaper, the ink twice blurred by smears and the tears standing in her eyes.

Grace knew death. Knew it well from following in its footsteps only minutes after they'd been made. She had learned how to trace its passage backward from knife wounds and bullet exits to the thought that had conceived of the act and in whose mind it had occurred. Death's less brutal faces were unfamiliar to her, but she learned their names in the stall, their portraits spelled out in blurry letters reeking of fish scales.

Tuberculosis. Dysentery. Cholera. Malaria. Typhoid. Pneumonia. Diphtheria. Scarlet fever. Brain fever. Whooping cough.

In her room that night she rubbed her eyes to free them from the words that still seemed to dance on the backs of her eyelids, the names of the remaining family members listed as if to stand in defiance of death, proof that their blood would continue. But none of them had the prefix *Dr.* attached to them, and Grace had returned to her room without informing Thornhollow of her failure.

Grace stretched under her bedcovers, her eyes returning to Alice's letter on the bedstand, her heart lurching. She'd been unable to find the words to respond; the only thing she burned to write was to tell Alice to get out, to run away and never return home. But that message would never be delivered, Grace knew. Falsteed wouldn't allow her to advise Alice onto a path that could deliver her into another breed of harm, or bring it home to roost on Grace's doorstep if she declared herself the author.

With blurred newspaper print still dancing in her eyes, Grace tossed and turned, the smell of rosewater following her down to sleep.

Plaster trickled onto her face along with the first rays of the sun. Grace pulled away from the wall as Joanna pounded on the other side, her leather mitts dulling her impact but reinforcing her determination. Grace sighed and sat up, her hands going to her scars for reassurance and bringing the lingering scent of Lizzie's mother's perfume with them. Her eyes still ached from deciphering columns of newsprint the day before. Her heart was heavy with futility, and Alice's fate hung like a sword above her head. For the first time, the walls that held her felt less like safety and more like imprisonment, binding her to an existence where she could witness suffering but do nothing to help.

The rosewater stayed with her as she pulled her hair up, glancing into the cloudy mirror as she did, her town dress reflected alongside her own face. Without thinking, she pulled curls down to cover her scars, pinning them in place along with the matching hat. The dress followed, and Grace surveyed herself in the mirror, every inch a normal girl with no cares in the world, her surroundings screaming out the opposite.

She snuck into Elizabeth's room, tiptoeing in her boots so as not to wake the other girl. Grace riffled through Elizabeth's dresser until she found the little bottle of perfume, carefully easing Lizzie's door shut behind her when she left. Joanna's constant thumping covered Grace's footsteps as she slipped down the stairs and out the door long before the rest of the asylum was awake.

Fresh flakes of snow fell on her as she crossed the grounds, catching in her hair and filling the footprints she left behind her. With Nell on her mind and Elizabeth's bottle in her pocket, Grace followed the path the Irish girl had shown her down to the frozen river. She crossed easily, the ice firm beneath her feet, and soon she was on the edge of town, the sun waking up the residents and shops just opening their doors.

Grace shook the snow from her shoulders and walked through the streets, nodding greetings to those she met while her eyes roamed the storefronts for what she needed. She found a chemist's shop on Hudson Street, the midmorning sun lighting up the colored bottles in the window and drawing her to them.

She opened the door, a bell dinging overhead as she did so. The man behind the counter was in conversation with another customer, so Grace browsed the shelves. Colored bottles in various sizes lined the walls, their labels promising cures for everything from chicken pox to dandruff. A table set with everything a fine lady would need for her toilet caught Grace's eye, and she made her way to it. She removed the stoppers from the perfumes to take experimental sniffs.

None quite matched Elizabeth's scent, their much heavier tones almost overpowering Grace. She put the stopper back on one, barely restraining a sneeze when she noticed a small, hand-lettered sign on the table.

Custom Fragrance Matching Available
Inquire With Chemist

Grace's fingers tightened on Elizabeth's bottle as she waited for the man ahead of her to finish his business. His voice carried as he turned to leave. "We're glad to have you back in regular business, Beaton. The wife swears by your glycerins, says she won't put anything else on the baby's bum. Begging your pardon, ma'am." He tipped his hat to Grace. She nodded in return as the bell dinged over his departure and approached the counter.

"Excuse me," she said, "I was wondering if you could—"

Her words died in her mouth as she faced the man across the counter, his massive shoulders spanning the width of a sign above him that read:

`Physicians Prescriptions Carefully Compounded`

"I . . ." Grace's voice was as forgotten as it had been in Boston, her mind losing all words as she regarded the man whose portrait she and Thornhollow had been drawing for so long without any defining characteristics.

The vague shape of what they had anticipated filled out in flesh and blood provided a rush of details that her mind locked on to. He was tall and broad, his shape more what one would expect behind a blacksmith's hammer than a chemist's counter. His eyes were bright, avoiding hers at all costs as a flush crept over his face. Grace turned to pull Elizabeth's bottle from her pocket and felt them dashing over her body, his curiosity devouring her in the only way he was capable. When she glanced up and locked her eyes with his for the barest of moments she could see his intelligence, no less quick than her own. She reminded herself to be wary and clenched her fingers as they itched to touch her scars.

"I apologize," she said, fanning her face. "I think some of the perfumes may have overwhelmed me for a moment."

"Quite all right," he said, eyes rooted on the counter, cheeks still flushed red in her presence. He cleared his throat and seemed to steel himself before he raised his gaze. "What can I help you with, Miss . . . ?"

"Madeleine Baxter," Grace said. "I'm in town visiting an old friend and her mother has run out of her favorite scent. Since they're putting me up for some time I thought I'd try to make a little gesture of thanks by refilling it, but you don't seem to have anything with quite the same fragrance."

She set the bottle on the counter and he removed the stopper, sniffing it. "Seems to be a simple compound of rosewater, although there may be a touch of bergamot as well." He held it up to the window, the tiny blue of the glass nearly lost in his hand. Grace watched him as he sniffed again, dabbing his palm with the stopper, all confidence restored when he was lost in his work. The bottle went back to the sunlight, followed by the stopper, and he frowned.

"I can't make out any manufacturer's mark on the bottle, so I won't be able to order a replacement, but I can mix up something similar for you, Miss—" His eyes returned to her. His voice dropped off and there was the slightest tremor in his hand when he set the bottle back on the counter. He cleared his throat again. "Miss Baxter," he said, nodding toward the ground as if to confirm that he'd finished his sentence.

"That would be lovely, thank you," she said. "Have you been away? I couldn't help but overhear the gentleman in front of me saying how glad he was that you've reopened, and I must say I'm rather pleased myself." She smiled, hoping to put him at ease.

"No, no, not closed up entirely," he said, eyes drifting over her shoulder. "My mother was feeling poorly at winter's beginning, so I spent a few days with her every week. She lives down in Pomeroy, so I wasn't able to keep regular shop hours."

"I'm sorry to hear that, Mr. Beaton," Grace said, waiting to see if he'd correct the name she'd picked up from the first customer. "I hope she's quite recovered," she added when he didn't. "When should I return for the scent?"

He avoided her eyes, looking to the ceiling as he stammered for an answer. "I—I can prepare it in about a day, but I've been returning to Mother over the weekends. Could you come back on Monday?"

Grace was set back for a moment herself, all days of the week having no meaning to her in the asylum. "Is it—" She broke off, her indecision evident. "Is it Friday today?"

Her broken composure seemed to stream into him, and he managed a small smile as he held her gaze. "Yes, Miss Baxter. Today is Friday."

"I'm sorry," she said, feeling her blood rising to her cheeks to match his. "One loses track of time when on a holiday."

"I understand." He nodded, his smile wider at the sight of her blush. "I will see you on Monday then, Miss Baxter."

"Monday," she agreed, eyes still locked with his.

THIRTY-TWO

Thornhollow was not in his office when she returned, so Grace went to work at the blackboard alone, filling in the missing pieces. The puzzle fell together with ease, holes neatly filled. She heard the office door open behind her, and Thornhollow's step as she continued to scratch away with the chalk.

"Grace, why are you wearing your town dress?"

"Doctor, come here," she said. "I've found something."

"Grace," he said more slowly. "Why are you wearing that dress?"

She turned to face him, chalk still in hand. "It hardly matters," she said. "I've found our killer, seen him face-to-face. It's just as you thought—a large man, definitely flustered interacting with women, he even mentioned his moth—"

"Grace!" Thornhollow pulled the chalk from her hand. "Why are you wearing that dress?"

"I . . ." She felt her shoulders sag under his scrutiny, and she corrected her posture before answering him calmly, her tone icy. "I went into town, Dr. Thornhollow."

"For the love of—" He walked away from her, flinging the chalk across the room.

"I won't say I'm sorry," Grace said, following close behind. "When you hear what I—"

"When I hear what, Grace?" He turned to face her, fuming. "When I hear that you left the grounds without telling anyone, I'll jump for joy? When I hear that you came face-to-face—your words, Grace—with our killer, a man who knocks women senseless and then—" He broke off, his face contorted against emotions he never allowed himself to feel. "Dear God, woman, please tell me what is the point of keeping track of your father when I can't even keep you in the building!"

He threw himself into the wing chair, hands buried in his hair.

"Doctor," Grace said. "You must hear me out."

"And you must not tax my nerves," he muttered to the carpet.

Ignoring him, she continued. "You were right in most respects, Doctor. He's a large man, easily capable of crushing a rag against a woman's face and holding her against her will until she succumbs."

"Which he could have done to you."

"In broad daylight in his own shop?" Grace countered easily. "Doubtful."

"A shop?" Thornhollow asked, drawn in despite himself. "What kind of shop?"

"Chemist," Grace said. "With the tools and the knowledge to mix ether, no doubt."

"A chemist." Thornhollow groaned at the floor, stamping his foot. "Damn me for a narrow-minded fool. Why were you in a chemist's shop in the first place?"

"I was getting some perfume for Lizzie. He's going to match the scent for me."

"Oh, of course. How foolish of me not to assume that. Go on." He waved a hand in the air. "I might as well know it all since you've gone and learned it."

"As to his feelings toward women," she continued, "there was a marked difference in his behavior with me as opposed to the male customer I saw him interact with. He's definitely nervous around women, although when I showed some hesitation myself he seemed to gain strength from that."

Thornhollow glanced up, one hand still buried in his hair. "Interesting. Perhaps he feels more confidence around women he perceives as weak-willed. A positive alternative to his mother, perhaps."

"Whom he mentioned," Grace said. "He said she's been feeling poorly this winter and he's been giving her care in her home, leading

303

to him only having the store open certain hours."

Thornhollow rose from his chair, hair standing on all ends as he surveyed the notes Grace had added to the blackboard. "Abandoning his business solely to see to his mother seems a bit extreme."

Grace nodded. "Leading one to assume that the mother is rather demanding."

"And"—Thornhollow held one finger in the air—"also confirming that he's an only child, as I said."

"Only *possibly* confirming that," Grace said, eyes narrowed. "I didn't ask."

"No man would weaken his livelihood to care for a parent if there were other siblings capable of taking on that load," Thornhollow insisted.

"He very well could have a sibling who lives farther away than Pomeroy and can't offer assistance," Grace said, irritation heating her words.

"Now you're arguing for the sake of argument."

"As are you."

"Nonsense. How does Pomeroy come into it?"

"That's where the mother lives," Grace said, moving to his desk and a map she had spread out before his arrival. "I checked, and the road—"

"To Pomeroy passes right through where the kitchen girl was

found," Thornhollow interrupted.

"Where Jenny Cantor was found," Grace amended.

"Regardless, I'll make a trip to Pomeroy over the weekend, ask a few questions. I think it's safe to say that they've seen at least one body like ours, no doubt their deaths occurring during our lulls."

"I'll come with you," Grace said, still leaning over the map.

"You won't."

She looked up. "Excuse me?"

Thornhollow sighed heavily. "Grace, there's no plausible reason for you coming with me, beyond some base conclusions that the staff would readily jump to for the sake of gossip."

"Then let people think base things," Grace said. "I'm past the point of caring what others think."

"I do," Thornhollow snapped back. "How would it reflect on me, on my career, if the staff believes that I'm . . . I'm . . ."

"Having sex with your patient?"

"Yes!" he burst out. "That kind of thing can end a man, you know."

Grace closed her eyes, hands flat on the map. "You're right," she said. "I can't help but be upset, though. I've been unable to accomplish anything at all these last few months, and now I'm being left behind."

"Left behind?" Thornhollow nearly laughed. "You're traipsing about in the snow at the crack of dawn and smiling at killers across counters while I'm dead to the world in my bed. Who's the one left behind?"

Grace rolled up the map, her heart still low. "So what now? When will you inform the police?"

"Inform them of what?"

"That we've found the man guilty of three murders here and who knows how many in Pomeroy."

"*Guilty* is a very strong word, one that we have no plausibility for."

"What are you saying?" Grace asked, confusion furrowing her brow and a familiar defeat brewing in her chest.

"What shall I show the police, Grace? Our blackboard? It's a sheer mess that only you and I can read. If I were to march George in here, he'd laugh and say I belong in the men's ward, not an office."

"Davey would believe you."

"Excellent, a patrolman who can barely grow whiskers on my side. I'm sure the arrest will be forthcoming. Grace . . ." The doctor broke off, his tone losing all sarcasm. "Grace, I'm sorry. We've never pursued anything so far, and I haven't prepared you for this part."

"What is this part?"

He sighed, eyes on the labyrinth of their shared writing that covered the blackboard. "This is when we know we're right, and have nothing in the way of proof."

Grace came to his side, the weight of futility resting heavily upon her once again. "What can be done?"

The doctor shrugged. "Nothing, I'm afraid. If I were in Boston I'd have the same men I trust to watch your sister tailing this man, but I have no contacts here that I know are discreet. If this chemist—did you get his name?"

"Beaton."

"If this Beaton hears that the killings have been linked or suspects he's being followed, he'll be gone in an instant. A man with his intelligence and a trade as well can go anywhere, set up under a false name, and begin anew. Go to a fresh town with women who won't meet the gaze of men and whose disappearances matter little to skulk among. No, Grace, we must be very careful now. I'll go to Pomeroy this weekend. You must promise me that you'll behave yourself while I'm gone."

"I will," Grace said.

"Good. When will he have the scent ready for you to pick up?"

"Tuesday," she lied.

The snow fell steadily all weekend, giving the grounds a pristine covering that Grace despised. She wanted to maul it with her footsteps, hook up an asylum carriage, and beat a path to Pomeroy, where she would watch over Beaton from a distance, protecting other women like a vengeful dark angel.

Instead, she played checkers with Elizabeth, who seemed depressed by the weather. Her head kept pulling to the right, String whispering things to her that she wouldn't share as her countenance became more troubled. Grace won every match easily, despite starting at a disadvantage with three fewer pieces.

She knocked the table to gain Lizzie's attention and raised an eyebrow, gesturing at the board.

"No, I don't think I'll play again," her friend said. "I may go and have a lie-down, actually."

Grace watched her go, then packed up the board. Time stretched before her, and she returned to the west turret, where the quiet was so intense she could hear the snow falling. She pushed inches of snow from the three chairs and sat watching the flakes reclaim them. The sun sank and lights in town appeared one by one. Grace sat alone in the dim until night fell completely, the two empty chairs sentinels on either side of her.

Janey intercepted her in the hall, and she curled her fist around the key for the turret, eyes wide with innocence.

"Don't you look at me like a babe in the woods." Janey shook a finger at her good-naturedly. "I know you didn't take any dinner. This weather's got us all in a bit of a mood, but not eating won't do you a lick of good."

Grace nodded and Janey went on. "Dr. Thornhollow's sent a telegram, says Ned won't take the horses out in this weather and he's stranded in Pomeroy until sense returns to the man. Which, we may never see the good doctor again if that's what we're waiting on."

Janey handed a telegram to Grace. "This one's meant for you. I can't make head or tail of it."

```
Have found at least two STOP Am delayed
by Ned's sentimentalism STOP Will return
whenever possible STOP Elizabeth smells fine
without improvements END
```

Janey watched Grace's eyes flick over the message. "I guess you know well enough what he's saying?"

Grace nodded, thanking Janey with a pat on the shoulder.

"All right," the nurse said. "Now I want to see you head to the kitchens instead of to your room, you hear? Joanna's chewed the laces through on one of her mitts, and I've got to see if I can't mend it before she tears into someone. But the kitchens may have a bite or two left, if you get down there."

Grace moved as if in a fog, the familiar veil dropping between herself and reality as she walked, body in the present, mind working furiously toward a point in the future and all the elements required to make it her own.

He was startled when he saw her, as she opened the shop door just as he'd been about to lock up for the evening.

"Miss Baxter," Beaton said, nearly dropping his keys. "I had thought perhaps the weather delayed you."

"Not the weather, but my own disarray," Grace said, raising the carpetbag she'd pulled from under Lizzie's bed, her asylum clothing inside. "Packing for a journey always leaves me in a fuddle. I'd hoped to catch you on my way to the depot. Is the scent ready?"

"It is," he said, returning to the counter with his head down. "If you'd like I can deliver it to your friend's mother with your compliments, since you are leaving town."

"That's very nice, but I'd rather send it along myself with a thank-you note for their hospitality."

Beaton produced the bottle and Grace took a whiff, the familiar scent of Lizzie's perfume reinvigorated with the bloom of freshness. "That's . . . really quite extraordinary. It will mean a lot. Thank you," she said honestly.

He blushed at the compliment, and Grace hesitated as she paid with the money she'd stolen from Thornhollow's desk, the moment before her now if she chose to take it. "I . . ." Her voice broke as she deliberated, the tentative manner of a well-bred young lady conveyed all too easily in her tone.

"I hope you won't think me too forward, Mr. Beaton," she went on, her voice gaining strength. "I delayed much more than I meant to and have missed my train. I'm sure I can catch the next, but I'm wary of walking to the depot alone now that night has fallen. Would it inconvenience you greatly to accompany me? I'd feel so much more confident with a man of your size alongside me."

It was easy to read the thoughts flickering behind his eyes, his own scale of indecision weighing the opportunity versus the risk. In the second before he accepted her proposal, his gaze raked her body and the freely offered sacrifice was too tempting to deny.

"Of course, Miss Baxter," he said with a true smile. "If you'll give me a moment I just need to lock up the back room."

He returned with the barest scent of ether on him, and they stepped out into the darkness together.

THIRTY-THREE

"Grace, wake up. Grace." Janey was shaking her roughly as she came into consciousness, rolling to face the nurse. "Thornhollow's just now got back. The horses weren't even unhitched before he got a message from town. There's another body found, and the doctor's wanting you."

Grace dressed quickly and climbed into the carriage to find an exhausted Thornhollow facing her.

"I was looking forward to my bed, but that's a comfort that will have to wait," he said. "I'm sorry for my delay, Grace. Ned refused to take the horses out, and I didn't want to upset him needlessly. Though if it's another doll we go toward it'll be on my conscience for not insisting we return sooner."

"Don't borrow trouble," she said coolly as they rattled into town.

They traveled in silence to the park, where Davey and George waited, gas lamps raised. "Not a woman," Thornhollow said as they approached, eyeing the form of the corpse. "There's that relief, at least."

Grace didn't even nod, the practiced mask of insanity appearing the moment she exited the carriage.

"Well, if it ain't our pleasure to see you again," George said the moment they came into the light. "Oh, and you too, Doctor," he added, tipping a wink.

"Yes, the joy of your company cannot be overstated," Thornhollow said, removing his gloves to lean over the body in the snow.

Davey moved to stand next to Grace. "Are you warm enough? It's been some bitter cold we've had here lately. I can stand it, though, if you need my coat."

His sincerity was wasted, all her attention focused on Thornhollow. Her nerves steeled for what was to come, her vision tunneling to include only him and the blood congealing in the snow.

George stamped his feet, breath fogging in front of his face. "Seeings as we've got to stand here and freeze our balls off I'd appreciate you explaining how your voodoo is so much better than our regular police work."

"Not voodoo, simply logic," Thornhollow said. "And if you're truly interested I have no objection to broadening your horizons."

"And if I'm not, the good laugh might at least keep me warm," George said.

"You can tell me yourself how amusing it is once I'm finished," Thornhollow said, rising to pace around the victim. "Starting with the body facedown as it was found—we obviously have a male, rather large in stature, who was killed only hours previously. The body is cool and the blood is frozen, but I can tell you by the spray pattern and pooled blood that the carotid artery has been severed. Also, by the tracks all around the body—and I'm noting to myself here your inability to leave the crime scene unaltered—none seem to match the size of the victim's shoe so we can assume that he was killed while the snow was still falling in enough earnest to fill his steps. Unfortunately, it also filled those of his killer."

Thornhollow bent to the body again, bare fingers touching the man's overcoat. "However, the body was still warm enough to melt most of the snow that fell on it. There's moisture on him here, but no accumulated snow, which means he lay here not terribly long before the snow stopped."

"Heat and snow and moisture," George muttered. "You sound like the weather column in the papers."

"Perhaps I do, but it's all toward establishing a time of death, which I doubt you see mentioned in the forecasts," Thornhollow said. "I'll add that even though he fell forward his hat remains on. Before you roll him over I'll postulate that we'll see a single neck wound delivered from the front, deep enough to kill with one stroke, and no defensive marks on the hands."

"How do you get all that from his hat still being on?" Davey asked.

"Physics," Thornhollow said, approaching Davey. "Pretend I were to stab you, right now, quite unexpectedly, in the throat. What would you do?"

"I imagine I'd lie down and die," Davey said. "Though I'd thank you for not doing it."

"Yes, you would, but there are steps to get you there. First, your hands would instinctively go to your wound in a futile attempt to stop the blood from flowing instead of warding off your attacker. Instantly weak from blood loss, you'd sink to your knees, perhaps one at a time, slowly getting yourself to the point where you in fact, lie down and die."

"With my hat still on," Davey added.

"Yes, with your hat still on because you were taken by surprise. You didn't grapple with your killer or have it knocked from your head in an attack from behind."

"So . . . ," Davey said, looking to the doctor for approval as he spoke each word. "He was walking with someone, a person he had no reason to think meant him harm."

"It's a possibility," Thornhollow agreed.

"A possibility," George echoed, hawking spit into the snow. "You don't sound too confident."

"Not the only option, but definitely a contender," Thornhollow went on, ignoring the heckling. "Whoever killed this man did not jump him from the shadows. The killer stood face-to-face with him and drove a knife into his throat without him having any idea it was about to happen. So yes, I'd say a companion or an agreed-upon meeting are both excellent deductions."

Davey stood a little straighter, ignoring the dark look from George as he rolled the body over. "All right, we'll see, then. A single knife wound, coming up."

George's sarcasm died in his throat when the corpse was turned, a bloody gash at the base of the throat all that marred the bone-white skin.

"By God, that's Beaton," Davey said. "The man what's got a shop up on Hudson. Oh, my ma won't be too happy about this. She says his powders is all that helps her eczema."

"It's who now?" George asked, raising his lantern to the victim's face.

Grace locked eyes with Thornhollow, her blank gaze betraying nothing while his face solidified into his own mask of impartiality, although his eyes blazed as bright as George's lantern.

"It's Beaton," Davey said again. "You know the fellow. He makes up the medicines for the whores—" He stopped, face flushed. "I mean for the ladies that serve up at the tavern when they get . . . when they get a cold."

"Don't spare your language for Grace's sake," Thornhollow said.

"She's heard and seen worse things than you, I imagine."

"Done them too, from what you've said," George added.

"Yes," Thornhollow agreed. "Yes, she has."

Grace bit the inside of her cheek until blood flooded her mouth. Beaton's face in the moonlight had not affected her, the dark spray against the untouched snow had not given her pause, and the hot, coppery scent of flowing blood had not brought her to gag. But one look from Thornhollow in the arc of the lamplight had clenched her stomach, her convictions weakening with the weight of his heavy glance that sank straight into her soul.

"So this man Beaton, he mixed medicines for prostitutes?" Thornhollow went on.

"He did, was the only man that would service them. Did it free of charge as well," George added. "Said he wouldn't take money from them that had so little to spare, though perhaps he took payment otherwise."

"Somehow I doubt that," Thornhollow said to himself.

"This'll be a blow to his mother," Davey said. "She lost her other son just a few months ago at Wounded Knee."

Grace felt her mouth twist as Thornhollow's brow came together in confusion. "He had a brother?"

"Yeah, few years older if I remember right," George said. "He joined up soon as he could, no doubt to get away from their mother. I wouldn't shed too many tears over Beaton, Davey boy, except over

317

his medicines. He's happier wherever he's gone. Those were the two most browbeaten men I ever seen."

"He may be happier dead, but who would kill him?" Davey asked.

Grace watched Thornhollow, the twitch of his jaw muscles the only indication of his inner struggle. "His medicines may have been the end of him," he finally said. "Whoever drove this blade knew how to cut and did so with no hesitation whatsoever. There's a complete lack of human compassion at work here."

Grace stood slack, eyes wide and uncomprehending, though a yawning chasm had opened inside her stomach.

"It's a professional job, then?" George asked. "You think he got mixed up in something over his head?"

"Possibly. The taxes on opium imports are high—I can tell you as a doctor that uses them on the most violent of patients. When it's wanted for recreational purposes the cost can go sky-high unless you can find someone homegrown with the capabilities to maximize the effect of the drug. And of course you'd have to pay them well for their services and discretion."

"So Beaton got greedy, you think?" George asked.

Thornhollow shrugged. "Or said too much to the wrong person. We'll probably never know."

"I can at least check at the depot, see if there was anyone behaving oddly on the last train out," Davey suggested.

"You can if it'll make you feel thorough," Thornhollow said.

"Though someone with the training to kill with that kind of precision can undoubtedly stand right next to you without giving away a thing, they're that adept at mimicking true feelings. Gentlemen, I am freezing." He turned to leave, about to take Grace by the elbow when he found that Davey's hand was already there. The policeman handed her up into the carriage and Grace fought to keep her face calm as Ned brought the horses to a trot, and they left the gaslit lamps of the park behind them.

"Please tell me you already burned your clothes." Thornhollow's voice came from the darkness, devoid of all inflection.

"I did."

"And the ether rag?"

"Thrown in the river."

Silence stretched between them and Grace sat stiffly, ready to combat any argument that he would use against her actions.

"Grace, do you have any idea what you've done?"

"I've killed a man," she said. "One that deserved to die."

"And what of yourself, Grace? What part of you had to die in order to take this drastic step?"

She expected to feel the heat of her rage at his words, but there was nothing but the darkness that yawned inside her. "I don't want to speak about this anymore," Grace said, her voice shaky.

Thornhollow slammed his foot onto the carriage floor. "Whether you will or not does not dictate the course of the conversation. I'm speaking to you now as your doctor, and I do not like what I've seen before me these past few months. It was human nature to rant and explode at Nell's death, but this—this is something entirely new. You've cut off your emotions to the point where you could look a fellow human being in the eye and drive a knife into his throat."

"A fate he well deserved," Grace said.

"And was not yours to deliver!" Thornhollow shot back. "Can you not see it? Only your sister's name can evoke any emotion from you, that or a new break in our case—one that you've very thoroughly closed. The ends neatly tied up with butcher's string."

"*I'm* the butcher?" Grace asked. "With so many bodies in his wake?"

"Bodies that he covered," Thornhollow reminded her. "Bodies that he positioned so that he may believe them alive and absolve himself of guilt, not with their throats open to the world as if to proclaim no guilt could be had from the action!"

"None can," she asserted, though he had planted a seed of doubt that had found traction somewhere inside her hollowness. She searched for words to appease Thornhollow without giving ground. "I want to say that in many ways he seemed so very normal."

"As do you, Grace," Thornhollow said. "As do you."

THIRTY-FOUR

"Doctor," Grace said quietly as she watched him erasing the blackboard. "I need to speak with you about my sister."

"Yes," he said. "I know."

Grace had kept to herself in the week since Beaton's death, giving Thornhollow a wide berth and processing her own actions. There had been a veil over her mind when she killed, her blade striking true, the sharp edge of the asylum kitchen's knife slicing through Beaton's neck easily. The spray of blood had not alarmed her, having seen so many crime scenes. His face as he went down, the confusion in his eyes, the ether-soaked rag in his pocket—none of these things had slipped into her nightmares.

The killing itself was easy, her removal from it in the moment, complete. But Thornhollow's words had torn the veil away, and

Davey's words of Beaton's kindness haunted her. Little memorials began to appear in the newspaper from private citizens who posted in their mourning. Beaton had treated prostitutes when no one else would. He had mixed a substitute powder for an infant who would have died after refusing her mother's milk. He delivered medicines to elderly patients in their homes so they need not wander out in the weather. Except for one glaring exception he had been a lovely man.

Thornhollow had left her to mull her actions in private, granting her wish to not speak of it again, which she now realized was in fact a harsh punishment. It was not guilt precisely that plagued her but a nagging realization that while her actions had saved lives, it was clear that some of Beaton's had too. And she'd removed him from the world with a flick of her wrist. Their chalkboard had always consisted of black and white, but the reality was gray, and she struggled with the pain of learning it.

Breaking Thornhollow's silence was not easily done, but time was passing. Each day brought her father closer to home and to Alice, with a present he would demand something infernal for in return.

"I'll be blunt with you, Grace," Thornhollow said, back still to her. "I've not been able to come up with a plausible way to remove Alice from the household. Even if anonymous letters were written to the Society for the Prevention of Cruelty to Children, your father is powerful enough to see it brushed under the rug. There are possibilities for delaying his return further, but I can see nothing that will separate the two of them for good."

"I can," Grace said.

He turned to her, his features drawn. "I won't let you kill him."

"I won't have to," she said, willing some calmness into her face as she watched Thornhollow carefully. "We have dead women with no one convicted of the crimes, the true killer no longer among us. The blame can be shifted."

Thornhollow mulled this, his mind working. "True, but your father was only in the area when one of the crimes was committed."

"Yes, I know," Grace said, moving to the chalkboard to create a new picture. "Jenny Cantor's time of death was never fully established due to the temperatures. She could easily have been killed when he was here."

The doctor pulled the chalk from her hand to make his own notations. "We can hardly pin him with one murder because he was here and ignore the connection to the others. He was nowhere near when they were committed."

"Why can't we?" Grace said. "Mellie Jacobs wasn't murdered, according to the police. You never shared your suspicions about Jenny and Anka Baran being done by the same hand."

"No I didn't, because I knew no one would listen to me," Thornhollow admitted, tossing the chalk from hand to hand in thought.

"Or the two from Pomeroy, either. Beaton had one hell of a method, I'll give him that. Even a good coroner might come to the conclusion of natural causes once the ether evaporated."

"And now we put it to our own use," Grace said, snatching the chalk as it sailed from one of his hands to the other. "Accuse my father of Jenny Cantor's death. If he's convicted, he'll hang."

"Grace, do you hear yourself?"

"I do, Dr. Thornhollow, and I don't see shame in it." She groped for words, unwilling to let her fought-for voice fail her now. "Jenny Cantor is dead, Mr. Beaton with her, and no one but the two of us knowing the reasons for it. Why not extend the hand of justice a little further? You know my father is a monster."

Thornhollow grimaced and walked away from her. "He is, undoubtedly. But even if I were to agree to this plan, we have no grounds whatsoever that would earn a conviction from a jury. Your father was in the same general area as the victim. That's all. He has no history of violence or sexual proclivities that are on record. You may as well accuse his coach driver of being guilty of the murder and have just as much evidence."

"Except the testimony of an expert witness, Dr. Melancthon Thornhollow, who would state that Nathaniel Mae is a deviant fully capable of this act."

Thornhollow went pale and he sat down abruptly. "You'd have me take the name of my science in vain, on my word, in a courtroom?

I cannot do that, Grace, not even for you."

Grace had expected the argument. "I know better than to ask. Rather I'd ask you to testify in the name of phrenology, a science you have no faith in whatsoever."

"To condemn a man for a crime he didn't commit."

"No, Doctor—I'm asking you to condemn him for the crimes you know he *did*." Grace's voice grew thick as she fought back the emotions that longed to well up inside her, bringing with them all of the memories she'd relegated to the dark. She cried out, doubling over as she fought to keep them away and sliding to the floor in her misery. "It's not only for me, though I'm the one you see in front of you. There have been many. So many, Doctor. I see their faces and it can't be undone, only rectified."

His face went into his hands, and for long moments the only sound was the clock as he pored over her arguments internally. Grace waited, her spine crackling with nerves as he deliberated.

"I can't do it, Grace," he said, hands still covering his face, his words sending her heart plummeting. "The risks involved are so great. Your father would be tried here, where the crime occurred, bringing him near you again—something I would avoid at all costs. Even with my testimony there is very little to condemn him and your father would have the best lawyer money could buy. We would lose, Grace. He'd see my career ruined, and God knows what would happen to you if that were the case."

"Your career," she said, her tone cold though her voice quaked with emotion. "Science," she said, her volume rising. "These things mean nothing to me held in balance with my sister's fate."

"Did you not hear me mention your own?" Thornhollow yelled back.

"Also meaningless!"

"Christ, Grace. You're not yourself. You haven't been since—"

His office doors banged open and Thornhollow jumped to his feet, arms spread in front of Grace. Lizzie swooped in, color high and eyes burning.

"No, she's not been herself, Doctor. Not since Nell died and she killed a man."

"Elizabeth!" he sputtered. "You . . . you . . ."

"I what? I know things I shouldn't? Of course I do. String tells me. You might as well let Grace come out from behind you. She doesn't need your protection—she needs you to do as she says."

Grace pushed Thornhollow's arms away to look at Lizzie.

"Out with it, Grace," Lizzie said. "I know you've got a voice, same as the rest of us. String says so, and tells me more than you ever would even if you used it."

"Elizabeth," Thornhollow said quietly. "String did not tell you these things. You've learned them on your own by watching Grace and—might I add—eavesdropping outside my office for who knows how long." He closed the doors, giving Lizzie a dark look as he did.

He tried to usher her to a chair but she shook him off.

"Enough with manners. I've had manners my whole life, and they've done nothing for me. I know things, things that most everyone would rather not have said aloud in public, and I keep my mouth shut. I do it to keep the peace and let everyone have their secrets. But no longer!"

She stamped her little foot, the same ferocity that would flash itself occasionally at Nell now out in full force. "I know what he did to you, Grace. Thornhollow can have his ideas of how I learned it, but I know it all the same. I'd rather you told me yourself, Grace. Time and time again I gave you chances to speak, to let me hear your voice and share your woes with me the way I did mine with you. But *you*—" She turned on Thornhollow so quickly he stepped away from her. "You've got her shut up tight like a drum for fear of bringing a storm down on your head. Don't you *ever* accuse her of not thinking of how her actions affect your career, sir. She's more loyal than you'll ever know, her very tongue stoppered against her only friend left living, her troubles hers and hers alone just to keep your deception safe."

The girl suddenly slumped, all her energy poured into her words and leaving her body a drained shell. "Say something to me, Grace Mae," Elizabeth said, tears streaming down her face. "Let me hear your voice, and I swear I'll see that man hang for you."

Grace stepped forward on shaking legs, past the dumbfounded

Thornhollow. "Hello, Lizzie," she said. "I've been meaning to give you this." The tiny blue bottle went from her hand to Lizzie's, and it was the other girl's turn to be surprised as she removed the stopper, the smell of rosewater and bergamot filling the doctor's office as the two friends embraced.

THIRTY-FIVE

"It's a circus in town," Thornhollow said, hand brushing idly over the tips of the new spring grass. "Every newspaper in the state has a reporter here, and I heard someone say a fellow from the *Times* has taken permanent residence at the inn ever since the indictment."

"It got worse after Mr. Pickering said he'd seek the death penalty," Elizabeth said, picking over the sandwich she'd packed for their picnic by the lake. "I could hear the carriages rattling into town from my room." She unwrapped another sandwich, holding it out to her friend. "Grace, put that down. It doesn't say anything different since the last time you read it. You need to eat."

"I know it," Grace said, eyes still on Alice's most recent letter. "It's so very difficult to bear. She doesn't understand why her father's

329

not come home, and Mother is so frantic trying to dispel the rumors that she has no time for her child." Grace folded the worn letter and put it back in her pocket, turning her attention to food, though she had no appetite.

"Will your mother come for the trial?" Thornhollow asked.

"I can't see that happening," Grace said. "She won't want to be anywhere near when they read the verdict. Deep down she knows it's true."

"Except, it's not," the doctor said.

"She's lived with him. And some of the women on that list I supplied for the grand jury were friends of hers at one point." Grace's lips thinned as she remembered putting their names to paper, digging up memories of women who had left parties at her former home with tears on their faces and bruises forming on their arms. "Years of seeing women used and disposed of when no longer entertaining tells her it very well *could* be true. She'll not want to stand in public when the rest of the world learns what she's always known."

"She deserves her own punishment for blocking her ears against you," Elizabeth said, her feral side lurking closer to the surface in the days before the trial.

"And she'll have it, Elizabeth," Thornhollow said, tossing what remained of his food into their basket. "I've moved in society long enough to tell you that a stain of this magnitude will spread to Grace's mother as well. She'll not be received anywhere."

"Which for her will be worse than any hangman's rope," Grace agreed. "Tongues will wag and her name will be on them. A punishment to fit her crime of stopping my own."

"I do so love your voice," Lizzie said, reaching out to touch Grace's arm. "String said it was there, and hearing it these past months has been nearly worth the wait."

Thornhollow cleared his throat. "You do know not to mention String when—"

"Yes, Doctor," Lizzie snapped. "How could I forget with the constant reminders?"

"All right," Grace said, patting her friend's hand. "He's only trying to ensure that everything follows the course we have planned."

"And speaking of that," Thornhollow said, "what are your plans for tomorrow, Grace? I hope it goes without saying that you'll be nowhere near the courthouse."

"It seems my plans are in direct opposition with your own, then."

"Grace, be reasonable," Thornhollow said. "I understand the importance of this for you, but having you anywhere near your father is out of the question. Not to mention the logistics are ridiculous. A mental patient can't simply attend a court proceeding, first of all, and secondly if your father spotted your face in the crowd, the game would be up."

"Of course a patient would attract attention," Grace agreed. "But a widow in the press of the crowd wouldn't. And under her veil could be any face at all."

"And where do you propose to secure widow's reeds?"

"Your sister had them sent to me. She's also been in correspondence with Janey, and they've agreed that with my aversion to crowds it would be best to get me out of town, with your blessing—which, of course, she provided a signature that really was remarkably like your own. You've been so busy preparing for the trial Janey's been far too intimidated to question you about it.

"Adelaide's coming to get me tonight, supposedly whisking me off to happy seclusion. Really we'll be at the inn, right alongside the *Times* fellow. Adelaide said he's quite handsome and has promised good seats for herself and her widowed friend for the trial. I'll undoubtedly have an excellent view of the witness stand."

Thornhollow sighed and threw a stone in the lake. "Introducing the two of you was one of my larger mistakes. I should tell Janey I've changed my mind and have you thrown in isolation until this whole mess is through. You'd have plenty of privacy there."

"Try it," Elizabeth said, baring her teeth.

"You're a rather stunning widow," Adelaide said as she pinned Grace's veil on the next morning. "We'll keep that face covered for more reasons than one. I'll be thumping fellows left and right just to clear a path for us otherwise."

Grace smiled, though it felt weak even to her, as she tried to keep a calm face in front of her friend. "I don't think you'd mind thumping them."

"A few," she agreed, fixing her own hat in the mirror. "Though if I were to go after my prime target I'm sure the bailiff would wrestle me down."

"I'd very much like to see you toe-to-toe with my father," Grace said. "He's not much for women's rights."

"We're all lucky the judge is, otherwise I don't think this would have ever made it to trial. Although, Melancthon tells me as soon as whispers of trouble spread to Boston your father's political enemies were here to make sure the right voices were heard. Guilty or not, they weren't taking chances on it being hushed up.

"Regardless, as much as I'd like to take a swing at your father, I think dear little brother would be my first victim."

Grace laughed, the sound tinged with desperation, her veil puffing out with her breath. "You love him dearly and him you. Why neither one of you acknowledges it I don't know."

"Because we're Thornhollows," Adelaide said. "Emotions are not in our blood." She turned from the mirror, face suddenly serious. "I'll have you know my intentions for helping you, Grace. I think it'll do you good to see your father put away for all the demons he's brought upon you. You've earned the right to that, and I'll see you have it. But you also need to know that I share my brother's opinion that you've removed yourself too thoroughly from your own feelings. It doesn't come naturally to you as it does to myself and Melancthon. I fear you're nearing a precipice, and I'd rather be next to you when you go over."

"There is nothing wrong with me," Grace said as they left their room, ignoring that her hands trembled inside each other. "But I appreciate everything you've done. You've gone to great trouble just to help me, and I have no way to repay you."

Adelaide rolled her eyes. "Going against Melancthon's wishes is its own reward."

They had to walk to the courthouse. Mr. Turner, Adelaide's gentleman friend from the *Times*, joined them. The streets were packed with carriages, most of them headed for the same destination. Newspaper boys yelled from street corners, and prostitutes called from alleyways, hoping to distract a few of the novelty seekers with something more pleasurable than rhetoric.

Mr. Turner cleared the way for them once inside the courthouse, his press badge bringing them closer to the front than otherwise possible and his glib tongue explaining the need of seats for the two women as well. Grace settled in, her black skirts swishing around her as she crossed her ankles, grinding them together almost painfully to give herself something to focus on other than the fluttering of her stomach.

Even though it had bordered on cool outdoors, the inside of the courtroom was uncomfortably warm, the press of bodies adding heat. Words flew through the air, blurring together in a din that filled Grace's ears and had her retreating inside herself despite the physical veil in front of her face. She sat still and stony while Adelaide made conversation with Mr. Turner.

The courtroom erupted when her father was brought in, everyone around her rising to their feet, some screaming about the ridiculousness of the charges, while others jeered him. Grace stayed in her seat with Adelaide's hands on her own, only too glad to have her view blocked by a man's back at that moment.

The judge banged his gavel repeatedly, only gaining order once he threatened to bar the public from the proceedings if they couldn't control themselves. A dark murmur passed through the crowd but they found their seats, the man in front of her one of the last to rest. Grace felt her breaths coming shallow and quick as she saw Nathaniel Mae close up for the first time since being dragged screaming from her own home, her belly heavy with his child.

He seemed no worse for wear, his black mustache trim as ever, no hair on his head out of place. He rested easily at the defense table, calm as if he were taking in a ball game on a summer's day. He turned to speak to Mr. Atkinson, his lawyer, and Grace felt even the smallest of inhalations catch in her chest as his eye passed over her.

She had wanted to be here, she reminded herself. She had wanted to see him squirm and quiver under the stern eye of the law, but she had forgotten his panache, his absolute certainty in his divine right to behave as he saw fit. Grace had stilled her tongue in part to forget language and the sound of speech, but the sight of him brought his voice into her head as if she were back in their home, watching him fix his hair in her bedroom mirror.

"Appearances are everything, Grace," he had said. "As long as no one suspects something, it didn't happen."

"Appearances are everything," she whispered to herself now, as he shared a laugh with his defense team. If he had a shred of doubt as to his own victory he would not show it. Grace's breathing evened out. "That works both ways, Father," she said quietly.

"What was that, Madeleine?" Adelaide asked.

"I asked what happens now?" Grace said.

"Ah, well, today are the opening statements and if we're lucky, the prosecution presents their case. With Pickering aiming for the death penalty it could go into more than one day if there's a lot of cross-examining. You may change your mind about wanting to be here. I guarantee you with the heat, half this room files out by lunchtime. It's all fun when we're speculating from the comfort of our homes about sex and murder, but when we're smelling each other's stenches while the coroner goes on about body temperatures and timetables it loses most of its shine."

Adelaide was right in some respects. The facts of the case were presented from both sides, each with their own interpretation. That Jenny Cantor was dead could not be denied, and Atkinson—a small man with a full head of white hair—made much of the tragedy of that fact. But that his client was the one that murdered her, the very presumption of accusing an outstanding citizen of such a crime was an outrage in itself.

Beside Grace, Adelaide huffed into her fan. "Sorry, old boy," she muttered. "But the grand jury charged him. They don't do that on whims, you know."

Grace leaned to speak to her friend, irritated by how easily their assertion of her father's innocence had ruffled her. "I almost think he believes what he's saying."

"He believes what he's paid to believe," Adelaide said.

The prosecution kept their opening statement brief, saying only that the facts would speak for themselves, and that Nathaniel Mae's public facade was very different from the real man, whose dark appetites were only now coming to light.

After that the prosecution called its first witness, the coroner.

"I knew it," Adelaide said to Grace. "This will take us straight up to lunchtime and boring as bull piss."

So it was. Adelaide was right in that the coroner shared his opinion about the effect of temperatures on the body, the behavior of viscous blood, and so on, until even Grace lost interest, allowing her gaze to be drawn instead to the faces in the crowd. People shifted, eyelids drooped, and someone even passed gas at one point, which brought a hearty laugh from those around him. It was the most interesting part of the morning, and Grace found herself dozing on Adelaide's shoulder, sweat running down the inside of her stays as Adelaide shook her awake.

"Madeleine, they're breaking for lunch. Mr. Turner has offered to bring us lemonade. Some enterprising youths have set up a stand on the courthouse steps. They'll be millionaires by week's end. Shall we contribute?"

Grace nodded eagerly and Turner returned with sandwiches as well, offering to hold their seats if they wanted to eat theirs in the fresh air.

"Mr. Turner must be rather taken with you," Grace said as they sat on the grass, the breeze a blessing on her face now that she could have her veil up. "He's going to a lot of trouble for our convenience."

"I don't dislike him," was all Adelaide said.

"High praise from a Thornhollow," Grace said, her attempt at a light tone failing miserably. "I'm sorry for falling asleep. What did I miss?"

"Nothing, as I suspected. Facts about bodies and blood that no one but another doctor could make head nor tail of. I'm sure the jury was quite flummoxed. Then Mr. Atkinson went after the coroner like a terrier at a croquet match, but even that was rather boring. In the end, the only thing we learned is that the poor girl lay dead in the snow for quite some time, and it could have been during the time when your father was in town."

"Sounds rather anticlimactic," Grace said.

"It was, but they pulled their hooks out of the coroner, and I guarantee you the entertainment bar is raised a bit higher after lunch with all these women on parade. Oh, and by the way, I've changed my mind."

"On what?"

"I think I would very much prefer to thump your father before my brother. I'll sit through eight days of old coroners to see that smug smile wiped off his face."

"Let's hope it happens," Grace said, her stomach fluttering as she tossed the dregs of her lemonade into the grass.

She put her veil in place as they pushed their way back into the courtroom and to Mr. Turner's side just as the judge was returning. The crowd settled with the banging of his gavel, eyes bright and attention reawakened after the break.

The women whose names and faces Grace had scavenged her memory for were called one at a time, although there were notable absences. Not all of them would take the stand against a powerful man, no matter what he had done to them. Society faces she recalled from brighter days stonily recounted unwanted advances, pressed too far. Mrs. Vivanti, a regal woman who had once been their neighbor, testified, her voice chilly as each word dropped like ice from her lips. Her eyes never left Mae, and though her tone was controlled, the rage that burned under them reached for Grace as well, threatening to ignite her own wrath.

The concise sentences of the society women melted into the wary voices of servants roughly mistreated, then dismissed. Through it all Grace remained calm beneath her veil, too aware that her own control must be complete for the last, most dear face.

"Call your next witness," the judge ordered the prosecution.

Mr. Pickering stood, cleared his throat, and said, "The prosecution calls Elizabeth Martin to the stand."

Elizabeth entered the courtroom on a storm of whispers. People stood on tiptoe, some pointing, and Grace swelled with pride as her friend walked to the stand with her head held high.

"She looks rather nice in that dress," Adelaide whispered to Grace. "I ordered that print special from New York City. Sets off her hair nicely. You'd never guess she's crazy."

"Maybe she's not," Grace said.

Adelaide tapped Grace's arm with her fan. "She is to everyone else in this room."

After Elizabeth was sworn in she stated her name and residence, murmurs going through the crowd at the mention of the insane asylum, which quieted immediately when the judge glanced up.

"All right, Miss Martin," Pickering said, "I want you to tell the jury what you've told me."

"The jury?" Elizabeth asked, her voice so quiet the court descended into a dead calm.

"Those people right over there," Pickering said, pointing.

"Oh, all right," Elizabeth said, a sweet smile breaking over her face. "Um, hello."

More than a few of the jurors smiled back. One raised a hand in greeting.

"She's golden," Adelaide said, but Grace didn't hear. Her hands were crushing each other in anxiety for her friend, whose childlike innocence was no playact.

Elizabeth looked back to Mr. Pickering. "Where should I start?"

"With the night of the reception, if you please."

Elizabeth looked back at the jury. "All right, the reception." She cleared her throat. "There was a reception up at the asylum for Mr.— I'm sorry—Senator Mae when he was here in town. We've got the loveliest ballroom, you see, and the food isn't half-bad, either."

A chuckle rippled through the crowd, and Elizabeth looked mystified at what the joke could be. Her breath hitched in her chest before she continued, this time with wide eyes taking in the whole courtroom. "I've always been so proud of the asylum. It's a beautiful place, and I knew that we'd do right by Senator Mae when he was there. They didn't want any of the patients near him, but I thought maybe a peek wouldn't hurt anybody.

"I watched the carriages come from my window, all the fine people walking up the steps that I use too, and I picked out Senator Mae right away. You can't mistake someone who walks with that kind of pride."

Another titter swept the room, this one more restrained.

"I sat in my room and I listened," Elizabeth went on. "I'm close to the stairs on the women's wing so all their voices sort of float up to me. I couldn't make out words of course, but people got louder as the night went on. I help in the kitchens, so I knew there had been ever so much alcohol ordered in. I thought this was my chance. If I wanted to sneak down and take a look at all the fine people, I should go when they were distracted by drink."

Elizabeth fell quiet for a moment, the hush of the courtroom so still everyone could hear her draw her next breath. "I went down a flight of stairs, thinking I'd come to the ballroom through a side door, when Mr.—I'm sorry—Senator Mae himself turned the corner. I felt all nervous straightaway, knowing that they didn't want him bothered with having to see mental patients. So I tried to excuse myself, but he said he was looking for . . . he needed—" Elizabeth broke off, her face scarlet.

"He needed what, Elizabeth?" Pickering prompted.

"He was looking for the privy, sir," Elizabeth blurted out, her embarrassment sending the court into peals of laughter. Her flush faded after she took a drink of water, then continued. "He asked whether we had indoor plumbing—and we do, sir, the asylum added it new just a few years ago. It's ever so very nice."

Mr. Pickering leaned against the witness box, a patient smile on his face. "And what happened next, Elizabeth?"

"I told Senator Mae that I didn't dare take him over to the men's wing to their privy, but he said he'd use the women's so long as I didn't tell anyone, and he wouldn't tell anyone I was out of my room. Then he kind of winked at me, and I thought maybe it would be okay to help a senator, even if I was out of bed and taking him into the women's side. He's . . ." Elizabeth paused, her eyes dropping. "He's got that way about him, sir. The senator, he can talk you into doing things you wouldn't consider otherwise."

"Objection," Mr. Atkinson called lazily from the defense.

"Sustained," the judge said, and Elizabeth glanced up at him, alarmed.

"Did I do something wrong?" she asked.

"You can't say things that aren't facts, Miss Martin," he answered, his voice low and kind. "You're here to tell us what happened that night, not to make conjectures about Mr. Mae's personality."

"Senator Mae," Elizabeth corrected him.

"Yes, of course, Senator Mae," the judge said. "Please go on."

"All right." Elizabeth took a deep breath. "Well, I took him to the ladies' room. All the while we were walking he was ever so nice, asking me about my life at the asylum, what my name is, how old I was. And then we get to the . . . to the privy and I wished him a good night and—" She stopped, her lips quivering. "Do I have to, Mr. Pickering?" she asked, eyes pleading.

"I'm sorry, Lizzie. Yes, it's very important that you tell the court what happened after you wished him a good night."

"He . . . he grabbed my wrist, sir." Elizabeth's face contorted, her eyes shiny with tears and focused on nothing. "He grabbed and twisted it and dragged me through the door after him. He'd been so nice, so kind and polite, that I thought I had to be confused, that this fine, important man would never touch me like that and I couldn't imagine a reason for him doing it. And then . . . then he shoved me down to the privy floor and pushed my nightgown up and I guess I knew pretty well what his reason was then.

"I started fighting, sir. Yelling and crying too. But the fighting only seemed to make him like it more, and yelling and crying isn't anything new in an asylum. Nobody came to help, and he had his way with me, right there on the floor."

Elizabeth was crying freely. Mr. Pickering reached for his handkerchief and she took it but left it unused, her tears as much a part of her testimony as her words.

"And the next part, Lizzie?" Pickering said quietly, his voice carrying in the dead silence of the courtroom.

Lizzie bit down on her bottom lip, hands twisting Pickering's kerchief. "Near the end the senator, he put his hand over my mouth and my nose and pushed down real hard. The dark was coming in around the sides of my eyes and all I could think was 'Let me die, so this is over.' But I didn't die, and he was through with his pleasure. And he pulled his hand back and put his face down close to mine and he said . . . he said, 'You're lucky you'll be looked for, or I'd see you turn blue like that bitch out on the Pomeroy road.'"

A gasp rolled over the courtroom, followed by a swell of whispers and Elizabeth's rolling sobs as she wiped away her tears, while Grace's flowed unseen beneath her veil.

THIRTY-SIX

"Where are they taking her?" Grace asked Adelaide moments later as Lizzie was escorted from the courtroom by the bailiff.

"I imagine they're giving her a bit of a breather before she's cross-examined," Adelaide said, her face pale and pinched.

Grace only nodded slightly, retreating back into herself before Elizabeth was ushered to the stand. The crowd was buzzing, and still her father sat unperturbed at the defense table, his smile flashing out at whoever looked at him. She averted her eyes, focusing instead on the moons of her fingernails and the drying teardrops that had landed on her hands.

When Lizzie returned the hush came with her, the courtroom falling silent in respect as if the corpse had arrived at the wake.

Mr. Atkinson glanced at his notes while Elizabeth situated herself on the stand again, leaving them behind on the table as he approached to question her.

"Hello, Miss Martin."

Elizabeth nodded. "Hello, Mr. . . . Lawyer." Grace noticed a few jury members covering their smiles.

"That was a terrible tale you just shared."

"Yes, sir."

"Any man who did that to a girl as sweet as you ought to be hanged, whether another's murder came into it or not."

Lizzie watched him warily. "That's not for me to say, sir. I'm supposed to just tell what happened. That's it and that's all."

"Right, right," he said, his smile taking on an edge. "But the thing is, I'm not so sure it happened."

Lizzie's brow came together in confusion. "It did, though, sir."

"That's the thing, Miss Martin. It's your word against my client's, just as it has been with all the other women who walked through here today. They're easily dismissed, with scores to settle or imaginary slights to return. But you're playing a dangerous game, little girl. You've added the detail that makes this a federal case, and one with the death penalty attached. I hardly need to remind you—or the jury—that if what you say *isn't* true, then there's no reason to believe Senator Mae had anything whatsoever to do with Jenny Cantor's death. The only reason we're even here today is because of *you,* little Elizabeth Martin. You *claim* that Senator Mae raped you and during the course of raping you confided that he'd done the same to Jenny Cantor, asphyxiating her in the process. A man's life hangs on the question of whether or not you are lying."

"I know that, sir," Elizabeth said. "And I'm not."

"Where is it that you live again?" Atkinson asked, brow knit in mock confusion.

"I live up at the insane asylum, sir."

"Ah, up at the insane asylum. Thank you for repeating that. Now, why, may I ask, do you live there?"

Elizabeth's lips thinned. "I suppose I live there because I am insane."

"A simple enough assumption," Atkinson agreed. "Yet somehow we're still here today, listening to you slander a well-respected man. I can't help but wonder if you're saying these things not because they happened but because you were told to say them."

"Objection. Unless the defense would like to actually ask a question to the witness?" Pickering said from his seat.

"Sustained," the judge said.

"Very well," Atkinson said. "Miss Martin, did Senator Mae rape you?"

"Yes," Elizabeth said, nodding her head along with the word.

"Did Senator Mae imply to you that he had raped and killed Jenny Cantor?"

"Yes," she said again, seeming almost pleased that the questions were so easy.

"And why should the jury believe the word of an insane girl?"

"Because String would never let me tell a lie, sir," Elizabeth said quickly, invoking the most powerful reference she knew.

A bewildered hum swept through the courtroom, and Grace's heart fell as a blackness that was not her veil seeped into the edges of her vision.

"String?" Atkinson asked. "Who might that be?"

"Objection," Pickering said, rising to his feet.

"Surely he can't object to my questioning the sanity of an insane asylum inmate?" Atkinson said, eyes never leaving Elizabeth's bewildered ones.

"Sustained," the judge said. "You'll have to answer the question, Miss Martin."

Grace leaned against Adelaide, the hollowness that she'd invited willingly inside of her being burned away by the rage Falsteed had smelled out long ago, the familiar crush of helplessness and defeat following close behind.

"Grace," Adelaide whispered to her. "Do you need to leave?"

"Yes, tell us, Miss Martin," Atkinson pushed on. "Tell us about this String? Who is he?"

Elizabeth was on her feet in a second, small hands curled into fists. "String is *not* male! String resents the assumption."

An expectant quiet fell over the court. "Your Honor," Pickering said in a tired voice, "I request a recess until tomorrow morning."

"I'm so sorry, Grace," Elizabeth said, her face still streaked with tears, though they were in the safety of Thornhollow's office. "That man, he came after me so, I didn't know what to do."

"It's all right, Lizzie," Grace said, handing her friend a glass of water. "You did wonderfully."

"Yes, Adelaide said you were really something," Thornhollow said, though his eyes lacked enthusiasm. "I can't be in court myself as a fellow witness, but she said you may have turned the jury."

"And then turned them back," Lizzie said, shaking her head. "You're all very nice, but I know I made a mistake by mentioning String." Her hand went up to her ear protectively. "I'm not ashamed, but I do wish String needn't have come into it."

"You need sleep, Lizzie," Thornhollow said. "They'll finish your cross-examination tomorrow."

"Yes," Grace said. "I told Adelaide I'm sleeping here tonight, if I can be some comfort to you."

Elizabeth sniffed. "The whole idea was for me to help you, Grace." She went meekly to her room, hand curled in a fist near her ear.

"Tell me honestly," Grace said after the door shut behind Lizzie. "How badly did that hurt us?"

"Badly," he admitted. "The whole case hinged on Lizzie's

testimony being convincing. Which it was."

"Unfortunately, she's also convincingly insane," Grace added.

"Yes." Thornhollow looked at his drink, nearly finished. "I can testify as an expert as to what I believe your father is capable of, but Elizabeth is the only one who can testify that he specifically did something."

"He did," Grace said, her voice thick. "Only not to her."

Grace went to bed with the same dread that she'd felt long ago, her footsteps dogged now not by a man but a memory. She lay in bed, eyes on the ceiling. Then took a deep breath and remembered. She let them come up from her center, the pictures she'd stowed away for so long in the darkness so that their details would never plague her again. They'd been jammed beside her emotions, each losing importance as they rotted away inside her. And now she needed them both to deliver herself. She let them come.

Hands and sounds. Pressure and pain. Flash of flesh and her throat closing against the words as his eyes stared down at her, blank as the ones she saw in the mirror. She covered her eyes, even though Grace knew it would bring no relief. The scenes played out, each one to the end until she had known every terror again, each fresh memory of a new night revisited upon her as she caressed her scars for comfort.

Air rushed into her lungs as she let all the feelings flow, face twisted in agony. Rage came first, an impotent cry against the unfairness of the world, followed by a broken sadness and the black guilt of Beaton, staining her soul forever.

She knocked on Lizzie's door and was met with likewise tearstained eyes. "Lizzie, I need to tell you something."

"You're sure you want to do this again?" Adelaide asked as they took their seats the next day. "I thought for sure you would faint."

"I'm fine, thank you," Grace said, squeezing her friend's hand.

Adelaide's eyes narrowed. "You almost sound it," she said.

The defense and prosecution entered, Grace's father looking well rested and perfectly groomed, assured in his acquittal. Grace bit on her lip at the thought of him spending the previous night in premature celebration while she had writhed through her memories. The judge entered and banged his gavel, bringing the second day to its beginning. Lizzie took the stand again and Atkinson approached her like a hawk spotting a timid mouse.

"Now then, Miss Martin," he said. "Your testimony as to being raped by Senator Mae was rather memorable, but I'd also remind the jury that you're a ward of the state who lives in an asylum."

"Just because I'm insane doesn't mean it didn't happen," Elizabeth said.

"I didn't ask you a question," Atkinson snapped at her, and Elizabeth pulled back as if bitten.

"Objection." Pickering jumped to his feet. "Defense is intimidating my witness, who is in a delicate state as it is."

"Sustained," the judge barely had time to say before Atkinson rolled on.

"Delicate state? I can't blame her. She's brought people from all over the country here to listen to lies and vulgarity, to tell an alluring story that took place only in her perverted little mind. She has no proof!"

"But I do," Elizabeth said, her voice unsteady after being attacked.

"What was that?" The judge leaned in as Atkinson pulled in another breath to continue.

"I said she has no proof!" he repeated.

"*I do!*" Elizabeth cried, pounding her tiny fist on the rail. "I do have proof, Mr. Judge, sir. Senator Mae, he's got a birthmark right above his—" She broke off, her face a picture of perfect misery.

"Where, child?" the judge asked gently while Atkinson struggled for words.

"It's right above his privates. A port wine stain, in the shape of a heart."

"Bailiff," the judge said, rising to his feet, "if you would please escort Mr. Mae to his holding cell, where I will determine whether he does or does not have this mark."

"I . . . I object," Atkinson said.

"To what?" the judge asked. "You can take his pants down yourself if you like, but I *will* know."

Grace watched as her father was escorted through a door, his head held high, but tension keeping it unnaturally still as his defense team and the judge exited with him. Adelaide reached over and wordlessly squeezed her hands. Alone on the stand, Elizabeth wiped her face, head inclined ever so slightly to the right.

The courtroom was silent when the men reentered, everyone filing back to their places. The judge placed a hand on Elizabeth's shoulder as he passed behind her. He settled himself in his chair, and Pickering took the floor before him.

"Prosecution would like to enter into evidence that the defendant does indeed have a port wine stain in the shape of a heart above his privates."

The courtroom erupted and Grace's heart flew into her throat as the rage that had belonged to only her poured from their mouths. She caught the barest glimpse of her father's face, pale and peaked, before the man in front of her rose to his feet shouting that he should hang.

"How is Lizzie?" Thornhollow asked that evening in Adelaide and Grace's shared room at the inn.

"Janey sent a note, said she's resting," Grace said, accepting the cup of tea that Adelaide handed her.

"As should you," Adelaide said. "This trial must be taxing for you."

"Which is why I didn't want her there," Thornhollow reminded them both.

"She wants to be there, and that's what matters," his sister said. "I feel as if the two of you could jaw over the whole thing all night, each of your morbid brains imagining each pitfall through to the end rather than just seeing it out. I'll take myself to bed, thank you very much."

Grace and the doctor sat together quietly for a moment after the door shut behind her. "Do you still want to be there?" he finally asked.

"It's not been easy," Grace admitted. "But yes, I want to come tomorrow. You're testifying for my sake. Not being there would be an abandonment of sorts."

Thornhollow sighed. "It's clear I can't stop you, but the courtroom was a circus for the notoriety of the thing. Now that there's a true scandal involved, it will only escalate."

"Doctor, I—" Grace broke off, searching for words that wouldn't come.

"I know that face," Thornhollow said. "It usually comes before you admit you were wrong about something."

"Then you can't know it very well," Grace shot back, and the doctor threw back his head, laughing.

"It's good to see you riled," he said. "I much prefer it to this cold, thoughtful thing that used to be Grace."

"I know," she said, eyes on the floor. "I had to remove myself when we went through Nell's room with the policemen, and there was a comfort to the emptiness. I held on to it too long. It was all I had when I killed Beaton and I didn't feel it, Doctor, I swear. I didn't feel a thing when I cut his throat."

"I believe you," Thornhollow said.

"And that was so frightening," she gasped, her voice cracking. "But it gave me power, to feel nothing. Me, who was so powerless. And I reveled in it for a time, but last night I knew I had to give Elizabeth something for the jury in the way of proof. So I let myself see. I saw my father, and I saw it all, right into the depths of his eyes, where there was that same nothing. I won't do that. I won't become him."

Thornhollow leaned forward. "Good. I would have you be Grace, whichever side of her you're using in the moment. But, Grace."

Grace's tea sat in her hands, untouched and cold. "I know you have reservations, Doctor," she said quietly. "I know you don't want to dirty your theories by using them to falsely accuse my father. Everything you've done for me culminates in this. It's the right thing to do, and I thank you for it."

"Wait until tomorrow to thank me," he said, resting back into his chair again. "Much like Jenny Cantor at Christmastime, we're not out of the woods yet."

Grace resumed her seat the next day with Adelaide and Mr. Turner, rising with the sun in order to make sure they were assured a place in the courtroom. Dr. Thornhollow was right; now that Elizabeth's testimony had brought a senator that much closer to the gallows, everyone wanted to be there when it was decided whether he would hang. The closeness of bodies was worse than the day before, those in the balcony pressed up against the railing, those in the back leaning against the walls when it became standing room only.

Dr. Thornhollow took the stand, his gaze never once going to Grace or his sister.

"I understand, Doctor, that you are formally trained in the science of phrenology, is that correct?" Pickering asked.

"Yes," Thornhollow said, though Grace knew he was dying to correct the terminology to *pseudoscience*.

"If you would take a moment to explain to the jury in layman's terms, please, what phrenology is, and how it works."

Thornhollow turned to the jury, his speech precise as if teaching a class of toddlers. "The concept behind phrenology is that the human brain is divided into seven main sections, each with a broad scope such as domestic or intellectual. These sections are further divided into areas that represent different specific functions, like hope or friendship. The more each of these sections is used, the more it grows. Likewise, if a section is not used often, it can shrivel. These undulations of the brain cause the skull itself to change form, allowing a trained phrenologist such as myself to read the bumps on a person's head to determine their emotional or intellectual leanings."

"Very good," Pickering said. "And you have had a chance to examine Mr. Mae, is that correct?"

"I have."

"And what were your findings?"

"Mr. Mae had pronounced bumps in the areas associated with combativeness, destructiveness, and suavity."

Adelaide leaned into Grace. "I bet he added that last bit for Elizabeth. If she couldn't get it on record that your father is a sly son of a bitch, by God, he will."

"Likewise," Thornhollow continued, "there were definite concavities in the areas represented by benevolence and conscientiousness."

"And in your professional opinion," Pickering asked, "does this indicate that Mr. Mae would be capable of raping Elizabeth Martin and doing the same to Jenny Cantor, asphyxiating her, and blithely leaving her body in the snow?"

"Oh yes," Thornhollow said, his voice heavy with conviction that hadn't existed until then. "He's capable of that and more."

"Objection," Atkinson said from his chair. "Unless Dr. Thornhollow would like to widen the umbrella of crimes my client has been pushed under by defining what he means by 'and more'?"

"Sustained," the judge said.

"Dr. Thornhollow," Pickering tried again. "In your opinion is Mr. Mae capable of the crimes he is accused of?"

"Yes."

"They've irritated him," Grace whispered to Adelaide. "His jaw muscle is ticking."

"I saw," her friend agreed. "He'll never make a living at the poker tables, will he?"

"Furthermore," Pickering continued, "in all your studies of the human brain, have you found that someone with proclivities such as Mr. Mae's can ever be rehabilitated?"

Grace's brow furrowed. "Why is he asking that?"

"He's trying to tie up his argument for the death penalty," Adelaide whispered. "If Melancthon says that not only did your father commit this crime but that he's likely to do it again, the jury will almost have to recommend the gallows, senator or not."

"Dr. Thornhollow, did you hear the question?" Pickering asked.

"Why is he not answering?" Grace asked, a lump of fear forming in her stomach.

Adelaide only shook her head, her own confusion evident.

"Dr. Thornhollow—"

"Yes, I heard you," Thornhollow said, his voice biting. He swallowed hard, his eyes not leaving the jury. "In my professional opinion, Mr. Mae's brain function is not only irreversible but is indicative of criminal insanity."

Mr. Pickering froze, his mouth still half-open to pronounce his next question. At the defense table, Atkinson was scribbling madly. The courtroom milled, a heavy buzz of whispered conversation gaining steam as those who understood explained what had just happened to those who didn't.

Grace's grip on Adelaide's arm was crushing. "What has he done?" she whispered, panic rising.

The older woman's gaze was cold as she stared at her brother. "He gave the defense grounds for an insanity plea." She disengaged Grace's clenched fingers from her arm. "I'm sorry, Grace. He just saved your father's life."

THIRTY-SEVEN

"Why?" Grace screamed, the single word so full of betrayal she could hardly pronounce it. "Why? Why?"

"Grace, please, don't shout," Thornhollow said.

"Let her shout, Melancthon," Adelaide argued. "Let her bring down the whole inn around your ears and you'd deserve every splinter driven into your traitorous skin."

"I would not," Thornhollow said. "I was under oath. It was my word—*mine*—that would send a man to his death, and I could not let that be."

"He's not a man," Grace choked. "He's a monster—you said so yourself. You knew what you were doing, Doctor. You knew and you said the words anyway."

"Yes, I did. Grace, please. Listen to me." He held out his hands as he crossed the room toward her. "I wanted to see him dead, I swear. But when I examined him as ordered by the court I couldn't see it through."

He reached for her, one hand resting on her shoulder as she quivered with rage. "He *is* mad, Grace. A lifetime of unmitigated power has left his mind skewed and warped. He truly believes that he can do no wrong, building on false logic to legitimize any action, no matter how heinous, as long as he wants it to be so. He's a spoiled child, Grace, with the appetites of a man, who answers any questioning of his actions with 'Because I want to.'

"I've seen people do horrible things, Grace. You yourself know the depth one can sink to when distanced from emotion. But in your father I see not a chasm between the man and his feelings but simply man and chasm joined as one. There is no empathy for him to draw upon when he sees another in pain. Society regards those who are insane as less than human, and in his case I could nearly agree as he has lost all qualities that would deem him human.

"Before you rage at me, before you renounce everything we've worked toward and any claim I may have on your friendship, consider his actions through this lens. My lens. The one I view life through, in which I have taken the responsibility for the mad on my shoulders. I speak on their behalf, Grace, always. And I saw a madman in front of me when I questioned your father. It's a madness so discreet that it can walk the streets and be applauded in some circles, but it is madness nonetheless."

Grace closed her eyes against his words. There had been no shame in her father, ever. Never in all the times he'd left her room had he been anything but confident and satisfied. He had wanted something and had taken it, needing no more reason than that to defile his daughter.

Grace shook her head, the shadow of his betrayal still upon her. "It is not my place to pick and choose the mad that you defend. But I cannot agree that he is among them. If it's childish reasoning that brings him to his actions, it is reasoning all the same. A child learns the difference between right and wrong, and violating that is exactly what brings him pleasure. He knows what he does, Doctor. He knows and revels in the doing."

"I cannot agree, Grace," Thornhollow said. "If I am to have any faith in humanity whatsoever, I must believe that no man could do what he has done to you and be in his right mind."

"What will happen to him?" Adelaide asked.

"Atkinson will jump at the chance to use my testimony to plead insanity. Elizabeth turned the jury soundly against your father, the description of his birthmark the nail in that particular coffin. I'll recommend he be remitted to the Wayburne Lunatic Asylum of Boston, under the care of Doctor Heedson."

"At least there will be a familiar face," Grace said, her mouth twisting as she saw his logic. She knew those halls, knew the dispassion of those within them. Her father's emptiness would be met with the same, his infection treated with nothing as his apathy met with like. There would be darkness too, a pitch to match his sins that had paraded for so long in the light.

"A rather fit punishment for both of them, I thought," Thornhollow said, with a ghost of a smile. "Regardless, you are safe, I promise you. And your sister as well. You need never see that man's face again."

"Except I want to, Dr. Thornhollow," Grace said. "And I want him to see mine."

THIRTY-EIGHT

She slipped into the courthouse the next evening in her widow's reeds, Adelaide by her side. They pushed against the tide of the crowd that milled outward, disappointed in such an anticlimactic ending to the trial.

"Excuse us, excuse us," Adelaide said repeatedly, a pie plate raised above her head. Grace linked arms with her so that they wouldn't be separated, finally climbing the steps to the double doors where the last of the thrill seekers had gathered to rehash the day's events.

"Whew," Adelaide said, inspecting her plate. "The pie made it."

"You're sure this will work?" Grace asked.

"The pie? No, I bought the cheapest I could find. But people like to talk about themselves, if you give them the opening. Just follow my lead."

They went into the courthouse, the air still redolent with the accumulated breaths of so many. Adelaide pushed the double doors of the courtroom open, and they saw only the bailiff shutting the door to the holding cells behind him.

"Hello." She waved, confidently making her way up the aisle. "We're from the Federation of Women's Clubs, here to bring a little something to the poor senator."

"Oh, no, ma'am," the bailiff said, straightening his shoulders. "I can't allow that."

"Nonsense," Adelaide said, with a flick of her hand. "It's just a pie. We heard that the man is quite insane, and even if that's the case he's still a senator, isn't he?"

"I suppose so, but I don't see—"

"And we'd hate to have the hospitality of our town fail him, mad or not. It would reflect negatively, don't you think?"

The bailiff shook his head. "I don't know about that, ma'am. All I know is that I can't let you go back to the holding cells."

"Holding cells," Adelaide repeated. "That sounds quite dangerous and exciting, doesn't it, Madeleine? Of course, I imagine it's all old hat to you, isn't it? You must have such stories."

"I do, ma'am. I do at that," the bailiff agreed, a small smile blossoming at her admiration.

"I'd love to hear some," Adelaide said. "I understand if we can't take poor Mr. Mae the pie—after all I might have baked some instrument inside it, mightn't I?"

"Oh now," the bailiff said, shuffling his feet. "I'm not saying you did anything of the kind."

"Good," Adelaide said. "But nonetheless, if we can't, then we can't. How about you tell me a story or two over a slice while my friend goes back and has a word with the poor oppressed?" She leaned toward the bailiff, voice dropping conspiratorially. "She's lost her husband recently, by his own hand. Told me she couldn't live with herself if she were to hear that another such travesty happened here in our town. If she has a word or two that might settle the man's heart, it can't hurt for him to hear it, am I right?"

"I suppose," the bailiff agreed, his attention more focused on Adelaide than Grace. "But I can't let you back there no more than a few minutes."

"One slice of pie, each," Adelaide said. "Then we'll both be quite out of your hair." She nodded to Grace, who didn't wait for permission from the debating bailiff before opening the door and slipping past him.

The hallway was short and empty, with two cells, only one occupied. Grace walked up to the bars and raised her veil before her courage failed. "Hello, Father."

He came unsteadily to his feet, eyes wide and jaw slack. "I am mad then," he said to himself as he stepped toward her, hands outstretched. "They said it was so, and I must be, to see the dead and talk with them."

"I am not dead," Grace said. "And you are not mad. It's easier for

Dr. Thornhollow to believe it, and I will let him. But I know better, don't I?"

He reached the bars, his hands encircling them. "The dead know nothing," he insisted.

"And the living have secrets."

"Grace." He said her name for the first time, and she could not help but flinch. "Grace," he said again, reaching for her. "How can this be? You died."

She smacked his hands away, and the physical contact brought the truth crashing home. His eyes, which had been wide in wonder, now narrowed. "What is this? What lies have been told to me?"

Grace laughed, the sound of her mirth jagged in her throat. "So many, Father. But they cannot match the ones you've told, accumulating over a lifetime to bring you here, face-to-face with the daughter you betrayed in the most shameful of ways."

His face contorted, rage twisting his handsome features into a sneer. "That filth Heedson! I'll have his job!"

"On the contrary, Father. Your very existence now supplies him with one. He'll be in express charge of your care, I'm told."

"Damn you, Grace!" he shrieked at her. "What have you done, girl?"

She leaned into the bars, her face a mask of anger. "What needed doing. You locked me away, Father, but had no key to my mind. I found it, there in the darkness. I found it and I've used it to your undoing, and I'd crow about it to the world if I could."

"I will, by God," he screamed, striking the bars in an effort to get to her. "I'll tell everyone what you've done, you lying bitch!"

"Go ahead, Father," she said. "Nothing you say will be believed. You're insane."

His futile wrath erupted in a wordless flow as she turned her back and left him behind her.

EPILOGUE

The wind whipped the pages in her hands as Grace stood on the west turret, the familiar handwriting of her sister no longer sending spikes of fear through her heart.

Dearest Fair Lily—

I worried that you would not know where to find me, but you are truly magic. Living with Aunt Beth is rather nice. I found a kitten in the garden, and she let me keep her. She has a saucer of milk each night and sleeps on my pillow. Aunt Beth says I can visit Mother on the seaside if I would like, but I think sand is itchy. She says that Father is gone and I will not see him, even at the beach. I am sad, but I pet my kitten at night and she purrs. I look for your letters and I know I am not alone.

Write Back—

Alice

P.S.—My kitty's name is Grace.

Grace's mouth twisted into a sad kind of smile as she moved on to Falsteed's letter.

Dearest Grace—

You'll see by the enclosure that your sister is in the best of care, and that you are remembered. It may not surprise you to learn that I have a new neighbor here in the darkness. He had words with Heedson and your name came up, earning him a spot among the forgotten. I do not regret to inform you that he has a certain smell about him, one that my nose treasures above all others. I haven't told him yet, as he seems to be under some stress. Someday I'd love to see your shining face again, and learn how this gift was delivered to me.

Yours—

Falsteed

"Grace!" The trapdoor flew upward, Thornhollow emerging from the stairwell. "I thought I might find you up here," he said, catching his breath. "Janey was half-frantic searching the grounds for you, when I remembered that you'd never returned the turret key to me."

"You never asked for it," Grace said.

"Good news?" he asked, gesturing toward the pages in her hand.

"Yes." She smiled. "All."

"Excellent!" He smacked his hands together. "Now, I'll have to tear you away from happiness and this stunning view to come to a murder with me."

"Of course," Grace said, folding her letters. "Give me one moment?"

"A moment only," he said as he descended the stairs, his voice floating in his wake. "There's fresh blood spilling, Grace. And we must see which way it flows!"

Grace shook her head at his words, glancing down as she put the folded letters in her pocket to see a note scratched on the back of Falsteed's.

One more word, if I may. The original meaning of the word asylum is, in fact, "protection." I hope you have found it to be so in your bright surroundings, as I have found my own niche here in the dark.

Grace leaned against the railing, her gaze taking in the rolling grounds, Elizabeth's silhouette by the lake, Thornhollow's carriage rolling to a stop in the roundabout, and Nell's empty chair beside her.

"Indeed I have," she said, her scars flashing brightly in the sun. "I am Grace Mae, and I have come home."

AUTHOR'S NOTE

The history of insane asylum medicine is not pretty. Even the well-intentioned sometimes caused great harm through ignorance, and in the worst cases, harm was caused for the sake of harm.

That being said, if a person was unfortunate enough to be declared insane in the 1800s, there were plenty of institutions that treated their patients with respect. The Athens Lunatic Asylum in southeast Ohio was one such place and is the basis for the asylum where Grace and Thornhollow live.

This asylum—popularly called the Ridges—gets a lot of unwanted attention for its supposedly paranormal aspects and not enough credit for its original intentions. Now it is owned by Ohio University and used as both art gallery and office space. You can visit the asylum today and see the original woodwork, staircases, and mosaic floors by touring the Kennedy Museum of Art, located in Lin Hall.

Although the patient wards are off limits to the public due to the major renovations necessary to keep the building safe, a walking tour of the outside of the asylum is sometimes offered through the Athens County Historical Society. You can visit their site at www.athenshistory.org for more information. If you're interested in learning more about the asylum Grace calls home, definitely check out *Asylum on the Hill: History of a Healing Landscape* by Katherine Ziff.

Like so many things, truth can be stranger than fiction. Nell's alligator was indeed quite real, although I adjusted his time period a bit. You can see pictures of the affectionately named Jim Crocky at http://media.library.ohiou.edu/cdm/ref/collection/archives/id/867.

ACKNOWLEDGMENTS

Bringing this novel together took me to some dark places emotionally, mentally, and even physically. There were a lot of people who followed me there—sometimes in all three ways.

First, thanks needs to go to my acquiring editor, Sarah Shumway, who saw the potential in a dark piece and encouraged me to go with my gut. On the heels of that, I need to thank my new editor, Ben Rosenthal, who dove right into my darkness without flinching. I also must thank my amazing agent, Adriann Ranta, who had the experience of fielding an unscheduled phone call from me for the first time on this one. I believe she's still recovering.

Everything I produce goes through practiced authors before I put it before anyone else. For this one, I owe R. C. Lewis, Kate Karyus Quinn, Lydia Kang, Megan Shepherd, and Demitria Lunetta, who all responded to a somewhat panicked and time-sensitive email from me, complete with a weighty attachment.

Lastly, I need to thank people who spend time with me in real life, and sometimes suffer for it. First to my college pals, Amanda, Mel, Erin, and Debbie, who listened to a rambling diatribe about lobotomies on our way to see the Royal Shakespeare Company. I also need to include the people who deal with me on a daily basis—whether it's a good day or a bad one.

And finally, thanks to my family and boyfriend, who understand that a writing cave is a solitary place and love me anyway.

Read on for a sneak peek of

THE FEMALE
OF THE SPECIES

1. **ALEX**

This is how I kill someone.

I learn his habits, I know his schedule. It is not difficult. His life consists of quick stops to the dollar store for the bare minimum of things required to keep this ragged cycle going, his hat pulled down over his eyes so as not to be recognized.

But he is. It's a small town.

I watch these little exchanges. They evolve in seconds, from *I get paid to smile at you* to the facial muscles going lax when recognition hits, the price scanner making a feeble attempt to break the silence by making a *beep-beep* when his food goes past.

I know this pattern but watch it anyway. The bread, the cheese, the wine, and the crackers that sometimes he will crumble and put out for the birds—a tiny crack of kindness that makes him all the more hateful. Because if there's a version of him that feeds birds as winter descends, then there is a decency that he chose to over-look when he did other things. Other things that also fed the birds. And the hawks. And the raccoons. And the coyotes. All the animals that took mouthfuls of my sister, destroying any chance of proving he killed her.

But I'm not a court, and I don't need proof.

I know this road, the one that leads out of town. He'll take a right where the bridge has been out for a decade, then follow the gravel that shoots to the left, each path becoming more decrepit than the last. From two lanes to one, from paved to gravel, and then just dirt. Dirt leading into the woods.

I know all these things because I've seen them every day for months. I'm just a girl trying to get in shape this summer, shedding the last baby fat as my womanhood emerges. How clean I look. How fresh and hopeful and one with the outdoors as I strain to make it up the hill, and then exuberant as I fly down the other side, hair streaming behind, enjoying my earned reward. This is what people think when they see me.

The few people who live out here wave as I go past, awkwardly at first, but later in recognition. As the days get hotter, one elderly lady waits at the end of her driveway every day with a glass pitcher of lemonade. She knows exactly what time I will pass her house, and my drink is always cold, the ice cubes clinking against my teeth.

I do this at first so that it won't be odd that I'm there on *that* day. I've come to like it, the way my legs have become all muscle and how my hair smells like wind hours later. I like the lemonade, too. I almost look forward to seeing the old lady. But I never let it distract me.

Because this is not how I get in shape and make new friends.

This is how I kill someone.

And it's a simple process, really. His hand hesitates for a second when he sees me pause at the end of his driveway. Yes, he's one of the people who wave. He sits on his porch most of the day, a middle-aged man who might be handsome if you don't look closely into his eyes and identify what lurks there. Every day the sun rises and the wine bottle empties and he sits there wondering where his life went wrong until it sets again.

I know exactly where. I'll explain that to him.

He's lonely. So when I stop for the first time ever, I almost feel bad when his face lights up. Almost. Because immediately following that pure smile of a human being who craves the company of another human being, his eyes flick down to my tank top, where my breasts heave up and down as I catch my breath. And we're not two human beings anymore.

We're a male and a female.

Alone in the woods.

And I lie, say that I'm winded, need to sit down for a minute. And part of him knows he shouldn't do this. The part that crumbles up crackers and feeds them to birds knows that he shouldn't bring me out of the sun into the darkness of his house. But another part *wants* to.

And it's much stronger.

I go, smiling when he holds the screen door open for me. It makes my nose scrunch up and draws attention to my freckles, which everyone says make me so cute. They have no idea.

I walk inside, into the cool shadows, pretending not to hear when he flicks the lock on the screen door. Then I turn around, and tell him who I am.

This is how I kill someone.

And I don't feel bad about it.

2. JACK

The thing about Alex Craft is, you forget she's there.

I didn't give her much thought until we were freshmen, chomping at the bit to help with search parties for her sister. We enjoyed pretending to be adults, the feeling that we were actually doing something, even though most of us forgot to check the batteries on our flashlights and Park had a baggie in his pocket that stopped our searching cold once we were out of sight of the real adults.

Branley actually packed a snack, like we were going camping or something. To be fair, after the baggie was empty, we were totally thrilled and she was our hero, just like she wanted. She sat on my lap that night, happy to squirm right where she knew I liked it. And I didn't stop her. I've never stopped Branley. Still haven't learned how.

So our hero was the girl who brought Doritos to chase our weed, and a few yards away from where we sat, an actual hero found the body. Parts of it, anyway. We didn't even notice the gathering flashlights until the girl Park was with made a noise when he got her in just the right place, and they swung toward us.

I've thought about it a lot in the three years since, how we must've looked in that glare. Branley's "Find Anna" shirt shoved up over her tits, my pants around my ankles, all of us with red-rimmed eyes and big *oh shit* looks on our faces.

The guy out in front was all rugged-looking, dirty beard and a hat, a loose jacket. The kind of guy who I thought would laugh and tell us to keep on going while he kept the light on us. But he never even glanced at Branley or Park's girl while they yanked their clothes in place. Instead he looked right at me and said, "Get the fuck out of here, douchebags."

I was so busy tucking it all back in I thought everybody was pissed because of us, that their faces were set hard and their lights were pointing at the ground because they didn't want to know—for sure—what we'd been doing. But that wasn't it.

Her hand was sticking up out of the dirt, stripped to

the bone, the gnawed-on skin peeled back to the wrist. I froze in the act of pulling up my zipper. I didn't know then that once the area was cordoned off, parts of Anna Craft would be found all over the place. I thought it was a shallow grave she'd tried to dig herself out of, with me a few yards away doing my best to pound a different girl down into the ground.

"What?" Branley had said, eyes on my face as always, completely missing that they'd found what we were supposed to be looking for.

I left her. I did exactly what that guy said and turned around and got the fuck out of there. I ran because one of the faces in that circle of light was Alex Craft, a girl I'd gone to school with my whole life, a girl who sometimes you don't see. I saw her then, as she reached down to touch her sister's dirt-streaked fingers, like a kid digging up a toy that got mired in the sandbox. And I haven't been able to unsee her since.

This is what I think about when she brushes past me on the first day of our senior year, her dark hair swinging as she walks, face still wearing the hard mask I saw that night, like it's permanently set.

I wonder if she heard that guy call me a douchebag.

And I want to know if she agrees.

Because I sure as hell do.

3. **PEEKAY**

I have a name, but everyone just calls me Peekay because I'm the PK—Preacher's Kid. I'm thinking about this because my name—or at least my nickname—should be somewhere in the pic Sara just sent me, a screencap she snatched off my boyfriend's phone while he was passed out at a party. A screencap of increasingly dirty sexting that should alternate between *Adam* and *Peekay* but instead says *Adam* and *Branley*.

I toss my phone into the passenger seat and focus on not crying while I wait for the woman from the animal shelter to arrive and unlock the building. My leg is bouncing up and down while I burn off my anger, the car keys jangling against my knee. I yank them out of the ignition when I spot the beaded key chain that

says "Peekay & Adam 4-Ever." It's made out of letters
and footballs and hearts, the paint rubbed away in spots
from years of friction as it passed in and out of my jeans
pocket.

Years.

"Fucker," I say, and break the black cord that holds
them all together, sending letters and hearts and footballs all over my car.

I'm not supposed to say that word, because I'm a
preacher's kid. But I'm also not supposed to drink beer
or know what a dick smells like, so language is the least
of my sins. My phone makes a noise at me, one that used
to make me dive for it in the middle of the night, breath-
less and happy. A noise that used to send my stomach up
in my throat. Except now that organ is definitely going
another way, and I get out of my car so I don't have to
look at the screen all lit up with his name, hearts on
either side of it. Some beads roll out behind me and one
crunches under my foot as I get out.

It's the "&."

More pieces fall out onto the gravel and I hear
another car. I tuck my hands up into the sleeves of my
hoodie because it's colder than it's supposed to be today
(thanks, Ohio) and I'm ready to get inside the shelter
and start my Senior Year Experience.

On my grade card it will say SYE—Animal Shelter

Volunteer, and that will probably be followed by a capital A, nicely aligned with all the others. I have a very different idea about what constitutes a Senior Year Experience, and Adam was supposed to be a part of that. Until now.

I stomp my foot, telling myself I'm doing it to keep warm, and that the little heart charm that has now been ground into a fine powder had nothing to do with it. The other car pulls up next to mine, but it's not the lady from the shelter. It's another student, and it takes me a second to place her as she gets out of the car.

Actually, that's kind of a lie. I know exactly who she is, I just can't remember her *name*. So I'm standing there, my fists balled up in fabric and my feet smacking against the ground, when I say, "Hey, Anna. You volunteering here for SYE?"

She looks at me for a second before I realize what I just did.

"I'm Alex," she says.

"I know, right. Yeah, I totally know," I say, my words falling out all over one another. "It's just—"

"It's just that when you look at me all you think about is my older sister, so your brain offers that name instead."

"Yeah," I say, more than a little set back by her factual presentation, like I'm a science fair judge instead of a girl who just put her foot in her mouth.

"Yeah," she echoes back at me, then moves toward the shelter. Which, it turns out, was unlocked.

I watch her walk away from me, back rigid, and I think it's going to be a long Senior Year Experience. Then I hear my phone again, insistently making its Adam noise, and I think about those texts between him and Branley Jacobs and that word slips out of me again.

"Fucker."

It's cold enough that it makes a fog in front of my mouth when I say it, and even though I brushed good this morning I can smell stale beer. So there's the word and the beer, all hanging there together in the air, and my dad would probably be really disappointed in me right now. Also because I know what a dick smells like. Or what Adam's does, anyway.

But just his.

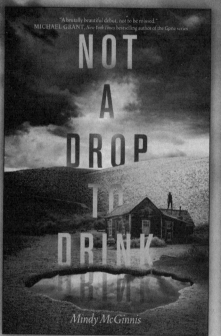

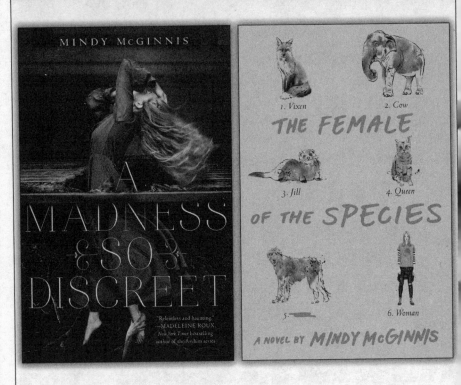

JOIN THE Epic Reads COMMUNITY